Thre

The first soldier who h sailing across the room by a brutal swing of Hogun's mace, Hridgandr. Fandral could see the ferocious intensity in Hogun's eyes, a vicious rapture more akin to the mania of a berserker than any normal man.

"You've tasted my arrows, now sample my sword." Fandral jeered at the mercenaries, "One at a time or all at once, as you prefer." The first soldier to react to his goading charged at him. The mercenary's blade was a monstrous sword that demanded both arms to swing. There was no question of trying to parry such a blow with his own rakish weapon. Instead, he dodged to the side at the last second, letting the heavy sword cleave through the space he'd so recently occupied. Before the foeman could recover from the ponderous attack, Fandral slashed at his neck. The soldier dropped his blade and stumbled away, clutching at his bleeding throat.

ALSO AVAILABLE

MARVEL CRISIS PROTOCOL
Target: Kree by Stuart Moore

MARVEL HEROINES
Domino: Strays by Tristan Palmgren
Rogue: Untouched by Alisa Kwitney
Elsa Bloodstone: Bequest by Cath Lauria
Outlaw: Relentless by Tristan Palmgren

LEGENDS OF ASGARD
The Head of Mimir by Richard Lee Byers
The Sword of Surtur by C L Werner
The Serpent and the Dead by Anna Stephens
The Rebels of Vanaheim by Richard Lee Byers

MARVEL UNTOLD
The Harrowing of Doom by David Annandale
Dark Avengers: The Patriot List by David Guymer
Witches Unleashed by Carrie Harris
Reign of the Devourer by David Annandale

XAVIER'S INSTITUTE
Liberty & Justice for All by Carrie Harris
First Team by Robbie MacNiven
Triptych by Jaleigh Johnson
School of X edited by Gwendolyn Nix

MARVEL LEGENDS OF ASGARD

Three Swords

C L WERNER

FOR MARVEL PUBLISHING

VP Production & Special Projects: Jeff Youngquist
Associate Editors, Special Projects: Caitlin O'Connell and Sarah Singer
Manager, Licensed Publishing: Jeremy West
VP, Licensed Publishing: Sven Larsen
SVP Print, Sales & Marketing: David Gabriel
Editor in Chief: C B Cebulski

Special Thanks to Wil Moss

© 2022 MARVEL

First published by Aconyte Books in 2022
ISBN 978 1 83908 110 1
Ebook ISBN 978 1 83908 111 8

All rights reserved. The Aconyte name and logo and the Asmodee Entertainment name and logo are registered or unregistered trademarks of Asmodee Entertainment Limited.

This novel is entirely a work of fiction. Names, characters, places, and incidents are the products of the author's imagination or are used fictitiously. Any resemblance to actual events, locales, organizations or persons, living or dead, is entirely coincidental.

Sales of this book without a front cover may be unauthorized. If this book is coverless, it may have been reported to the publisher as "unsold and destroyed" and neither the author nor the publisher may have received payment for it.

Cover art by Massimiliano Haematinon Nigro

Distributed in North America by Simon & Schuster Inc, New York, USA
Printed in the United States of America
9 8 7 6 5 4 3 2 1

ACONYTE BOOKS

An imprint of Asmodee Entertainment Ltd

Mercury House, Shipstones Business Centre

North Gate, Nottingham NG7 7FN, UK

aconytebooks.com // twitter.com/aconytebooks

*To Shauna, for her valuable
input over the years.*

ONE

The searing heat of day was but a distant memory as Vigdis moved through the darkened alleyways of Gunnarsfell. The Skornheim desert, an inferno while the sun was high, became as cold as Niffleheim by night. Her heavy cloak, adopted to conceal her identity when she left her workshop, was now even more appreciated for its ability to fend off the chill in the air.

While one hand held the clasp of her cloak tight, Vigdis kept the other curled about the knife hanging from her belt. Sometimes goblins burrowed up into Gunnarsfell and abducted anyone they could catch alone, but it wasn't thoughts of the troll-like creatures that provoked such uneasiness this night. Gruesome as the goblins were, Vigdis was more worried about running into King Gunnar's men. The tyrant's soldiers were as thick as fleas in the town and always trying to find someone they could turn over to collect the bounty offered for rebels.

It mattered little to the soldiers if those they caught were innocent. They had many brutal tricks for making someone confess to whatever they were asked. The overseers at the tin mines where rebels were sent were even less concerned with the guilt of their charges. Their only interest was in having enough workers to meet the harsh quotas set by King Gunnar.

Vigdis took some solace that whatever happened, at least she wasn't a hapless bystander victimized by circumstance. She couldn't have said that a few months ago. Then, she'd followed her father's example and tried to be indifferent to what was happening in Helmhold – the town King Gunnar had renamed in his own honor. She'd tried to stay blind and deaf to the tyrant's outrages. At last the despotism came too close to be ignored. Unknown to him, her father made barrels the rebels used to smuggle weapons. His protests of innocence had no traction with King Gunnar and he'd been sent to the mines.

Vigdis was ashamed that it had taken something so personal to finally get her to act. She tried to make up for her tardiness in joining the rebels by accepting the riskiest duties for herself. A courier, bearing messages from one band of rebels to another, was the most dangerous assignment. Slipping from one hideout to another, always having to be vigilant and with no one but herself to help her if something went wrong.

"But it will bring down the tyrant," Vigdis whispered. "By Odin's spear, we'll be free of Gunnar's boot." Even in the brief time since she'd joined the rebels, she'd seen their numbers swell and their equipment improve. The leaders had even engaged outlanders from beyond the sands of Skornheim to train them how to fight Gunnar and topple him from power. The rebellion was growing so big that she knew things must reach the crisis soon. Either they would rise up and overcome the tyrant or else his soldiers would discover them and strike before they could act.

Vigdis hurried on through the back alleys, eager to deliver the message and help speed the day of Gunnar's reckoning. Her haste was measured with caution, and when the sound of marching boots reached her ears, she slackened her pace and eased back against the alley's limestone walls. She shifted along until she was deep in shadow. The sounds came from just around the next bend. From the clatter of armor and the jangle of swordbelts, she knew she was listening to a group of Gunnar's soldiers.

The courier started to retreat the way she'd come. Too much depended on the message she carried to chance being discovered by the patrol. Now that she had some idea of their route, she could circle around them and reach her destination by a different path.

As she withdrew, Vigdis kept looking in the direction of the sounds. With her attention focused on the patrol she made the mistake of not paying enough notice to what else was around her. A vicious hiss and the rustle of something moving in the dark was all the warning she was given. Spinning around, Vigdis just had time to pull her knife before a shape rushed at her from the night.

"Back, you swine!" Vigdis snarled as her blade whipped through the air. The flash of steel caused her attacker to reel back. In doing so, the ambusher was revealed in the moonlight. It was a broad, squat figure, half a head shorter than Vigdis with long arms and bandy legs. Its skin was a reddish-orange and the shock of hair that rose from its scalp was black. Its head was flatter than that of a human, with a craggy brow and a protruding jaw. Sharp yellow eyes gleamed from either side of its pushed-in nose. She could see the malevolence in the creature's wicked gaze, every bit as menacing as the spiked mace it held in its clawed hand.

Goblin! Vigdis had seen them a few times before, but only in the light of day and after they had been killed by soldiers. It was a far different thing to meet a live one in the dead of night. Through her mind raced all the terrifying stories told of those who were captured by goblins. Dragged down into the Realm Below, never to see the sun again.

"You'll not find me easy prey, cave-worm," Vigdis vowed. She brandished her knife again, letting the moon shine along its edge. All the stories said that goblins were cowardly and would run from any fight where they didn't outnumber their prey. As yet, she'd seen only this one. She hoped that a show of force would make the creature retreat.

The goblin bared its fangs in a wolfish grin. It seemed it hadn't heard the same stories as Vigdis. Uttering a low growl, it lunged at her.

The knife raked across the goblin's chest, but most of the cut was absorbed by the scaly hauberk it wore. Vigdis only drew blood from the edge of its shoulder. The spiked mace, meanwhile, came cracking down with vicious force. Had she not twisted away from its path, she knew the creature would have split her skull. As it was, the spikes grazed her cheek. She could feel the torn flesh start to bleed.

The spiked mace came whipping back around and forced Vigdis to give ground before the goblin. The yellow eyes gleamed with vicious savagery as the creature surged relentlessly towards her. First it would swing for her head, then try to strike for her knees. All Vigdis could do was backpedal and try to keep out of the goblin's reach. Its arms were longer than those of a human, making it doubly difficult to gauge the distance it could swing.

Vigdis studied more than the reach of the goblin's mace. She noted a pattern to its attacks. When the creature tried to mash her head, she knew its next swing would be directed at her legs. She took advantage of that foreknowledge. As the mace came whipping around for her knees, she leaped over it and jumped towards her foe.

The goblin's eyes narrowed with alarm. The next instant Vigdis was plunging her knife down between its shoulders. The creature dropped its mace and staggered back, pulling the knife from her grip. The goblin's clawed hands slapped frantically at its back, but it was unable to reach the blade. Vitality gushed from the wound, and the monster slumped to its knees. It directed a last hateful glare at Vigdis before pitching forward onto its face.

For a moment Vigdis was paralyzed by the sight of the dead goblin, knowing it was her hand that had driven life from the creature. It was the first time she'd killed something even remotely human. She knew she should feel excited, but instead there was only a sickness deep inside her.

Harsh laughter broke in upon her thoughts. "The first one's always the worst, but once you get used to it you don't even notice any more." Vigdis turned to see five soldiers bearing the heraldry of King Gunnar spread out across the alley. The sounds of the fray must have drawn the patrol she'd been trying to avoid.

"It was a good fight," the soldier who'd spoken continued. He was tall and had a grizzled beard drooping down from his cruel features. "For a time it looked like even odds who'd win." That remark brought gruff laughs from the other mercenaries.

Vigdis' temper flared at the patrol's humor. "Don't expect me to be sorry you lost your bet," she said.

The grizzled soldier chuckled louder. "Not me," he said, jabbing a thumb against his chest and then pointing at Vigdis. "My gold was on you." Some of the amusement drained out of his smile and his eyes became as cold as a snake's. He slowly drew his sword. "You see, I figured anyone creeping about at night where a goblin could find her must be able to fend for herself. Rebels might be stupid, but they tend to be tough."

Vigdis darted a look at the goblin with her knife sticking in its back. There was small chance of her reaching it before the soldiers subdued her, but she intended to give it a try. It was better than going down without a fight.

"I wouldn't," the mercenary chided her. "Even if you make it, you won't win."

"Five armed men against one unarmed foe are the odds I'd expect Gunnar's dogs to favor." The voice that called out from the shadows had a sharp, audacious quality to it. Vigdis thought the tone had all the withering authority of a master scolding an apprentice.

The soldiers swung around. "Who dares speak to King

Three Swords 13

Gunnar's huscarls in such a manner?" the grizzled mercenary sputtered.

"The wonder is that more people don't." A man stepped into the light. The vestment he wore was much different from the light, pale clothes of Skornheim. He wore a padded green tunic over a loose shirt that was several shades darker. A voluminous cape trimmed in fur hung from his shoulders. His breeches were a deep brown and the stiff boots he wore came up almost to his knees. He was tall with a rakish build, but he moved with an assurance and grace that recalled to Vigdis the manners of a cat. He wore his blond hair cut short, just a wisp of mustache across his upper lip and a brief beard groomed to a sharp point growing from his chin. His face, Vigdis decided, was more handsome and noble than anyone she'd ever seen.

"Beg our apology, braggart, or we won't leave enough of you for the tin mines," the mercenary growled. His companions began edging towards the stranger. Each had a sword or axe clenched in his hand.

The stranger ignored the approaching soldiers and instead bowed his head to Vigdis. "My apologies, but I fear I must insist on dealing with these varlets for you." One of the soldiers, giving voice to a frustrated roar, rushed in on the man. Before the mercenary could swing his sword, the stranger whipped off his cloak. In the same motion he spun it at the charging enemy. The cloth wrapped itself around the soldier's head and the roar collapsed into a bark of startled confusion. Still holding part of the cloak, the stranger gave it a powerful tug before releasing it. The combination sent the mercenary slamming into the limestone wall.

"That's what comes from being so headstrong as to challenge Fandral the Dashing," the stranger scolded the stunned mercenary. Without pause he spun around to meet the attack of an axeman. He ducked beneath the sweeping blade, kicking out with his boot to trip his man up. While the axeman stumbled and tried to recover his footing, Fandral met the swordsmen who followed. Vigdis watched in awe as he dodged their thrusting blades and caught one by his cloak. With a kick and a shove, he sent his momentary captive crashing into the axeman. Both warriors fell to the ground in a tangle of curses and invective.

The grizzled sergeant and his remaining man converged on Fandral from opposite sides. Fandral reacted by unbuckling his belt. Keeping his scabbarded sword in one hand, he employed the belt like a lash, swatting the soldiers whenever they tried to get close. The mercenaries yelped when the leather stung their hands.

"The pox take you, knave!" the sergeant snarled. "Fight like an Asgardian!"

Vigdis noted a change settle upon Fandral's visage. Before, there had been a kind of eager enjoyment as though he were savoring the conflict. Now a severe quality came into his face. "Perhaps I have spent too much time among the people of Midgard," he conceded. "Perhaps they've taught me too much of the ways of indulgence and mercy." He circled the regrouping mercenaries, now putting himself between them and Vigdis.

"You tell me to fight like an Asgardian, then perhaps I will." Fandral ripped the scabbard away from his sword. The exposed blade glistened in the moonlight. "I'll fight the way five louts who think a lone woman with only a knife is a fair contest deserve to be fought."

"Kill the yapping cur!" the sergeant commanded. The soldiers surged forward, seeking to overwhelm Fandral in their rush.

The hero, however, didn't wait for them, but instead charged into their midst. His blade flashed in a shimmering arc as he sent his adversaries reeling. One axeman crumpled, clawing at the crimson stain growing from his belly. A swordsman collapsed with a hand clenched about his slashed throat. The others staggered back with more superficial injuries, the first traces of fear creeping into their eyes. Far from a boastful fop, Fandral had proven to ply his sword with blinding swiftness.

Vigdis stirred from her awed fascination. She ignored her knife and instead took up the goblin's spiked mace. Tightening her grip about the clumsy weapon, she moved to support Fandral against the remaining mercenaries.

"It's not too late to run away," Fandral warned the soldiers. A low sigh killed his smile. "I suppose stubborn pride won't let you, though. I don't know which is more foolish to sell one's life for: pride or a tyrant's gold."

Fandral's goading brought the soldiers swarming at him. He met the attack of a swordsman by darting around the sweep of his blade and then thrusting his own into the man's ribs, his gleaming steel seeming to effortlessly pierce the soldier's mail. Then he was turning to meet the enraged sergeant's assault. The crash of sword against sword rang out, echoing through the narrow confines of the alley.

Vigdis noted all of this only in passing, for she was soon

occupied with the last axeman. Coming upon him from the flank, she delivered a blow to the soldier's side. The clumsy goblin weapon, however, failed to drop her enemy. The mercenary reeled, crying out and grabbing at his bashed ribs. Then, with vengeance in his eyes, he struck at Vigdis. She caught the descending blade with the heft of the mace, but the powerful impact nearly jarred it from her grip.

The mercenary smiled and pulled back to bring the axe chopping down. Vigdis didn't try to block the attack, instead choosing to emulate Fandral's earlier antics to foil her enemy. She brought the heavy mace smashing down on the soldier's boot, crushing every bone in his foot. The searing pain caused the mercenary to stumble. Before he could recover, Vigdis struck him a third time. From the way he sprawled on the ground, she knew there was no need to hit him again.

Vigdis turned from her vanquished foe just in time to see the end of Fandral's duel with the sergeant. The soldier delivered a flurry of slashes that forced the hero to give ground. Sneering, the mercenary moved to exploit the opening, but in doing so left himself exposed. So quickly did Fandral move that Vigdis couldn't see the thrust that pierced the sergeant's heart, only its aftermath. The wounded soldier took a staggering step back, then the sword fell from his grasp. The next second, he wilted to the ground beside his discarded weapon.

"A sorry end to a sorry company," Fandral commented. He glanced around and retrieved his scabbard and belt. Vigdis approached him as he cleansed the blood from his blade with a bit of cloth.

Three Swords 17

"I am in your debt for helping me," Vigdis started to say. "If you hadn't come along…"

Fandral smiled and shook his head. "I didn't just 'come along,' and by helping you I've done us both a service. I have friends who were worried about another friend who was running a bit late. So, I went out to look for her… and lo, I find her embroiled in a spot of trouble." He bowed his head and sheathed his sword. "I'm only happy to have been of service to a charming and brave lady." His eyes gave a furtive glance at the alleyway. "And I can be of further service by suggesting we withdraw to more pleasant surroundings. Perhaps you might suggest somewhere safe."

At once Vigdis was on her guard. Might everything that had taken place be a ploy by King Gunnar to learn where the rebels were hiding? Her hesitation must have shown on her face, for Fandral gave her a disarming smile.

"Shrewd, too," Fandral complimented her. "Very well, then let me suggest somewhere safe," he said, starting to walk away.

Vigdis dashed after Fandral. "Where are we going?"

Fandral laughed. "By the Fangs of Fenris, you're a curious messenger. We're going to the Vanquished Dragon. The place where our rebel friends are waiting to hear your message."

Two

From the street the Vanquished Dragon was an unremarkable stone building nestled between a wainwright's workshop and a storehouse of the Ragnarsson clan. Its walls sported only a few narrow windows near the top of the facade, and a cloth awning shielded these apertures from the worst of the desert sun. A set of iron-banded doors afforded the only obvious entry and above them, fastened to the building by thick chains, was a sign depicting a warrior standing over a dragon's corpse, his sword bared and the wyrm's severed head held up in a triumphant display.

The mead hall had been a popular location for the people of Helmhold to congregate. As such, the mounting paranoia of King Gunnar had caused the despot to order the Vanquished Dragon closed. The doors had been nailed shut by his soldiers and a tin plaque inscribed with the royal diktat was fixed to the frame. Gunnar assured his subjects that his decree was to protect his subjects and prevent them from accidentally associating with rebel traitors. The tyrant emphasized the severity of his command by threatening imprisonment in the mines for those who defied his orders.

"If ever there was a man unfit to be a king, it's this trash," Vigdis cursed as she read the diktat.

Fandral sympathized with the woman's anger. He'd traveled widely, within Asgard and realms beyond the Rainbow Bridge. People were much the same everywhere. There were those who cared only for power and those who desired only freedom. When they met, conflict was the inevitable result.

"A dog barks loudest when trying to convince itself that it's a wolf," Fandral said. He steered Vigdis away from the door and towards a narrow gap between the tavern and the storehouse. "This way," he said after checking to see that there weren't any of Gunnar's soldiers around. All he could see was a ragged beggar with an alms bowl resting beside him and it seemed he was too sleepy to pay them any notice. Fandral weighed the chance that the man could be a spy but decided it was unlikely. Gunnar wasn't usually so subtle in his oppression of his people.

Fandral ushered Vigdis down a short alley, then directed her to a niche on their left. It seemed nothing more than an alcove at first, but once inside it turned sharply. A few feet along this and they came to a set of steps that led down to a door.

"I've visited the Vanquished Dragon many times and never knew about this," Vigdis told him. She gave Fandral a sharp look. "Any other time when I was met, I'd be blindfolded before being brought inside so I wouldn't know the way."

Fandral gave her an embarrassed smile. "A rather poor blunder on my part. We'll have to make doubly sure to keep you away from Gunnar's mercenaries now." He quickly shifted conversation away from his mistake. "I shouldn't be surprised you didn't know about this door. Old Hrolfgar who owned the tavern must have been a pretty bad sort. He'd pick out fellows who were alone in their cups and do his best to get them drunk. Once they were under the table, he'd have them taken out by this back way and sell them to caravans leaving town. The caravan masters are always in need of extra bearers to carry their goods. By the time Hrolfgar's victims woke, they'd be miles from town and told if they wanted any water, they'd have to work for it. A pretty sort of racket for the villain."

"Then there's at least one man Gunnar's put in the mines who deserves to be there," Vigdis stated.

"When Gunnar loses his throne, there will be two," Fandral promised. He rapped the pommel of his sword against the portal. Three sharp knocks followed by two soft ones. A pattern repeated twice. The designated sign by which those inside would know it was a friend seeking entry.

The sound of something heavy being moved could be heard from behind the door. Fandral pictured the rebels set as sentries removing the casks and boxes customarily stacked in front of the entry. The extra weight would make the door almost impossible to force from the outside.

When the obstruction was cleared, the door cracked open and a suspicious eye studied Fandral and Vigdis. "Lothgar, you know me," Fandral reproved the sentry, "and I dare say you've seen Vigdis before now. Open the door and let us in before one of Gunnar's jackals comes along."

The door swung wide and the sentry sheepishly stepped aside. "Sorry, Lord Fandral," he muttered. The guard was young, his cheeks bereft of even the first stubble of a beard. Lothgar's companion, still shifting some of the boxes out of the way, was several years his junior. It pained Fandral to see boys who should be whiling away their time in play and sport drawn into far more serious conflict.

Fandral kept his misgivings to himself and instead gave Lothgar a reassuring clap on his shoulder. "Never apologize for vigilance. It was wrong of me to chide you for treating your duty with the severity it warrants." He shook his head and wagged his finger at the youth. "However, I will chide you if you call me 'Lord Fandral' again. It's unseemly."

"But Lord Volstagg said–" Lothgar started to explain.

"I might have known." Fandral looked aside at Vigdis and laughed. He turned back to Lothgar. "You just don't pay any mind to what Volstagg tells you to call him. He'd have you addressing him as 'All-Father Volstagg' if he dared." The levity drained out of Fandral's expression and he pushed the door shut behind him. "Vigdis has a message for your father and it might be the word we've been waiting for. So get everything locked up again and keep watch as carefully as you have been."

Lothgar returned his smile. "Yes Lor… Fandral," he said, jumping to the task and helping the other boy rebuild the obstruction.

The sentries were posted on a small landing. A dozen or so steps descended still further. Fandral led Vigdis down these and swept aside a heavy curtain that blocked the entrance to the stairs. Beyond was the Vanquished Dragon proper, a basement fifty feet long and nearly half again as wide. Tables and benches were scattered around the room, and along one wall ran a stone-topped counter. Fandral was always impressed by the notable difference in temperature. Hrolfgar might have been a villain, but he'd known enough to burrow into the ground to keep away from the Skornheim sun. The mead hall was one great cellar sunk twenty feet below the street and a good ten degrees cooler than the buildings baking above it. Light from the narrow windows in the exterior facade filtered down to provide illumination.

Where once the mead hall would have been filled with raucous patrons, now its occupants were of a more severe demeanor. Tables had been shoved aside to create open areas. Places in which rebels could learn and hone their martial skills.

"You're one of the outlanders come to help my people," Vigdis remarked as she looked across the cellar at the changes that had occurred since she'd last been here.

Fandral nodded. "The people of Gunnarsfell have courage and determination in excess, all they need is finesse and discipline." He pointed to an area where five rebels were loosing arrows at empty barrels with targets painted across them. "Those are my pupils, who are trying to spite their teacher by showing better marksmanship when I'm away than they do when I'm here."

As they continued across the cellar, Fandral indicated a cleared space where several rebels had formed a wide circle.

Three Swords 23

A mix of men and women from every class in the community, they were united now in the obvious anxiety etched across their faces. Fandral could see Vigdis echo their concern.

"Don't for a moment think they're afraid," Fandral said. "They've shown more pluck than my own pupils by taking Hogun for their instructor."

"Come at me," a stern voice commanded from the middle of the rebel ring. The speaker was a broad-shouldered Asgardian with black hair and long mustaches. He wore a horned helm with a leather cowl covering the back of his neck and shoulders, the whole trimmed with the white fur of a snow lion. His tunic was dark, hanging loose about his rugged frame. Leather greaves, studded with steel, protected his forearms while a similarly reinforced hide tasset hung from his belt and skirted his waist. The expression on the warrior's face was intense, and there was an almost feverish light in his gray eyes. In his fist he clenched a broad-bladed sword. "Come at me," he repeated, goading the visibly intimidated man who stood opposite him. "If you can manage to hit me, know there isn't a dog in Gunnar's army you won't be able to kill."

Hogun's pupil rushed at him with a snarl, swinging his sword wide. Hogun twisted around and in an almost effortless motion slapped the wrist of his opponent with the flat of his blade. Stunned, the man dropped his sword. A kick of Hogun's boot sent it skittering along the floor. Before the student could react, the instructor had one arm locked around his neck and the point of his sword pressing against his ribs.

"Never let your emotions provoke you," Hogun explained

to the rebels around him. "Harness your anger, but don't let it control you." He shoved his captive to rejoin the others in the ring. "In a fight, the first one who makes a mistake is the one who dies. Remember that and you might have a chance against mercenaries who place more value on gold than they do on life." His eyes roved across the watching rebels. "Alright, who's next?"

Fandral turned Vigdis away as a hesitant pupil stepped forward to match Hogun. "They're fortunate he's using a sword," he told Vigdis. "If he was using his mace, there'd be a lot of broken bones."

"I thought the idea was to teach them to fight," Vigdis said.

"Some lessons come harder than others," Fandral replied. "They don't call my friend Hogun the Grim without reason, but however strict he might be, it's better he shows someone where their swordplay's weak than to have them discover it when they're fighting Gunnar's men."

They continued across the cellar to another circle of rebels. Cracks of wood striking against wood rang out in swift succession from their midst. As Fandral and Vigdis approached, they could see two rebels sparring against each other with quarterstaves. Their tutor sat on a bench and bellowed instructions to them when he wasn't biting into a roasted goat leg or taking a swig from a stein of ale.

"That's good!" he roared, then wagged the partly eaten leg at one of the combatants. "Not you, the other one! Your defense is too low! You'll get your skull cracked by anybody taller than a dwarf if you try that in a fight!" He dropped the leg onto a trencher and tore into a wheel of cheese.

"I see what you mean," Vigdis said with a frown. "Hogun's at least working to teach my people how to fight."

Fandral took a deep breath. He understood why Vigdis was annoyed. What she didn't understand was just how keen Volstagg's hearing was.

"I'm working. You just can't see it," Volstagg grumbled, dropping the cheese back onto the trencher and wiping his fingers on his leggings. He stood up, proving himself to be a hulking figure. Nearly seven feet tall, weighing three times any of the rebels around him, Volstagg seemed built on the scale of a troll rather than an Asgardian. The prodigious girth of his belly was paired with the brawny musculature of his limbs to present a figure not unlike that of a great bear. Massive as his frame was, his clothes boasted an opulent finery that even Fandral deemed ostentatious. The buckle of the belt that circled his waist was gold, the buttons of his tunic were emerald, the blue cape that hung from his shoulders was silk. He wore a silver cap that sported plumes from some bird so exotic few had ever seen its like.

Volstagg motioned the sparring rebels to part and lumbered towards Fandral and Vigdis. He stroked his thick red beard and gave Fandral a questioning look. Fandral rolled his eyes. It was Volstagg's humor to immediately assume any woman he saw Fandral with was a new paramour.

"Allow me to introduce Vigdis, the courier we've been expecting," Fandral said. "This is Volstagg, better known as Volstagg the Voluminous." He smiled and then added, "Or as the credulous sometimes call him, Lord Volstagg. At least until they know better."

The big Asgardian straightened to his full height and

stared down at Fandral. "Humility has ever been my weakness. By rights, I could be addressed as King Volstagg. I was declared such by the people of–"

"Until they wised up and thought over what they'd done," Fandral interrupted whatever extravagant claims would follow. Volstagg wasn't exactly a liar, but sometimes he'd tie the truth into such knots that it hurt Fandral's brain to try to follow the braggart's convoluted thinking. He'd always suspected his friend's bravado was Volstagg's way of bolstering his self-confidence whenever a glimmer of doubt started to nag at him.

Volstagg skirted past Fandral's interruption and instead addressed the accusation Vigdis had made. "I assure you, I am instructing these stalwart fighters in the most practical manner." He snapped his fingers, and one of his students tossed him a quarterstaff. He cast an appraising eye over it and nodded. "Good stout wood," he said. He leaned close and made a show of smelling the staff. "I'd say this was harvested in Hindi before last winter, in a grove not far from Ringsfjord." He leveled his eyes on Vigdis. "This is a good weapon and will serve an ordinary fighter well in battle."

Suddenly Volstagg took a step back and spun around with a speed that Fandral always found startling from someone of his size. The quarterstaff came smacking down against the floor and instantly exploded into splinters along half its length. Volstagg let the remainder of the shattered weapon clatter to the ground and turned back to Vigdis. "I was breaking too many staves and your rebellion doesn't have enough supplies to spare. So we decided it was better if I just sat down and coached my pupils from the side."

"Volstagg is very practical when it affords him a chance to eat," Fandral laughed.

"I have to keep up my strength," Volstagg objected. He nodded to Vigdis. "Which as you see is considerable. Considerable strength, considerable appetite. There's always a balance to these things. Besides, as leader of the Warriors Three–"

Fandral glared at his friend. "The what?" he demanded, mockingly reaching for his sword.

Volstagg made a placating gesture with his hands. "Alright, let's say instead the moral foundation of our association. The anchor, if you will."

Fandral could only maintain the pretense of anger for a few seconds, then laughed heartily. "By Nidhogg's tail, you disarm me there. You're certainly the anchor."

"Away with you," Volstagg smiled. "I've fighters here who are just beginning to show some real talent. I can't have you interrupting their lessons." He nodded to Vigdis, then turned and clapped his hands together. "Alright, you in the red! Yes, the one who looks like a sea serpent scared his mother. I want you to see what you can do with that lout in brown. Yes, I'm talking about you. I don't care if you've already sparred three times, now you get to go again. If you want to rest, then learn to do it right."

Vigdis looked back as Volstagg returned to his bench and the pupils he'd chosen squared off. "Maybe I was wrong," she said.

"Volstagg takes some getting used to," Fandral admitted, "but believe me when I say he's a good man to have on your side in a fight."

"But will it be enough?" Vigdis asked, a quiver in her voice. "Even with the Warriors Three helping us, can we really depose King Gunnar?"

Fandral was quiet a moment. He had often been accused of having a glib tongue, but not so glib as to give someone false hope. He'd seen for himself that Gunnar was ruthless and the soldiers who served him were equally vicious. Inwardly he was convinced that the tyrant would be overthrown. What he wasn't sure was if the price of freedom would be too dire for the town to endure.

"Let's get you to Haklang," Fandral told Vigdis. "Maybe once you've delivered your message, we'll all of us know better how the odds are stacked."

THREE

Haklang was an old man, his skin darkened by the desert sun, his hair bleached by the erosion of time, but for all his years he retained a powerful build and a robust manner. When he saw Fandral and Vigdis approaching, his eyes lit up with eagerness and he rose from the table where he'd been holding conference with some of the other rebels.

"By the grace of Frigga, you've made it through!" Haklang exclaimed. He hurried forwards and clasped Vigdis' arm in a warrior's greeting. "Gunnar's put more than the usual number of patrols out in the streets."

Fandral nodded. "Vigdis had trouble with some of Gunnar's dogs. They weren't too happy when the odds changed from one against five and became two against five." His tone shifted from light to somber. "There will be some empty beds in the tyrant's barracks tonight."

"They didn't get the message I bear from Arnfinn," Vigdis reported. She bowed her head to Haklang and ran her hands through her long hair. She soon removed a slip of parchment that had been pinned beneath her tresses and proffered it to the old man.

Haklang set the message down on the table and leaned over it, his nose only inches from the page. After perusing it for some moments, he looked up and regarded the rebels around him. His face was rigid with tension. One finger tapped against the parchment. "Arnfinn advises that the swords we're expecting from Ringsfjord will be arriving on the morrow."

Fandral's expression grew as grave as that of the rebel leader. "There's some trickery in that message. We shouldn't be receiving any swords from Ringsfjord. Why would Arnfinn..." He snapped his fingers as the answer came to him. "A warning, hidden in such a way that someone reading it might not recognize it as such."

"Exactly," Haklang said. "This can only mean Arnfinn has been discovered and was forced to write that message."

Vigdis turned to Fandral. "When I was given that message, Arnfinn told me something curious. He said I wasn't to come back and should stay with Haklang's group."

Fandral felt a wave of unease rush through him. He grabbed Vigdis' arm. "Do you remember his exact words?" he asked. "Did Arnfinn say 'stay' or did he say 'join'?" He looked to Haklang. "There's an important distinction if what I fear is true."

Vigdis closed her eyes and thought about her last meeting with Arnfinn. "Yes," she said at last. "He did say I was to join Haklang's fighters."

"Loki take me for an idiot," Fandral berated himself. He gave Vigdis a sympathetic look. "I'm afraid we've both been

Three Swords   31

taken advantage of. That patrol we fought was just a decoy. Something to speed us on our way."

"You're always a cautious one, Fandral," Haklang objected. "Surely you didn't let anyone follow you."

"No," Fandral conceded, "but Gunnar might have some small idea of where this hideout is by this time. He might have spies scattered around the district to keep watch." Even as he said it, his mind turned back to the ragged beggar in the street outside. Spinning around, he dashed back across the cellar and up to the barred main doors. Drawing back a small aperture, he was able to see the lane outside. The mendicant who'd been there before was gone, though Fandral could see the alms bowl lying there abandoned.

Fandral turned back to the basement hall, every speck of his being filled with foreboding. His race through the cellar had provoked alarm among the rebels. When he turned, he found that they'd broken away from their training and congregated at the base of the steps. Hogun and Volstagg were at the forefront of the group.

"I'll assume you've a good excuse for denying my pupils the expert training only Volstagg the Heroic can bestow upon them," Volstagg's boisterous voice rang out. The humor of his tone didn't reach his eyes, however. Fandral could tell his friend was well aware something serious was happening. His pretense of boastful confidence was to ease the alarmed rebels. At least until they knew what was going on.

Fandral saw no use in keeping the truth from anyone. "A few minutes ago, there was a beggar outside," he said, projecting his voice for the whole cellar to hear. "He's gone now, but he left his alms bowl behind. Now, I don't know about beggars in Gunnarsfell, but I've never known one so prosperous that he'll forget to take his bowl when he moves on."

"A spy," Hogun declared. "Gone to summon the king's soldiers."

Frightened murmurs spread among the rebels when they heard Hogun. Fandral thought it a credit to both their fortitude and discipline that their alarm didn't go further. There was concern, but no panic.

"What'll we do?" one of the archers asked, his question rising above the tumult.

Haklang forced his way to the front of the crowd and looked back at his people. "We do what we've been training to do," he announced, raising his hand and clenching it into a fist. "We fight Gunnar's dogs and send them into Hela's keeping!" The old man's words were greeted by loud cheers from his people.

"No!" Fandral shouted. He waved his arms, commanding attention from the rebels. "You court disaster to fight Gunnar's men here." He pointed at Haklang. "When the Warriors Three came to Gunnarsfell to help you, we did so not merely to teach your people how to fight but also to advise you when to fight. Listen to me now when I tell you that this is not the place to meet the tyrant's dogs."

The crowd fell silent as Fandral continued to speak. Their weeks of training under the Warriors Three had impressed in them a deep respect for the heroes. They attended Fandral's words with rapt focus.

"Gunnar certainly knows we're in the Vanquished Dragon

Three Swords 33

now," Fandral said. Unconsciously his gaze drifted to Vigdis. He saw color rush into her face and knew the courier was feeling guilt that she'd played a part in exposing the hideout. "If you fight his soldiers here, then you'll be fighting them on ground of their choosing."

"What then are we to do?" one of the rebels asked.

Hogun set his intense gaze on the man, then turned his eyes across the crowd. "Temper your pride and retreat," he stated. "Escape the trap. Later you will fight. Fight at a time and place that you've chosen, not Gunnar."

Fandral pointed at Haklang. "Have your people start slipping out the back in small groups. Scatter across the town. Find other places to hide and bide your time." The old man nodded, seeing the wisdom in Fandral's advice.

Vigdis stepped forward, suspicion in her eyes. "What about you?" she said, gesturing at the Warriors Three.

Volstagg laughed and gulped down the rest of the mead in his stein. "Someone needs to act as a rearguard while the rest of you get away." He puffed himself up and looked aside at Hogun and Fandral. "Now, I could do it myself, but I wouldn't want to deny my friends a share in the glory."

"There's more at stake here than glory," Fandral said, annoyed at Volstagg's choice of words. If there was anything that would make the rebels hold their ground against any other advice, it was the promise of glory. "You've a tyrant to topple. Knowing the town, you also know how to keep clear of his soldiers." He waved his hand to indicate himself and his friends. "We're outlanders and far less able to remain inconspicuous. Therefore, in the crisis of the moment, we're the most expendable."

"Odin watch over you," Haklang said, taking Fandral's hand before turning to start sending groups of rebels out the back.

Vigdis walked up to Fandral. "If you need to stay, let me fight beside you."

Fandral slowly shook his head. He leaned close to Vigdis. "I know you can fight," he told her in an undertone, "but if I let you stay, others will want to as well. The only chance your people have is to escape this trap, reorganize, and strike back when opportunity favors your side, not Gunnar's."

For a moment, defiance shone on Vigdis' face. Then she nodded. She knew Fandral was right, that if she stayed to fight, others would insist on doing the same. She pressed her lips against Fandral's cheek. Her eyes glistened with emotion when she drew away. "For luck," she told him, before hurrying away from the steps.

Fandral pressed his hand to his cheek and watched as Vigdis disappeared into the crowd. "Thank you, good lady," he whispered. "We may just need all the luck we can get."

"Well, maybe I wasn't so wrong at that," Volstagg chuckled, slapping Fandral on the back. "Don't worry, you'll see her again soon enough. Once these sellswords see they must strive against the Warriors Three, they'll turn tail and run!"

Hogun didn't offer a rejoinder to Volstagg, instead rushing up the stairs to keep watch at the aperture. Fandral stopped one of the archers before the rebel could join the throng dispersing by the back way and relieved him of his bow and quiver. He tested the tautness of the string and then evaluated the angle from the base of the steps to the door.

"Our enemies might be more impressed by Gunnar's

gold than they are by your boasting," Fandral softly chided Volstagg. "I rather fear we'll have to be more forceful with them."

Volstagg drew his sword, the blade crackling with an enchanted light. "Let them come. They'll join all the others in Hel who've cause to rue crossing blades with me." He looked askance at the bow in Fandral's hands. "If you leave any to cross blades, that is. How many of them do you plan to drop with that thing?"

Fandral ran his hand across the feathered shafts protruding from the quiver. "I've twenty arrows, so I'd be presumptuous to think I could kill twenty-one," he joked. "Even if I bag my limit, I suspect Gunnar will still have enough men to keep you and Hogun busy." He wished he felt as confident as he sounded. Intent on destroying a hideout of the rebels who'd caused him so much trouble, the tyrant would send a large force to spring his trap. Enough soldiers, perhaps, to overwhelm even the Warriors Three.

Hogun turned from the aperture. "They're coming," he said.

Fandral glanced back at the rebels. Only about a quarter of them had been sent out the back way. Haklang was trying to keep the groups small enough to avoid being spotted once they reached the warren of alleyways. Fandral caught Haklang's eye. "Whatever happens, keep them moving," he told him. He spotted Vigdis and added words in an even firmer tone. "If your people don't escape, everything will be undone. If we fall here, it will be up to you to avenge us by deposing King Gunnar."

Nocking an arrow to his bow, Fandral stood at the base

of the steps and faced the door. Soon enough, he knew, the Vanquished Dragon would change from a training ground to a battlefield.

The first sign of movement on the street almost went unnoticed even by Hogun's wary gaze. But eyes that have spent their childhood watching for ice trolls and snow lions become especially sensitive to the least hint of motion, the only warning of predators who blend completely into the snowfields they stalk. Hogun spotted the head that briefly emerged from a darkened alley to stare at the Vanquished Dragon. He reached to his belt and untied his mace from the loop it was attached to. Still keeping his gaze on the aperture, he wound the bindings around his wrist. In the battle that was coming, he didn't want to risk losing his weapon.

"They're here," Hogun called down. He glanced at the cellar. Less than a third of Haklang's rebels had been able to slip away. That would mean a lengthy defense to hold Gunnar's mercenaries back, and a fair bit of luck that they could fight their way past any soldiers sent to cut off the other exit.

From his vantage, Hogun now saw the enemy clearly. No more slinking in the shadows. Ready to assault the tavern, the mercenaries marched openly in double ranks. Those in the forefront carried iron bars to wrench aside the boards across the doors. Hogun could also see men carrying a steel-headed battering ram to smash through the portal and the beams the rebels had used to bolster it from the inside.

Hogun turned from the door and dashed down the steps.

Three Swords 37

He nodded to Fandral and joined Volstagg at the foot of the stairs. "I could see about forty, but there are certainly more." He paused as they heard the sound of the boards that sealed the door being wrenched away. "Of course they have a ram," he added. The next instant the cellar echoed with the boom of the ram being driven against the doors. They could see them shudder in their frame. Flecks of plaster fell from the ceiling as the impact rippled through the mead hall.

"How long?" Fandral asked. Hogun was always surprised by the different moods the handsome Asgardian entertained. Jocular and irreverent in the thick of a fray, it was in those moments immediately before a fight that he grew tense.

"Haklang's people reinforced those doors well," Hogun said. "I don't expect them to break through before the fifth hit."

Volstagg glanced back at the provisions stacked behind the bar. "Not enough time to empty another keg," he sighed. "Inconsiderate of the dogs. I hate to leave so much good food and drink for Gunnar's ruffians."

"Then you'll just have to make sure there aren't so many of them around to enjoy it after the fight," Fandral said. He kept his bow drawn and fixed on the doors. The panels now suffered their third hit from the ram and the wood began to crack.

Hogun felt his own blood begin to stir. His heart beat like a war drum, whipping up the ferocity that was locked beneath his controlled and reserved mien. He felt the call to battle as a drunkard knows the temptation of the bottle. It took all his self-restraint to keep from rushing up the steps and throwing aside the barriers that held back the enemy.

"Soon," he whispered to the violent urging. "Soon there will be blood enough."

The next hit from the ram splintered the doors and drove a hole through the panel. Fandral loosed an arrow almost the instant light shone through from the street. A cry of pain told that he sent the missile speeding into one of the soldiers outside. "That should give them pause," he commented as he nocked another arrow. "And buy our friends more time to get away." Now that he was in the fight, his humor was returning.

"Just don't go scaring them off and hogging all the glory," Volstagg complained. "It would be criminal to deny these rats the chance to end their miserable lives crossing swords with Volstagg the Mighty." He looked over at Hogun and smiled. "I'm sure you want to crack a few skulls with that egg-smasher of yours as well."

Hogun just nodded. He looked back to see how the rebel exodus was progressing. Almost half of Haklang's people were out of the cellar now. With the soldiers almost inside, the rebels were being sent out in larger groups, the threat of being caught in the streets lessening before the danger of being trapped in the cellar.

True to Fandral's suggestion, the arrow he'd sent through the hole did curb the eagerness of Gunnar's soldiers. Their attack on the door faltered, and Hogun could hear an angry officer shouting at his men. Though his lust for battle railed against the pause, Hogun knew they were gaining something more valuable than dead enemies. They were giving the rebels more time to escape.

Soon enough the battering ram was back in action. As it smashed into the doors, Fandral sent another arrow through

Three Swords

the hole. His unerring aim was borne out by a wretched scream from outside. Whatever threats or promises made by the officer kept his troops on the attack, however, and the ram immediately crashed into the doors again. Bracing beams fell away as they broke loose.

"I overestimated the sturdiness of those doors. The next strike or the one after should break them," Hogun told his companions.

The door groaned as the ram was driven home once more, its metal head punching through. A third arrow sped into the widened hole as the steel-capped ram was withdrawn. Hogun could see it hit one of the men bearing the ram, sinking into his thigh. The soldier tumbled away, but his place was instantly taken by another mercenary.

With a booming crack, the doors buckled and were driven inwards. Fandral sent an arrow into the chest of the soldier at the forefront of the siege crew, spilling him back into those behind him. The disruption caused the rest of the mercenaries to drop the heavy battering ram. There was a sickening crunch as the steel-headed log landed on one of the men knocked over by Fandral's shot.

The mercenaries unlimbered swords and axes. More soldiers swarmed through the broken doors and onto the steps.

Hogun glared up at the invaders, a wolfish smile on his face. He wondered if Gunnar's thugs had any idea how much trouble they were in.

FOUR

Fandral sent arrows speeding up at the mercenaries as they breached the door, knowing there was no better opportunity to strike them than while they were clumped together. The arm gripping his bow was rigid while his right hand was a blur, pulling arrows from his quiver and drawing in a continuous motion. His eye merely lighted upon a target before he loosed, each missile slamming into a soldier and pitching him to the floor.

"Come along!" Fandral shouted defiantly. "I promise you'll earn your blood money this day, my friends!" He shot an arrow into a mercenary charging down the steps. It pierced the mail the man wore and the shaft sank up to its feathers in his belly. With a groan, the soldier crashed onto his side and his dying frame tumbled down the steps.

For just an instant the attack faltered, then the soldiers took up the battering ram once more. An arrow punched through the helm of one of the men, but there were still enough to lift the metal-headed log. With a mighty heave, six mercenaries sent the ram clattering down the steps. The Warriors Three were forced to disperse as it came hurtling down into the cellar.

"You'll suffer for that indignity!" Volstagg thundered. In his retreat he'd blundered against one of the tables and upended it. The sight of the big Asgardian rising from the wreckage was, as he said, far from dignified.

Hogun brandished his spiked mace at the rebels still in the cellar. Many of them had turned to rush back to help. "Out with you, or all of this is for naught," he growled at them, his voice as vicious as a wolf's snarl. The warning sufficed. Fandral saw the rebels turn back to the Vanquished Dragon's hidden exit.

Mercenaries were racing down the steps in the wake of the ram. Fandral leaped onto a table and took aim, sending more arrows into the throng. Men shrieked as their bodies were pierced and they careened from the stairs. "That's it, you knaves! Get closer so I can't fail to hit you!" The taunting shouts were bluster that would have stood Volstagg in good stead. Fandral knew the moment was before him when he'd have to throw aside the bow and take up his sword, Fimbuldraugr. On the steps, with arrows whipping among them, the very numbers of their enemy worked against Gunnar's soldiers, but when it came to melee it would be a different matter. Three against fifty or sixty were long odds, even for the Warriors Three.

The first soldier who lunged into the cellar was sent sailing across the room by a brutal swing of Hogun's mace, Hridgandr. A second and a third converged on him only to meet an equally savage finish. Fandral could see the ferocious intensity in Hogun's eyes, a vicious rapture more akin to the mania of a berserker than any normal man. More soldiers rushed in to take the place of the fallen, and while they couldn't bring down Hogun, they were forcing him back. Foot by foot, they were gaining ground.

"You've tasted my arrows, now sample my sword," Fandral jeered at the mercenaries. He jumped down from the table, landing before a clutch of soldiers trying to flank Hogun. Fimbuldraugr snarled through the air in a jaunty flourish that startled his enemies. "One at a time or all at once, as you prefer," Fandral grinned. The first soldier to react to his goading charged at him. The mercenary's blade was a monstrous sword that demanded both arms to swing. There was no question of trying to parry such a blow with his own rakish weapon. Instead, he dodged to the side at the last second, letting the heavy sword cleave through the space he'd so recently occupied. Before the foeman could recover from the ponderous attack, Fandral slashed at his neck. The soldier dropped his blade and stumbled away, clutching at his bleeding throat.

Other soldiers came at Fandral in a wild surge then. One after another, he darted among them, avoiding their attacks while delivering cuts of his own. The press of enemies made it impossible to deal the sort of wounds he'd have preferred. Forced to give each soldier only the most momentary consideration, Fandral simply blooded each one before turning to the next, stunning them for the moment rather than removing them from the fray entirely. Such weakening tactics could prevail, for he knew his stamina could surpass that of most fighters, but Gunnar's troops had fresh reserves running down the stairs to join them.

A bench went flying through the air, smashing the skull of the soldier it struck and knocking down two of his comrades. Volstagg's voice boomed across the mead hall. "What, is everyone in this rout such a coward he'd not test himself against Volstagg the Fierce!" His dwarf-made sword glowed with a bright blue light as he shook it at the mercenaries. "Valhalla isn't for the likes of such feckless scoundrels," he grumbled. "Oh for an adversary worthy of my time!"

The press of soldiers around Fandral lessened as many of them submitted to Volstagg's insults and angrily rushed to give battle to the towering warrior. Fandral seized the advantage, not knowing how long this reprieve would last. He spun away from one enemy's axe and darted back to thrust his sword into the chest of the soldier coming at him from behind. The man dropped, blood bubbling from his mouth, his blade clattering to the floor. Fandral completed the corkscrewing twist he'd adopted and slashed at the legs of the axeman, cutting them to the bone and leaving the mercenary writhing on the ground.

More soldiers swarmed down into the cellar. Fandral was beginning to wonder if Gunnar hadn't sent his entire army to attack the tavern. Every sellsword he cut down seemed to have his place taken by two more. Sooner rather than later, their numbers would prevail over the heroes.

"The last rebels are out!" Hogun's shout reached Fandral. He saw the champion bring his mace whipping about in a sweeping wave that crushed the bones of those who failed to leap aside. With the area immediately around him cleared, he withdrew from the melee and hastened towards the rear exit.

Fandral took the opposite approach. Instead of driving off his foes, he now used their numbers to assist him. Darting between the men with the facility of a weasel, he forced them to show restraint lest they strike their own comrades. A few pained cries told of mercenaries who were too slow to arrest their swings.

"Volstagg! We're leaving!" Fandral shouted to the enormous swordsman.

"Don't be hasty!" Volstagg shouted back. He brained a soldier with the pommel of his sword, then snatched a second mercenary by the neck with his free hand. Shaking the man like a terrier with a rat, his captive was soon senseless. Volstagg held him forth like a living shield as he plowed into the soldiers, scattering them to either side as he forced his way across the cellar.

"Interesting tactic," Fandral nodded at the insensate human shield.

"You may now call me Volstagg the Inventive," the huge warrior declared. He frowned at his captive and spun around. Soldiers were regrouping to charge them. Volstagg decided to disrupt their plans. "You want him back so badly, you can have him." He flung the unconscious sellsword into his comrades. The man struck as though he'd been launched from a catapult. Mercenaries were bowled over by the impact and those still standing were thrown into confusion.

"They'll get their bearings soon enough," Fandral said. He drew aside the hanging and rushed up the back stairs. Hogun and Volstagg hurried after him.

The back door stood open and Fandral could see bodies sprawled in the alcove outside. Both those of mercenaries and rebels. At some point, Gunnar's men had noted the withdrawal and sent part of their force to cut off the escape. There weren't enough dead rebels for them to have succeeded, and, as the Warriors Three hurried down the winding path, Fandral considered that most of Haklang's people had profited by the rearguard's delay.

"Gunnar will have to set more dogs to sniff out his rebels now," Fandral laughed as they neared the street. Then his eyes fell upon one of the bodies. A youth who'd been mangled by an axe. His heart sickened to recognize Lothgar among the dead. He paused in his steps and stared down at the slain sentry. His fingers tightened about the grip of Fimbuldraugr. "I've a mind to stay right here and kill every murderer who takes the tyrant's coin."

"Tarry here and you'll get your chance," Hogun snapped. He grabbed Fandral by the shoulder and pushed him towards the street. Fandral could hear mercenaries rushing into the alcove behind them. Others would be charging down the street to cut them off. To linger would be to court disaster, and to no purpose.

"You will be avenged," Fandral promised Lothgar's ghost as the heroes dashed out into the street.

"Across to the alley!" Volstagg enjoined his companions. There was already a swarm of soldiers hurrying away from the tavern and charging towards them. The ones who'd chased after them up the back stairs wouldn't be far behind. Fandral's plan had worked so far as letting most of the rebels get away, but all things considered, he thought a bit more attention could have been paid to how they were going to make their own escape.

Hogun and Fandral rushed past Volstagg as they left the street. The huge Asgardian found the narrow passage a tight squeeze. He had to expel his breath to push through and held it until he was at the next juncture. He found his friends waiting for him. "These Skornheimers didn't build to suit my kingly frame," he complained after refilling his lungs.

"You'll forgive them. They only have a snake like Gunnar to play on their notions of what makes a king," Fandral said. Volstagg had expected some friendly quip about over-indulgence, instead there was a cold fury in Fandral's tone that surprised him.

"Once we're clear of our pursuit we can start thinking about how to shorten Gunnar's reign," Hogun said. He gestured with his mace to a turn off to their left.

"How do you know that's the best way?" Volstagg asked.

"I don't," Hogun replied, already running towards the turn. Fandral jogged after him.

Volstagg shook his head. "It's certain enough we can't go back and can't stay here," he muttered. Already the clamor of pursuit was at their heels. He hurried after his companions, sticking to their tracks.

The turn suggested by Hogun led into another juncture of narrow lanes. "I wish we'd had thought to keep one of the locals with us," Volstagg observed. "Vigdis seemed to know her way pretty well."

"She's well out of it," Fandral said. "I hope she's found a

safe place and has sense enough to stay there until things quiet down."

Hogun gestured with his mace, again to the left. The choice made, the three heroes started down the passageway.

"We keep running blind like this, we're sure to trap ourselves," Volstagg told his friends. He gestured with his thumb at the pursuers who were just around the last turn. "They've probably already sent soldiers to cut us off."

"You saying you want to give up?" Fandral asked.

The question irked Volstagg. "Give up? This is Volstagg the Valiant you're talking to! Did I suggest giving up when we were surrounded by fire demons in the vaults of Melthion? Did I suggest we run away when the ice giants were after us in Cragmire Cavern?" He drew a deep breath and sighed. "What I'm saying is we need a plan."

"Agreed. What is it?" Fandral tossed the problem back to him.

Volstagg stumbled, shocked by the turnabout. He quickly recovered, following his companions as Hogun brought them around another turn. "Me? I was counting on you to have an idea this time. I can't do all the planning."

"I thought you were the leader," Fandral said.

Volstagg smiled. "Nice as it is to hear you admit it, you should also know that a capable leader recognizes the talents of those he leads. Your knack is coming up with plans, so let's hear one now."

"I've only one idea, but you won't like it," Fandral told him.

"How do you know that until you've told me what it is?" Volstagg retorted.

Fandral turned his head and gave him one of his sly grins. "My plan is that we make it up as we go along."

"I don't like it," Volstagg frowned.

Fandral shrugged. "I said you wouldn't."

Another turn ahead. This time as they started down the alley, Volstagg spotted a doorway on their right. It was suddenly thrown open. He whipped around with his sword, ready to strike down an ambusher, but instead he saw only an old man with a long white beard who beckoned to him with a withered finger.

Volstagg whistled, drawing the attention of his friends. He nodded at the old man in the doorway.

"Quick, this way. Before the soldiers see you," the white beard called to them.

Hogun swung back, his mace gripped tight in both hands. "How do we know it isn't a trap?"

Volstagg stepped over to the door. Before the old man could move, he closed one of his big hands on the elder's shoulder. "If this is a trap, you'll be the first to regret it."

Maintaining his hold on the elder, Volstagg followed him through the door. Inside was a room of unremarkable size but most remarkable furnishings. Bundles of dried herbs hung from the ceiling, bottles of strangely colored fluids filled a set of shelves, the mummified body of a dwarf or goblin grinned from where it leaned against a wall. Most telling of all was the curious design picked out on the floor in vibrantly hued powders. Where each line of the design crossed, the meeting was marked by a smooth stone on which a rune was etched.

Volstagg heard Fandral and Hogun follow after him,

Three Swords

heard the door slam shut behind him, heard the sound of the soldiers rushing down the alleyway. He knew he should be worried that the mercenaries would discover where they'd gone, but at the moment all he could do was stare at the old man. As though the shoulder he held had turned white-hot, he drew away his hand.

"Are... are you a seer?" Volstagg stammered.

The old man bowed his head. "Indeed, I am Onund Gerisson." He stepped away from Volstagg and looked over at Fandral and Hogun. The two were still by the door, weapons at the ready. "There's no need to fear. Gunnar's men cannot hear anything that happens here. Indeed, they cannot even see the door through which you came."

Hogun turned to face Onund, Hridgandr still at the ready, the fierceness in his eyes burning even brighter. "Sorcery," he spat.

"Magic," Onund corrected him. "Magic that has enabled me to rescue you from Gunnar's ruffians."

"You've done us a good service," Volstagg laughed, both to allay his own uneasiness and to mitigate Hogun's hostility. "Not that we couldn't have fought our way through a few hundred of Gunnar's ruffians, mind. Why, against Volstagg the–"

"It has been my experience that magic is seldom used frivolously and never without a cost," Fandral interrupted Volstagg. "Might we inquire why you've done us this good turn?"

Volstagg was annoyed by the intrusion but admitted Fandral made a good point. Seers were mysterious in their methods and rarely generous with their spells. "If you're an enemy of Gunnar, your magic would be greatly appreciated by the rebels."

Onund stepped around the design on the floor, careful not to disturb the colored powders. "I care nothing of King Gunnar, either for or against," he said. He pointed at the runestones arrayed between the lines. "My concern is for what my art has revealed to me. A peril that threatens all Asgard and perhaps the whole of the Nine Realms."

The seer let his dire words linger for a moment before locking eyes with Volstagg. He saw now that they were mismatched, one being a dull gray while the other was a deep brown. Both were alike in the sense of power they evoked.

"I foresaw your coming to Gunnarsfell and prepared for it," Onund said. "I have helped you, Warriors Three, because I need your help. I need you to help me save Asgard."

FIVE

"Help a wizard?" Hogun fixed Onund with a gaze that was intense with hate. The fury boiled up inside him, needing only the least excuse to be unleashed. His family had been killed, his homeland conquered and despoiled by a wizard. These were events that had branded themselves upon his very soul. Trusting the wizard Mogul was a mistake that had doomed his people. Hogun would not make that same mistake.

"He helped us get away from Gunnar's soldiers," Volstagg reminded Hogun. He shrugged and shook his head. "The least we can do is give him the courtesy of hearing what he has to say."

Hogun kept his attention riveted on Onund, estimating how many steps it would take him to reach the seer and crush his head with Hridgandr. "A snake's tongue isn't so forked as that of a wizard. They speak only in lies."

"I know what Mogul of the Mystic Mountain did to your

homeland," Fandral reminded Hogun, "but there are some who use magic for good instead of evil." He nodded at Onund. "So far the seer has given me no reason to suspect ill of him." Fandral sheathed Fimbuldraugr and folded his arms across his chest. "Let him speak and we'll judge the merit of what he has to say."

Onund bowed to Fandral, then turned to Hogun. "Your loathing of wizards stands you in good stead," the seer declared. "Most who practice magic become intoxicated by the power they can command and decide to harness it towards their own ends, no matter who suffers." He pulled at his beard and smiled. "Even your hate, Hogun the Grim, may find something to interest it in what I have to say."

"My companions have agreed to listen, but don't think to court my indulgence," Hogun cautioned Onund. "Speak your piece, and then we'll be on our way."

"On your way indeed, but to where is what we must discuss," Onund said. "I did not misspeak when I told you that there is a menace that even now threatens all Asgard. A menace that you, Hogun, will appreciate more keenly than your friends."

"Forget the preamble," Hogun growled. "What is this menace you claim is so perilous?"

The seer slowly circled the arcane design on the floor. "You call yourselves the Warriors Three. In your travels, have you perhaps heard talk of a cabal who style themselves the Enchanters Three?"

Volstagg laughed at the question. "Enchanters Three?" he chuckled. "Audacious swine, aren't they? Though I suppose if they're trying to imitate someone, they couldn't have chosen a braver warband than ours to copy!"

Onund didn't share the big Asgardian's humor. "I assure you they are anything but imitators. The Enchanters are powerful sorcerers from Ringsfjord." He turned and looked at Hogun. "Combined, they are mightier even than the dread Mogul who has inflicted so much harm upon you."

"Who are these Enchanters?" Fandral interjected.

"Three brothers, each deeply versed in the black arts, the most ruthless forms of magic." Onund pulled at his beard while he described the enchanters. "Magnir has focused upon the enchanting of objects, endowing blades with devastating powers and crafting armors capable of withstanding any blow. Brona's specialty is the transformation of living things, to shift the properties of one organism into another and make creatures that are neither." The seer paused, and for an instant a shiver of fear passed through him. "The eldest of the brothers is Forsung and his is the most terrible power of all. By his sorcery he is able to siphon the essence of demons and set it into mortal beings, changing them into ravening monsters."

Hogun was unimpressed by the catalog of horrors Onund described. "When Mogul conquered my lands, he commanded an army of demons and monsters. Your Enchanters sound no worse than he."

The seer raised his hand, motioning for Hogun to wait. "The Enchanters possess something no other wizard in any of the Nine Realms has. With it, their powers far surpass those of Mogul or any other sorcerer. Indeed, Forsung once challenged Odin himself and was only narrowly beaten by the All-Father."

Onund folded his hands against his chest. He spread

his fingers to create a diamond-like shape. "Each of the Enchanters wears a Living Talisman, a magical artifact they can employ to strengthen their spells. The Living Talismans endow them with the might of gods. They can use them to command reality itself and to manifest powerful elementals."

"So what you're asking us to do is chase down these warlocks and destroy their trinkets," Volstagg said. He snapped his fingers. "As easily done as that. Be sure to have a triumphal feast ready for us when we return!"

There was something very close to panic in Onund's visage. "No!" he enjoined Volstagg. "You must get the Living Talismans away from the Enchanters, but don't even think of destroying them! They represent such a concentration of raw magic that if you did manage to destroy one it would send fissures through the Nine Realms that would shake the World Tree to its roots! At the very least there would be earthquakes and tidal waves on an unimaginable scale." The seer fixed Volstagg with a frightened gaze. "Or the destruction of the talismans would set off a chain reaction of cosmic energies that would snap the bindings of time and space. Worlds and eras would fold into one another, consuming each place and moment in a spiral of primal chaos."

"We get it," Hogun said, "don't damage the talismans." He couldn't quite tell which vexed him more: Onund's fear of what could happen if the power contained in the talismans were unleashed or the notion that the Enchanters had been reckless enough to create things capable of causing such destruction. "Just don't try to tell me to be careful about damaging the wizards wearing them."

"You must get the Living Talismans away from the Enchanters," Onund answered. "How you do so is of no consequence provided the talismans aren't damaged."

Fandral stepped to the edge of the design on the floor, glancing at it for a moment before returning his attention to Onund. "You place a great deal of importance on these talismans. What will you have us do with them when we take them from the Enchanters? Since we're forbidden to destroy them, what will be done with them?"

"Aye, seer, what becomes of these infernal things?" Hogun echoed. He moved away from the door, drawing closer to Onund so the mystic would be within reach if he didn't like how he answered.

Onund closed his eyes and bowed his head. "They are too terrible to be trusted with anyone." He turned and pointed to an iron chest resting against the wall. "When you bring the talismans back, they will be put into that box."

Volstagg lumbered over and gave the chest a closer inspection. It was heavier than it looked, forcing the huge warrior to strain to lift it from the floor. He eventually gave up the effort. "What've you got in there, the Midgard Serpent?" he grumbled.

"There is nothing in there," Onund stated. He looked across at the other heroes. "The dwarves of Nidavellir crafted this chest, and I speak truly when I say that it contains nothing. An all-consuming nothing, an infinite emptiness."

"Why, there's no lock or hinge." Volstagg scratched his beard and stepped back, perplexed by the box. "How does it open?"

"It cannot be opened," Onund said. "To do so would undo the dwarves' work and destroy the emptiness they've trapped within."

Hogun scowled at the explanation. There was far too much magic about such things. "If it can't open, how will you use it to dispose of the talismans?"

Onund stepped past Volstagg and indicated a design on the top of the chest, a broad swirl of twisting knots that reminded Hogun of a maelstrom on the Sea of Fear. "Observe," Onund instructed. He removed a silver torc he wore on his arm and set it upon the design. "I will send it into the nothingness." His hands wove before him in arcane passes, and eldritch words rasped across his lips. Though the power of Allspeak was innate to every Asgardian, Hogun could make no sense of the litany. It was a facet of their trickery that mystics obscured their incantations in ways that confounded even the gods.

The result of Onund's spell wasn't obscure. The design on the box began to stir, writhing as though it were indeed a whirlpool and not a thing of metal. As it revolved faster and faster, the torc was drawn down into it. Like a sinking ship, the silver band was pulled beneath the surface to vanish into the chest.

The seer staggered back once the feat was accomplished, sweat dripping from his brow. "It is not so simple to send something into nothing," he said. He wagged a finger at the top of the box as the maelstrom design grew still once more. "It would take a magic far greater than mine to draw something out again. If it could be done at all." He smiled at the Warriors Three. "In there, the Living Talismans could cause no harm to anyone and the menace of the Enchanters would be broken for all time."

Hogun lunged at the seer, wrapping one arm across his neck as he seized him. He let Hridgandr drop from his hand and drew the knife from his belt. He pressed it against Onund's throat. "Bring it back," he hissed.

"By Ymir's beard, what do you think you're doing?" Volstagg bellowed, shocked by Hogun's sudden attack.

Fandral grabbed Volstagg's arm before he could try to intercede and pulled the huge warrior back. For just an instant, Hogun saw a sly gleam in Fandral's eyes.

"Bring it back," Hogun hissed again. He prodded the seer with the tip of his blade. "Bring it back, or there'll be one less wizard in Asgard."

"You'd better do as he says," Fandral encouraged Onund. "Hogun has little enough liking for magicians already."

Volstagg tried to pull away from Fandral's grip. "What are you..."

Fandral jabbed his elbow into Volstagg's side and gave him a warning look. Understanding quickly came into the big Asgardian's eyes.

"Better listen to him," Volstagg shouted at Onund. "There's nothing Hogun likes better than sending a wizard to speak with Queen Hela."

The seer's face grew paler and his body trembled. "But... I can't," he sputtered. "It's impossible."

"Bring it back," Hogun insisted.

Fandral watched the fear growing in Onund's eyes. He also watched Hogun. He was trusting his friend's instincts.

His suspicion that the seer could restore the talismans once they were drawn into the strange chest was something they had to verify or deny. He only hoped Hogun wouldn't take it too far.

"Bring it back." Hogun's voice was as sharp as the knife he held.

"I can't," Onund moaned. "You must believe me."

"No," Fandral corrected him. "You have to convince us." He stepped closer and studied Onund's face. "I'm more sympathetic than Hogun. I know not everyone who practices magic is a sorcerer who treats with demons."

Onund clenched his teeth as Hogun pricked his skin with the knife. A little bead of blood formed under the blade. "I can't… what you demand is impossible. Once something's been sent into the chest it would need the power of Odin himself to draw it out again." He winced as Hogun turned the knife and extended the cut. A thin rivulet of crimson dripped down the seer's neck.

"Kill me… but I can't make something happen that's beyond my power," Onund gasped.

Fandral shook his head and motioned Hogun back. Reluctantly, the dour fighter released the seer and stepped away. Fandral clapped his hand on Onund's shoulder.

"I'm sorry we had to put you through that," Fandral apologized. "But we had to try and prove your sincerity." He glanced at the dwarven chest. "The way you described these Living Talismans, we had to know we weren't just taking them from one villain and giving them to another."

Onund pressed a hand to his neck. "I understand," he said. "Far from resenting your vigilance, I applaud it." He turned to Hogun. "Ask me to invoke whatever vow you want and I will swear the ability to return something from within the chest is beyond my magic." The seer faced Fandral again. "Once the talismans are within the chest, we will take it to Odin's hall and present it to the All-Father for safekeeping. Let that allay any doubts of my conviction." Onund's expression became almost as grim as Hogun's.

"I have had visions of what will happen if the Enchanters aren't stopped," Onund said. "Left unchecked they will return to Asgard and overthrow Odin. They will be able to open a gateway to other realms and release an unstoppable army against their enemies. Against such a host, even Asgard will fall. Under their rule the Realm will descend into darkness and terror. An eternal night from which there will be no new dawning."

Volstagg cracked his fist into his palm. "The best way to deal with tyrants is to knock them down before they can stand," he said. He looked aside at Fandral, then turned to Hogun. "I never doubted you for a moment, Onund. My companions are a bit too cynical for their own good."

Fandral brushed aside Volstagg's interjection. "It will be a hard journey to Ringsfjord," he told Onund. "First we'll have to leave Gunnarsfell, which will be no easy task."

Volstagg nodded. "I admit, I've no liking for that. I don't like leaving Haklang's people to fend for themselves. It feels too much like abandoning them to Gunnar."

"They'll suffer much worse should the Enchanters rule Asgard," Onund pronounced. He looked to Fandral. "And it would be useless to journey into Ringsfjord. The Enchanters are no longer there. Instead, they have used their magic to disperse across the boundaries of time and space, far beyond the borders of Asgard."

"How then do we find them?" Fandral wondered. He had a feeling he wasn't going to like the answer. Where magic came into play, the solution was sometimes as confusing as the problem.

"My divinations have shown me where they are," Onund said. He walked about the room and gestured at the design on the floor. "I have prepared an astral circle that will send you across the streams of the Nine Realms, through the skeins of time and place." He looked at each of them in turn and smiled. "If you've the courage to make the journey, I can send you to where the Enchanters are."

"A moment ago, we didn't trust you when you claimed you couldn't bring things back from the chest," Fandral pointed out.

"True," Onund mused. He stared at the astral circle. "Still, if I meant you harm, there are far easier ways than this to do so."

"Well, that convinces me," Volstagg declared. He swaggered towards the seer. "Alright, so you'll use your spells to send us speeding away from Asgard. If you're willing to annoy Heimdall, don't think that Volstagg the Bold is too timid to try."

Onund held up his finger in warning. "The Enchanters have employed their magic to slip into times and places even Heimdall cannot peer into." He pointed again at the design with its intersecting lines and runestones. "To send you where they've gone, I must use sympathetic magic. There will be no one who can help you and only I will know where you've gone."

"Enough talk," Hogun growled. "If we're going to kill these wizards, then let's be about it."

"Step into the circle," Onund invited, waving Hogun forward. "Don't touch the lines and keep within the outer ring."

"One moment," Fandral said even as Hogun started toward the circle. "We're supposed to bring back the Living Talismans as well as defeat the Enchanters. How will we recognize them?"

The seer smiled at the question and seemed on the cusp of laughter. "Forgive me," he said, "but if you had once seen the Living Talismans, even in a prophetic vision, you would know there's no confusing them for anything else." Once more he folded his hands against his chest and spread his fingers in a diamond pattern. "Each Living Talisman is a fabulous jewel about this size. The Enchanters are never without them and wear them fastened to their armor. The jewels themselves shift and change in color, but always they will display an animation, a presence that manifests as a malignant visage staring out from the depths of the stone. No, do not worry that you'll fail to recognize the Living Talismans when you see them."

Fandral was quiet for a moment, digesting the seer's description. "They sound as forbidding as the powers you ascribe them."

"They are far worse," Onund said. He watched as the Warriors Three carefully picked their way into the circle. "I must remain here to cast the spell that will return you to Asgard. My magic will alert me when you have captured a Living Talisman."

"Where exactly is it that you're sending us?" Volstagg had a tremor to his voice now. Fandral knew he was thinking of his family. It was one thing to be away from his wife and children in some other part of Asgard, but quite different to be separated by the incalculable gulf that Onund promised.

"I send you to the place and time where Magnir has hidden himself," Onund replied. "Of the Enchanters Three, Magnir is the least subtle in his methods. If you can overcome Magnir, then there's a chance you can overcome his brothers."

The seer started to walk around the outside of the circle. Fandral seemed to feel each step vibrate through his body. A strange cold seeped into the atmosphere, turning his breath to frost. He looked over at his companions, wondering if they experienced the same sensations. Volstagg bore a worried look until he caught Fandral's eye, then his expression quickly shifted into his usual bravado. Hogun, as ever, had an intense look to him with perhaps a tinge of eagerness. The prospect of fighting wizards was always to his liking.

Fandral turned back to see how Onund was faring in his conjurations. Even as he did, there was a blinding flare of light. The room, the seer, even his companions beside him vanished. Everything disappeared as though it had never existed. For Fandral, the only reality was the light that engulfed him and the terrible cold that numbed his very soul.

SIX

Once, when he was very young, Volstagg had been on a longship during a thunderstorm. The sea had been churned into undulating mountains of water with white-capped peaks and plunging valleys. Even after many centuries, he could still remember that voyage and how the violent motion had nauseated him to the point where he thought that any moment he'd cough out his stomach, not merely its contents.

The sensations that racked Volstagg's body as light engulfed the astral circle were far worse than that sea voyage of long ago. It was as though he were being pulled apart in body, mind, and soul. Was this the transition from Asgard to Magnir's plane, or had Hogun been right and this was all a plot by Onund to kill them?

As terrible as the excruciating pain was, it ended with such abruptness that Volstagg was left reeling. His knees buckled under him and he sagged to the ground, throwing out his hands to keep from falling completely. He was surprised to feel a cool, smooth surface under his fingers. It certainly wasn't the floor of the seer's refuge. This felt as though it was a great slab of metal beneath him.

Volstagg's other senses returned to him, one after another. The temperature was warm and acrid, far different from the searing heat of Skornheim. There was a panoply of strange noises that coursed into his ears, curious whirrings and whistles, sounds that he instinctively knew were artificial rather than natural. There was a weird smell as well, a kind of smoky metallic odor that he could liken only to a blade being quenched after leaving a swordsmith's forge.

When his vision returned, Volstagg found that he was indeed standing on what looked like a wide bridge of ruddy-hued metal. He could see that it was suspended over a great chasm, but it was the nature of that chasm that shocked him rather than the distance to its bottom. The walls of the gulf weren't raw rock, but instead represented constructions of some sort. He could see windows and balconies, even other bridges, opening from what must be gigantic towers built from strange metals and glass and other materials of a nature he couldn't begin to imagine.

A glance to either side showed him that Hogun and Fandral had successfully been transported by Onund to the metal bridge. The other Asgardians lifted their heads at almost the same time Volstagg did. Indeed, the walls of the chasm were the sides of towers, buildings of a size to stagger the giants of Jotunheim and in such profusion that counting them would have confounded the Norns themselves. Lights of every color imaginable crackled from the windows or sizzled across the open air to create strange glyphs and stranger images. The spires themselves seemed to stab the sky itself. Many of the towers ended in flattened ovals, but others narrowed until they were like the tips of spears. Beyond the colossal edifices, Volstagg could see the starry sky, but he could find no recognizable constellations, neither of Asgard nor Midgard.

"Friends, I think Onund sent us farther than we thought," Volstagg muttered.

Fandral caught him by the arm and turned him about. "If you think the stars are strange..." he said, drawing Volstagg's attention back to the bridge they were on. The Warriors Three weren't alone on the span. A cluster of beings unlike anything the Asgardians had seen before was watching them in silence. Volstagg was struck by their disparate looks. Some were almost human in appearance, though with more bulbous heads and slender limbs. Others were nowhere near human in their shapes. He saw creatures that resembled dogs with chitinous bodies and things he could liken only to eels with arms. However strange the beings, all of them were arrayed in similar raiment, crude brown cloaks that were threadbare and frayed. Around their necks, or whatever might approximate a neck, they wore metal collars.

"A rather motley bunch," Hogun commented. Volstagg saw some of the tension lessen as Hogun decided the beings presented no threat and he lowered his mace.

"They're probably as surprised to see us as we are to be here," Fandral said.

Volstagg nodded. "They might be able to tell us where

we can find this dog Magnir," he told his friends. Drawing a deep breath, and sheathing his sword, Brandrheid Undrsigr, he adopted his broadest smile and started to approach the creatures. "I'm Volstagg of Asgard," he said, extending his open hand in the Midgard fashion of displaying peaceful intentions. "I thank you for welcoming us to your city. It is as wondrous as it is beautiful."

Volstagg was confident the creatures, however curious they looked, would understand him. The Allspeak spoke to the mind more than the ear, which was as well because he couldn't see any ears on a few of the beings he was addressing. Some of them reacted to his speech, but none of them offered so much as a word in reply. At his approach they instead drew back. The eyes of the more human-seeming creatures widened with fright.

"You're scaring them," Fandral upbraided Volstagg. "Think for a moment. We've just materialized before their very eyes and the first thing you do is start lumbering towards them like a lovesick giant."

Volstagg paused and scratched his beard. "They do seem a timid bunch," he said. He glanced over at Fandral. "Alright, you try to make friends," he challenged.

"Give them a chance to calm down," Fandral said. "They're too afraid right now."

"They're afraid," Hogun interrupted, "but not of us." He pointed out that many of the creatures weren't even looking their way now, but instead were gazing up towards the tops of the towers.

Volstagg turned his eyes back to the heights. "Whoever's in charge must live up there," he said. He squinted as he caught a flash of light. At first, he thought it was a shooting star. Then the light began to descend. Rapidly.

"Looks almost like a sled," Volstagg considered as the light resolved itself into a puzzling sort of vehicle. It was a small platform with a raised section at its fore. As the flying sled turned to present its profile to him, he could see lights and buttons scattered about a panel on the raised section. Two enormous lights shimmered from the underside of the sled, creating a hazy distortion in the air underneath it. From the rear of the platform, two small flames were projected.

"Looks like a small dragon," Fandral said.

Volstagg shifted his attention away from the flying sled to the creature that operated it. It was roughly human in size and build, with two arms and legs, an upright posture, and a head set between two shoulders. There, however, the resemblance ended. The body was covered in bright green scales and its spine continued into a long, thick tail. The head was wedge-shaped, without a nose, only two nasal cavities set above the wide scaly mouth. The eyes were deep-set and as red as rubies. A shock of yellow hair created a crest along the creature's scalp.

The reptile didn't wear the crude cloaks of the beings on the bridge. Instead it had a blue tunic over which it wore a metallic harness from which were suspended a variety of curious tools for which Volstagg could provide no name. There was, however, no mistaking the outline of the sword that hung from its belt. His guess was right. Whoever ruled the city was somewhere in the heights. This flying lizard was either that personage or some representative.

Before any of the Asgardians could speak, the reptile

addressed them in a hissing voice. "State to which enclave you belong!" it demanded, poising its sled so that it hovered above the bridge. "Which enclave has been so irresponsible as to allow weapons to be carried by slaves!"

Fandral returned the reptile's glare. "Slaves? Now there's a word I don't like to hear. You've made a–"

The reptile's mouth dropped open in an expression of shock, its rows of needle-like fangs on display. Its eyes blazed with outrage. "Impertinence!" it raged. "You dare speak the tongue of your masters! What enclave has dared teach its slaves the speech of the Sssth!"

"We don't…" Volstagg started to correct the reptile, to tell it that it was the effect of the Allspeak that made it think they spoke its language. Fandral cut him off with a flick of his hand.

"No use trying to explain anything to this lout," Fandral said. His smile was no longer amused, but instead was edged with menace. "There's only one language someone who keeps slaves understands."

The Sssth hissed angrily and ripped the sword from its belt. The reptile's blade crackled with electricity and it dipped its sled towards the bridge.

"Violence is the speech of choice of any bully," Fandral continued. As the Sssth dove down at him, he met the lizard's swing with a parry that nearly sent the creature tumbling from its vehicle. "Unfortunately, my scaly friend, you'll find I can speak to you in your own language."

The reptile snarled and swung at Fandral's head. There was strength to the Sssth's arm and the shock from the

Three Swords 69

energized blade he imagined would have been ample to stun a being with a constitution less robust than an Asgardian. Fandral was a kind of foe the lizardman was unaccustomed to engaging: an enemy who could fight back. Darting aside as the Sssth struck at him, he delivered his own slash. The sword and the clawed fingers that held it went hurtling down into the abyss below the bridge.

"Now maybe you'll take a more pragmatic view," Fandral advised the wounded Sssth. The reptile veered its sled away from the bridge, hugging its maimed hand to its chest. Its other hand flew about the lighted panel. The sled soon emitted a shrill wail.

"That's a call to arms," Hogun declared. He took a few steps back then ran across the bridge, angling himself to face the Sssth's hovering platform. A great leap sent him across the emptiness. Hridgandr smashed into the reptile's skull, hurling it from the sled as the Asgardian landed. Fandral could see the lizard's body tumbling away into the urban chasm.

"Hogun! Quick!" Fandral shouted. Without the Sssth at the controls, the hovering platform lost its ability to defy gravity. The lights on its underside winked out and the distortion beneath it vanished.

Even as the sled started to fall, Hogun jumped back for the bridge. This time there wasn't any room for a running start and his lunge fell short of the span. Fandral dashed to the edge and threw his arms out. His hands caught Hogun's grasping fingers as the warrior hurtled into the chasm. The weight of his friend would have pulled Fandral over as well, but as he started to slide, he felt his legs seized in a mighty grip. Volstagg, his mass exceeding that of both his companions, used himself as an anchor. "Keep tight hold on Hogun and I'll pull you both up," he grunted.

Fandral saw more bright specks descending rapidly from the towers. More Sssth on their sky-sleds. Violent flashes blazed from the front of each vehicle and fiery flares slammed against the side of the bridge, blackening the metal.

"Dragons in truth," Fandral said as the flares sizzled past him. The moment he was back on the bridge, he noticed that the cloaked beings were fleeing towards a door on the far side of the bridge. It seemed they wanted no part in the fray between the Asgardians and the Sssth.

"I was tardy silencing the alarm," Hogun grumbled as he was lifted onto the bridge. He darted to one side as the place he'd been standing was scorched by a ray from the sky-sleds.

"Let the snakes get a bit closer and they'll rue tangling with me!" The huge Asgardian whipped his sword from its sheath and brandished it overhead. "Ho, you crawling vermin! Come down here and show me your mettle!"

Fandral would have given the reptiles credit for being too smart to submit to Volstagg's taunts. Certainly, the sophistication of their weapons marked them as intelligent. Yet they spurred their sleds to greater speed and swarmed down from the height at which they could have safely shot at the Asgardians. Then he recalled the arrogance of the first lizardman and realized the Sssth hadn't encountered serious opposition in such a long time that they didn't realize what it meant to be in a real fight.

Two sky-sleds charged toward Volstagg, their Sssth riders swinging their electrified blades as they came in for the attack. Volstagg raised his sword and bit down on the dwarven blade, holding it in his mouth and freeing his hands. The reptiles drove on, believing their enemy had gone mad and was now utterly defenseless. That delusion persisted only until the huge Asgardian seized hold of one of the sleds as it dove at him. For an instant his enormous frame shuddered as the sled's engines pushed him back. The Sssth growled and chopped at him with its sword, sending electricity crackling through Volstagg.

Far from wounding Volstagg, the shock seemed to energize him. Grunting his own battle cry, his hands crumpled the sled's metal. He spun about, hurling the machine as though it were a discus. The Sssth dropped its sword and clung to the sled as Volstagg sent it careening through the air to smash into his other attacker. Both vehicles disintegrated in a vicious explosion, pitching debris and bodies into the yawning abyss.

Hogun was matched by a reptile that took little interest in using its sword. The Sssth had a strange device that looked like a stein resting on its side. The lizardman held it by its handle and aimed the open mouth at Hogun. From that opening a ray of searing light flashed. Hogun brought Hridgandr around, shielding himself with the mace's spiked head. The beam crackled harmlessly against the weapon. By the time the Sssth was aware its attack was inefficient, its sky-sled had brought it within perilous reach of Hogun. The moment the ray faltered, the warrior swung his mace in a wide arc and shattered the lights underneath the sled. The machine hurtled onward, losing altitude as it sailed past the bridge to career into the chasm.

Fandral noted the successes of his friends even as he struggled to avoid his own attackers. Like the one that had confronted Hogun, the pair who set their sights on the rakish Asgardian did their best to burn him down with their rayguns. He surprised the reptiles with his speed, dodging the flurry of shots they aimed at him until, in their haste to get him in a crossfire, they were forced to break away lest they hit one another.

Fandral seized that moment as they spun away. Jumping at one of the sky-sleds, he managed to grab its underside. He felt his skin blistering under the heat from the suspending lights and the distorted air beneath the machine threatened to choke him. He could imagine that a human from Midgard would have been killed instantly by such exposure, but an Asgardian was made of much tougher material. He clung on as the Sssth, in a panic, tried to shake him free. "Now that was entirely too close," he muttered as a ray beam from the other lizardman crackled past his ear. The nearness of the shot rattled the operator of the sky-sled and for an instant it stopped trying to dislodge its unwanted passenger.

The instant was all Fandral needed. Firming one handhold, he swung his body around, describing an arc that put him firmly on the sled's platform and behind its scaly operator. He seized the reptile in a crushing grip. "What do you say we land this contraption?" he suggested to his captive.

Before the Sssth could answer, the other sky-sled swooped in. The blast from its rider's raygun sizzled into Fandral's prisoner, burning a hole in its chest.

"Now that was a churlish thing to do," Fandral snapped. He dropped his dead prisoner, but as the reptile fell, he drew

Three Swords 73

the sword from its belt. Throwing it like a javelin, he sent the blade slamming into the other Sssth as it came around for another shot. The lizardman was impaled by the sword and its uncontrolled sled slammed into the side of a building.

The machine Fandral was on was bent on a similar trajectory. He leaped from the falling craft, hitting the surface of the bridge and rolling almost to the edge before he caught himself. Fandral stared down into the abyss and whistled. "I rather think that was enough of that," he told himself.

A few sky-sleds remained, but these drew away to a safer distance. "It looks like the Warriors Three have taught this rabble some caution," Volstagg laughed. "Crawl back under your rocks and have nightmares about Volstagg the Indomitable!"

Fandral couldn't join in his friend's mockery. He was looking at the gateways on either side of the bridge. The cloaked beings were gone, but others had taken their place. More Sssth. Many more. And unlike those on the sky-sleds, these weren't the size of humans. These were larger. Much larger.

"Volstagg," Fandral sighed as he drew Fimbuldraugr. "Just once I wish you'd be careful what you say." He gestured at the reptiles on either side of the span. Even the smallest of them would tower over Volstagg. "There always seems to be somebody around who wants to make you eat your words."

SEVEN

Hogun fixed his steely gaze on the giant reptiles as they charged across the bridge. "Seems they don't very much like us," he told his companions. He shifted Hridgandr about so that its spiked head covered his torso. Though the lizardmen rushing them appeared to only have electrified swords, he wasn't forgetting the rayguns used by the reptiles on the sky-sleds.

"If we try to fight them here, we'll be overwhelmed," Fandral said. He waved his sword upward, illustrating that more sky-sleds were descending from the towers to support the attack.

"Now they've seen how I fight, they won't take us as lightly as they did before," Volstagg declared. He tilted his head and nodded at one end of the span. "If we fight our way through one of those doors, we can limit how many Sssth can come at us at one time."

Three Swords 75

Hogun knew the situation was dire when Volstagg suggested retreat. It was the best plan under the circumstances and there wasn't time to devise another. "A lot of lizards between that door and us," he growled. "Let's see about thinning their numbers."

Springing into action, Hogun raced ahead to meet the charging Sssth. He blocked the sword of the foremost reptile with Hridgandr's heft, then in a wide spin brought the spiked head whipping around. The lizardman was lifted off its feet and flung over the bridge's side. A second Sssth staggered back when Hogun smashed it in the chest, puncturing the creature's scaly hide. A third crumpled as the heavy mace crushed its ribs.

Fandral was beside Hogun, his sword stabbing at any reptile that tried to flank the grim warrior. The impetus of the Sssth charge faltered as their fighters stumbled back, bleeding from cuts and slashes.

Behind him, Hogun could hear Volstagg doing his utmost to hold back the Sssth to their rear. He risked a glance to see the huge Asgardian seize one of the reptiles by its tail. A blow from the flat of his sword knocked the lizard senseless, and in the next moment Volstagg was using the unconscious body to scourge the others, lashing them with the limp saurian. Several of the Sssth were swatted from the bridge while the others fell back several paces to avoid sharing such a fate.

"By Idunn's Apples, I think we may get through!" Fandral exclaimed as he pierced a reptilian throat and saw his enemy drop away.

"They must think so too," Hogun warned, glancing up at

the sky-sleds. Reinforced, the vehicles now came darting downward. Bright flashes erupted from the rayguns the riders carried. The surface of the bridge was blackened as shots narrowly missed the Asgardians. Then a searing pain in his shoulder told Hogun that not every blast had gone amiss. The smell of cooked meat and burnt hair was in his nose. He dreaded to look at the injury he'd sustained. As long as he could still swing his mace, he determined to wait before seeing the severity of his wound.

The fire from the sky-sleds didn't spare the Sssth on the bridge. Hogun saw one red-haired reptile cut down, its torso charred by the destructive ray. He seized the opening left by the shot lizard and threw himself into the very midst of his enemies. He felt the crackle of electricity race through him as the Sssth slashed at him with their blades, but he judged the swords to be less of a menace than the rayguns.

Fandral cried out as one of the lizards slashed his breast with its blade. He retaliated with a thrust to his foe's belly that saw it slump to its knees. Clasping a hand against his wound, he started to move past the dying reptile when the Sssth suddenly surged towards him, clamping its sharp teeth in his leg.

Hogun swung back at his friend's shout. A blow from his mace broke the Sssth's jaw and pitched it over the side of the bridge. "Don't count an enemy harmless while they still draw breath," he advised. Hridgandr crashed against the skull of another reptile as it leaped at him, vaulting the lizardman's body back into the press of its comrades.

"We can't win here," Fandral stated between pained gasps. He dove aside as one of the sky-sleds fired at him. "We've no cover and far too many enemies to get through to reach the gate."

Hogun blocked the blast from another raygun, then shattered the collarbone of a Sssth that charged him from behind. He looked past to see Volstagg surrounded by the giant reptiles. He was using his dwarven blade now, but even its sharp bite wasn't fast enough to keep some of his adversaries from slipping around him. Hogun saw one of the Sssth spin back, intent on driving its sword into the Asgardian's kidney.

"If we're to fall, best to fall together," Hogun snarled. He dashed back across the scorched span, hurdling scaly bodies. Before the backstabber could strike Volstagg, Hridgandr shattered its head like an egg.

"Many thanks," Volstagg bellowed. "I must have lost track of that one." He brought Brandrheid Undrsigr slashing through the arm of a Sssth and watched as the maimed reptile reeled away into its fellows. "You'd think it would be hard to miss something as big as one of these."

Fandral fell back to join Hogun. He fended off the attacks of the lizards who pursued him, causing one to lose its footing. The Sssth clawed frantically at one of its comrades to keep from falling, but only succeeded in dragging them both into the chasm.

"Falling together," Fandral mused, repeating Hogun's words. There was a gleam in his eyes that Hogun never liked to see. It meant Fandral was plotting something especially reckless.

"I know that look," Hogun warned as he diverted another ray blast.

Fandral smiled and Hogun could tell whatever crazy idea he'd devised had really taken root. "Are you so fond of this bridge that you insist this is where you'll die?"

A Sssth went sailing past them as Volstagg shook its body from his sword. "What?" he asked. "Are we leaving?"

That wild light in Fandral's eyes was now a raging fire. Hogun followed his gaze and saw he was looking at one of the sky-sleds.

"You aren't thinking...?" Even as he spoke, Hogun knew the madness Fandral planned.

"I'll be right back," Fandral told him as he drew away and sheathed his sword. Before Hogun could react, Fandral leaped off the bridge.

Fandral's jump took him twenty feet out from the bridge and straight into the path of one of the sky-sleds. Before the Sssth rider could turn, the Asgardian crashed into its machine. Fandral felt the impact shudder through his body, provoking a flare of pain from the wound in his chest. He gritted his teeth and snatched at the raised front of the sled, using it as a fulcrum to twist himself around and put himself on the platform behind the operator. One hand closed around the reptile's neck.

"Now, my scaly rogue," Fandral told the Sssth, "if you don't want me to wring your neck, you'll fly this contraption closer to the bridge." He'd already seen for himself that the reptiles, while somewhat indifferent to what happened to their comrades, had a marked sense of self-preservation. The lizardman did as it was told, directing the craft back towards the span.

"Come along, then!" Fandral shouted to his friends. Hogun whipped his mace around in a wide arc that drove back the Sssth converging on him. The instant he had space to move, he turned and jumped onto the approaching sky-sled. The machine dipped as he landed on the platform, sinking away from the bridge.

"Get back up there." Fandral tightened his fingers around the Sssth's neck.

The reptile groaned. "Too much," it protested. "We can't stay up."

A sick sensation swept through Fandral. He hadn't considered there might be a limit to how many people the sled could carry. Even as that horrible fact was related, he saw Volstagg leap from the bridge. He slammed into the sled like a living avalanche. Hogun scrambled to catch hold of him before he slipped away and pitched headlong into the chasm.

The sky-sled, barely able to hover with three riders, went careening down into the chasm. Other sleds hurtled after it, their operators firing rayguns as they pursued the captured vehicle. In one respect, at least, the crisis helped the Asgardians. Their plummet into the abyss was too fast for the Sssth to land a shot or close the distance.

"We'll crash," the reptile gasped as their sky-sled narrowly missed hitting a lower bridge. Its claws scratched frantically at the control panel, causing the vehicle to turn before it could glance off a projecting balcony.

"I'm depending on you to keep that from happening," Fandral said. He felt his gorge rise when he looked up and saw one of the pursuing sleds slam into a bridge and explode.

It was a stark taste of what they could expect if they didn't think of a way out.

"As escapes go," Volstagg yelled at Fandral, "this isn't the best you've come up with! What's the plan now?"

Fandral shot Volstagg a sour look. "The Sssth suggested throwing off some ballast. Don't make me agree with it."

Hogun nodded at a bridge several hundred feet below. "What if we tried to land there?"

At the rate they were falling, Fandral estimated they'd be there in seconds. "Land on that bridge," he ordered the Sssth. The lizard bobbed its head in acknowledgment and angled the sled towards the span.

A large cluster of cloaked slaves scattered as the sky-sled hurtled towards the bridge. As it came within a few dozen feet of the span, Volstagg and Hogun dropped from the vehicle and fell to the platform below. Without their weight, the Sssth was able to regain some control. The sled lurched upwards for a moment, then the reptile was able to bring the abused machine to rest on the metallic surface.

"Sorry, can't risk any trouble from you," Fandral apologized before slamming the Sssth's head against the control panel. The lizard's eyes rolled back as it fell unconscious. Fandral eased it away from the machine and left it lying on the bridge.

"We're not out of this yet," Hogun warned as he jogged over to Fandral. He pointed up. Three sky-sleds had maintained their furious pursuit and were closing in.

"I'll attend to this," Volstagg swore. He pushed past the other warriors and took hold of the sled. Much as he'd done before, his hands crumpled the metal frame as he tightened his hold. With a great heave, he flung the battered vehicle at their enemies.

The cumbersome missile flew past the sky-sleds, and Sssth rayguns flashed as they fired down at the bridge. Fandral groaned, thinking Volstagg's throw had missed entirely. Then the hurled machine struck one of the bridges above them, glancing off it and spinning back around. It smashed into one of the other sleds and both vehicles vanished in a fiery explosion.

The remaining Sssth lost heart and accelerated upward, quickly becoming little more than specks of light.

"They'll bring more back," Hogun stated. "We stay here and we'll be in the same fix we were up there."

Fandral looked at their surroundings. Though far lower in the city strata, the bridge was much like the one above, with two massive gates at either side and a yawning gulf below. There was one important difference, though. The slaves who'd scattered at their approach hadn't fled. Several of them remained, watching the Warriors Three with keen interest.

"This time things might be different," Fandral said, slowly walking towards the onlookers.

"You expect help from them?" Volstagg scoffed. "Last time they couldn't scurry away fast enough from a fight."

"Maybe that's because they didn't know it was possible to win a fight with the Sssth." Fandral continued to approach the cloaked beings. Two of the more human-seeming creatures stepped out from the crowd. He thought they were near enough to human to recognize the emotion in their eyes. It was an expression of awe.

"You've beaten the Sssth," one of them whispered, something like reverence in his tone.

Fandral glanced back at the unconscious reptile. "Some of them, at least," he admitted with a smile. "I'm afraid there's still a good many of them around. If we stay here, they're certain to come for us."

The other thin-limbed being nodded her head. "We can take you somewhere they won't find you," she said. She awkwardly tried to form her face to match Fandral's smile. "You will be safe there."

Hogun stepped forwards, studying the creatures closely. "Think we can trust them?" he asked.

Fandral shrugged, a gesture he immediately regretted when the cut in his chest began bleeding again. "We're in no position to do anything else. We're all of us in no condition for a fray like the one we just left. But that's what we'll get if we hang around here."

Volstagg grumbled into his beard. When his friends failed to respond, he repeated himself in a louder tone. "At least maybe they'll have something to eat," he said, a hopeful note in his voice.

"This isn't edible," Volstagg commented, letting his spoon slowly sink into the bowl of pasty-white muck. As he looked away from the bowl, he saw Hogun glowering at him.

"Did you stop to think that this is all they have?" Hogun wondered.

The reprimand stung Volstagg. He glanced about the dark chamber the slaves had brought them to. It was some sort of store house, with metal boxes stacked almost everywhere.

Three Swords

The amount of corrosion visible on the containers was testimony to how long they'd been left here and the general neglect that had ensued. Narrow pathways snaked between the stacks, and somewhere deep within the warren of boxes, the slaves had removed enough of them to create a kind of clearing. A refuge hidden from their reptilian masters. A handful of glowing crystals provided the only light, tinging everything with a bluish hue. Volstagg had noted that the crystals seemed to be the same as those ensconced in the large fixtures that were suspended in the roof dozens of feet above them.

About twenty slaves had remained with the Warriors Three, beings of several wildly different species. Now that Volstagg had a closer look at them, he could see some generalities they shared beyond their shoddy cloaks and metal collars. All of them had a weary appearance, drawn and emaciated by their oppression under the Sssth. Many bore scars, reminders of whips and brands. A few even bore ugly bites from when the lizards had resorted to even more savage measures to discipline their slaves.

"I talk too much," Volstagg said as he fished the spoon from the bowl and took a mouthful of the nauseating muck. If anything, it tasted worse to suspect what sacrifices their hosts had suffered to provide even this wretched repast. He turned to watch Fandral. The rakish Asgardian was talking to two of the slaves, one of the lean-limbed humanoids and a being that looked like a plucked chicken with a cluster of tentacles where its wings should be.

"We appreciate the food and shelter you've provided us," Fandral said, "but what we need is information. We're

84 *Marvel: Legends of Asgard*

looking for a man, an Asgardian like ourselves. A rogue who has made friends with your oppressors."

The slaves exchanged worried looks. "There is such a one," the bird clacked, its voice monotone as it left its beak. "Several cycles ago, the man you speak of came to Golden Star."

Volstagg shifted around on the box he was using for a chair. "Golden Star? Is that what the Sssth call this terrible city?"

The humanoid shook her head sadly. "It is the name of our world," she whispered, choking back her sorrow. She clasped her hands to her shoulders and for a moment pride asserted itself. "Golden Star is our world. The Sssth are alien invaders whose armada conquered the planet many years ago." The pride at last faltered and regret held her so firmly that she seemed to shrink. "Our society was too peaceful, too unused to war and fighting. The Sssth overwhelmed us easily."

"The Sssth use Golden Star as a base from which they raid other worlds for slaves," the bird-creature elaborated. "There are many peoples who have fallen to these monsters."

"Does no one try to fight back?" Volstagg asked. He wondered about a people who'd submit to tyranny rather than die fighting their oppressors. Then he thought of Gunnarsfell and the Asgardians who languished under their despot king. Survival was an instinct that could break the defiance of even the strongest.

"A few," the humanoid said. She drew back the sleeve of her cloak to show a ghastly depression in her arm. The outline made it clear that a bite had been taken from just

Three Swords

above her elbow. The wound was now a scar, but the missing flesh remained missing. Volstagg grimaced at the sight. An Asgardian could regenerate from all but the most severe wounds. Even now, the injuries they'd sustained in the fight on the bridge were fading. Other peoples didn't have such a boon to mend them after battle.

"When the one you're looking for came to Golden Star, he fought the Sssth," the bird said. "But he only wished to display to them his power and compel them into alliance with him."

The humanoid's face curled with contempt and she nodded upward. "He's the guest of the Sssthgar, the warlord who rules the Sssth." She turned and looked at Volstagg, an edge of suspicion in her eyes. "When you were first seen, it was thought that you'd also come here to make friends with the Sssth and to join the Enchanter."

"We're friends of no one who makes slaves of others," Fandral assured her.

Volstagg set down his bowl and rose to his feet. He was accustomed to his towering height inspiring confidence in others, but he noted the effect was lost on the slaves. Then he recalled the Sssth on the bridge and their own monstrous proportions. A seven-foot Asgardian wasn't going to be impressive to people used to eight-foot lizards. Still, he wanted to try to put some heart into the long-suffering inhabitants of Golden Star.

"We've come here to stop the Enchanter," Volstagg declared. The statement brought some excited whispers from the slaves. Encouraged, he warmed to his subject. "Volstagg the Inspiring has vanquished many a sorcerer and overthrown many a tyrant." He slammed his fist into his palm. "The moment I arrived on Golden Star, the hours left to these villains were numbered." He smiled at that turn of phrase, but from the way Hogun rolled his eyes, he knew some failed to appreciate his theatrics.

"Is this true?" the humanoid gasped. "Have you come to destroy the Enchanter?"

Fandral walked over to Volstagg and clapped his hand on his shoulder. "My friend tends to the grandiose, but his words are no mistake. We have come to rout this scoundrel Magnir and put an end to his power."

Volstagg's smile broadened. "The Warriors Three have bearded many a wizard in his own lair," he boasted. "Just show us where the Enchanter is, and you'll no longer have to worry about him."

The humanoid bowed her head. "I believe what you say. I will take you to see Terrok. He will be able to help you."

"How will this Terrok help us?" Volstagg questioned her.

"Terrok was a slave in the Sssthgar's tower," she replied. "The only slave to escape from there." Her gaze brightened and hope crept into her tone. "He will be able to show you how you can enter the tower and find the Enchanter."

EIGHT

Their hosts waited until the coldest part of the night before leading the Warriors Three from their hiding place. "The Sssth have developed or stolen much technology," one of the humanoids told Fandral, "but even with thermo-regulators to increase their body temperature, they retain the instincts of reptiles. Few of them are active when it is cold and those that are tend to be lethargic and inattentive. It is one of the reasons they're so keen on enslaving others."

"Is that how Terrok escaped?" Fandral asked as they left the storehouse and crept along the dim corridors of the city's lower levels. The three Asgardians had been given tattered cloaks to wear over their armor so that, at least from a distance, they might pass for slaves. As yet there had been no evidence of the Sssth in these neglected passageways, but the humanoids insisted the reptiles had ways of watching what happened on Golden Star even when they didn't send patrols. The devices that enabled the invaders to do so sounded to Fandral to be something between a Midgardian security camera and a witch's scrying crystal. Whatever they were, it was enough to know the Sssth had such an ability and to be careful not to alert them. Though he judged it would have to be a very inattentive lizard who was taken in by Volstagg's disguise.

"Terrok... went a different way," the lean humanoid said. There was a note of fear in her voice. Something seemed to frighten her even more than the Sssth. She decided to avoid even articulating whatever it was. "Terrok will explain when you speak with him," was all she would say.

"Is it far to where he is?" Hogun asked. He pointed as a lone slave came creeping down the passageway towards them. It was only the latest in a relay of scouts that had ranged ahead of them to ensure that they wouldn't run into any Sssth.

"After escaping the Sssthgar, Terrok can't show himself," the bird-alien told them. "He must always stay in hiding or he would be killed."

Fandral sighed in sympathy. He knew what it was to be an outlaw and fugitive, the threat of immediate death once discovered. From what he'd seen, the Sssth provided even more incentive to avoid their punishment than other oppressors he'd fought against.

Another scout drifted back to the tiny group. The dog-headed being reported that there were no Sssth between themselves and something it called "the Drop".

The information gave the humanoid a moment of pause. She trained her gaze on Hogun. "A moment ago, you asked

Three Swords 89

how far it is to Terrok. It would be several days if we were to stick to the corridors and hide when the Sssth are active. But if we use the Drop, we can reach him in only an hour."

"Then let's go there," Volstagg declared. "I'm eager to settle things with Magnir and these lousy lizards."

"There's a complication," Fandral observed, noting the anxiety of their escort. "Something that makes using the Drop inadvisable."

The canine alien's eyestalks twitched. "The moment the Drop is activated, the Sssth will know someone has used it."

"If they don't catch someone, they'll make a broader search," the humanoid said. "They might find Terrok and the rest of the Vanished if they do."

"Time may be crucial," Fandral said, thinking of Onund's portents and the threat to Asgard. "It is critical we stop the Enchanter as quickly as possible."

The thin-limbed native nodded in understanding. She glanced at the other slaves. "Since he arrived, the Enchanter has made things even worse for us. You're right. He must be stopped. And there is a way to divert the Sssth so that they won't follow you."

A forbidding silence settled over the slaves as they conducted the Asgardians through the empty hallways. Fandral was impressed by their determination to press on despite the fear he could see in their eyes. It was not long before they reached what he imagined must be their destination. A plaza-like space at a junction of several corridors. At the middle of the area, surrounded by lighted pylons, was a yawning pit dozens of feet across.

Fandral took a few steps towards the pit and saw that

not only did it plunge downward to an incalculable depth, but that the ceiling above it opened into a shaft that soared upward to incredible heights. "This seems to run through the whole city, from top to bottom."

"Indeed," the humanoid said. "These channels run throughout Golden Star and were designed by my people to facilitate travel across our planet."

"The Sssth destroyed many of these channels," the hound-alien said. "Those that are left they use to convey materials from one level of the city to another." The chitinous portions of its face split apart in a grimace. "They monitor each activation of the Drop and know when its use hasn't been authorized by the Sssthgar. It is one way the Sssthgar controls the enclaves, restricting their commerce so none of them become powerful enough to challenge him."

The bird-creature bobbed its head. "The enclaves sometimes smuggle materials anyway. They order a slave to activate the Drop when they move their goods, then deny any knowledge of what the slave has done when the Sssthgar's patrols investigate."

"There's a way to trick the Sssth," the native said hurriedly. "We can bring you to Terrok and divert them before they know where you've gone."

Volstagg clapped his hands and chuckled. "I always applaud a clever ruse." He stepped towards the pylons. "Now what do we have to do? Climb down the side of the pit?"

The dog-alien walked past Volstagg. It strode directly across the edge of the pit, then continued until it was standing at the very center of the opening. Seemingly there was nothing underneath its clawed feet. "A region of null gravity," it explained. "Until the Drop is activated, entering it is no different from walking across the floor."

Fandral stepped out and joined the alien. He stamped his foot. Despite the evidence of his eyes, it felt like he was standing on a solid surface. "What happens when it is activated?"

The other slaves stepped out onto the gravity field. Hesitantly, Volstagg and Hogun followed them, still not quite trusting the weird phenomenon.

"When activated, the Drop will cause whatever is placed within the pylons to ascend or descend however far is desired," the native said. She stood near the edge of the pit, one hand close to a lighted pylon. "Because the channel engages or reverses gravity, speed is not a hazard. Wherever something is sent, it will find a field of null gravity waiting to receive it." She gestured to Volstagg and Hogun. "The process is quite safe."

"I'm not convinced of that," Hogun said, kicking his boot against the unseen surface.

"I'm fool enough to try anything once," Volstagg smiled. "I just hope I live to try a second time," he added in a less assured undertone.

Fandral shook his head. "Are these the same Warriors Three who braved Onund's astral circle not so long ago? Surely this isn't half so perilous as being thrown across space and time." He turned and gestured to the humanoid. "Take us to speak with Terrok whenever you're ready."

The native slapped her hand against the pylon. Fandral saw the light change, a flash that rippled through it and subtly altered its hue. The moment he was aware of the change, a lurching sensation pulled at his stomach. There was a blur of motion as the world around the pit sped past. The impression of vast reaches racing away lasted for only a heartbeat. Then the feeling in his stomach was gone and he knew the Drop was still again.

To look at his friends and the denizens of Golden Star it was as though no one had moved at all. But when Fandral looked past the periphery of the gravity shell, he saw that they were no longer where they'd been. The corridors were no longer arrayed the same way and their illumination was dingier than it had been before. The walls were of a peculiar masonry rather than sheets of metal and there was debris on the ground. Only the pylons looked the same, standing guard about the edges of the Drop. Fandral tilted his head back and stared up into the shaft. Certainly, the view was different than it had been, conveying the sense of an even greater vastness above him.

"Terrok is that way," the humanoid said. "Cargaas will lead the way." At the sound of its name, the dog-alien loped out onto the floor. The other aliens followed in its wake.

"We've come too far to go back," Hogun stated. Hefting his mace, he marched out from the Drop.

Volstagg gave Fandral a sharp look. "Were you intimating back there that I'm not as brave as you are?"

"Never," Fandral responded. "I was only remarking that you were being a bit too suspicious."

"I'll accept a complaint about caution," Volstagg decided, "but not aspersions of cowardice. I'll remind you that I once tried to save my horse from Fenris itself. It needs courage to challenge the Great Wolf."

Three Swords

Fandral walked beside Volstagg as they joined Hogun and started to follow their guides. "As I recall one of Gunnhilde's cookbooks was in a saddlebag and you were more afraid of what she'd do to you than you were about Fenris."

"Fighting a monster is one thing," Volstagg said, "but breaking a promise to your wife is another. I'm still trying to make amends for losing that book." His chest heaved with a regretful sigh. "Without that book, Gunnhilde's never been able to make spitfried venison the same." He made a dismissive wave of his hands. "Bah, you don't have a wife. You don't know about these things."

Fandral felt the sudden pall that came over him. From Volstagg's expression, it was clear the huge fighter knew the mistake he'd made with his remark. "I was married once," Fandral said, his voice solemn. He let the emotions pass through him, both the happiness and the sorrow.

"I never knew that," Hogun said, surprise penetrating his gruff exterior. "Not the sort of thing I'd expect you to keep quiet about. What happened?"

"She died." Fandral felt the cut of those words in his very soul. He shook himself, refocusing on what was before them. It served no good to dwell on tragedies of the past.

Fandral afterward blamed his melancholy for being unobservant. The Warriors Three had nearly caught up to the aliens when Fandral suddenly realized someone was missing. A feeling of dread gripped him. "The woman, the native," he hissed to his friends. He spun back to face the Drop. The thin-limbed humanoid was beside one of the pylons. When she saw Fandral looking at her, she slapped her hand against the glowing fixture. In an instant she was gone, speeding somewhere along the concourse.

"We've been betrayed to the Sssth!" Hogun snarled, hurrying toward the edge of the pit.

"You're wrong," Fandral's voice was grave. "The Sssth know someone used the Drop. So she's going to give them someone to hunt. Someone to catch." He stared up into the shaft, wondering where in Golden Star's vast city she'd gone and how soon it would take the reptiles to find her. "She's sacrificing herself for us and we don't even know her name."

"Ulira," the bird-alien said, dipping its head. "She was called Ulira, but don't seek her among the living." The creature's eyes took on a vengeful aspect. "She won't risk betraying anyone. When the Sssth find her, she won't let them take her alive."

Desperate need created desperate measures. Ulira's action was clear evidence for Hogun how fiercely the denizens of Golden Star struggled against the Sssth. The perfidious hole Terrok and the other fugitives had adopted as a sanctuary was further proof. The place was situated in the middle of the city's sewers. The stink of waste was overwhelming, worse than the inside of a dragon's gut. Hogun found it difficult to endure even for the little time it took to open a conduit near the Drop and proceed from there to the confluence of pipes where the fugitives had their squalid shelters. That anyone, regardless of how alien their species, could endure such conditions for months and years bespoke an endurance almost beyond imagination.

The shelters were cobbled together from rusted metal

Three Swords

and a bone-colored plastic. They squatted around and underneath the enormous pipes that squirmed through the cavernous vault forming a veritable city of its own. Several hundred slaves emerged from the shelters when the Warriors Three and their escort arrived. Hogun judged there must be thousands more who remained in hiding. The scope of what they'd risked exposing by using the Drop to come here explained the drastic sacrifice made to preserve its secrecy.

Cargaas made a barking whistle, a call that echoed through the vault. More fugitives began to gather, forming a great crowd that completely surrounded the Warriors Three. Hogun watched them amass with some misgiving. The only other Asgardian these beings had seen before was Magnir, an ally of the Sssth. He could see from the hostile glares directed at them that many of the fugitives had already made that association. If they got ugly, if the crowd became a mob, he didn't like their chances of protecting themselves without hurting a lot of people.

"Comrades," Cargaas shouted, "these offworlders are enemies of the Sssth!"

A voice shouted back from the crowd. "They look to be kinsmen of the Enchanter, and the Enchanter is friend to the Sssthgar!"

Fandral stepped forward. Unable to pick out the fugitive who'd spoken, Hogun watched him instead sweep his gaze across the whole crowd as he spoke. "It is true we come from the same realm as the Enchanter, but that does not make us his friends any more than living on Golden Star makes you a friend of the Sssth." It was simplistic reasoning, but it gave the crowd something to mull over. Hogun knew when trying to quiet a mob, any appeal to logic that managed to gain a foothold was a victory in itself.

"We've come here to fight the Enchanter," Hogun told the crowd. He shrugged off his cloak and held Hridgandr high. "After that, he will trouble you no more." Logic had quieted the crowd, now Hogun sought to appeal to something far different. Hope.

Volstagg pushed his way forward and made a grand gesture of throwing off his cloak. The effect was diminished when it caught on his sword's hilt, but he strove to quickly recover his dignity. "I am Volstagg the Victorious," he bellowed. "The Enchanter is our enemy as much as he is yours. But be heartened, for the villain's hours are numbered now that we are here to visit justice on him. He will not be the first wizard we smite. Nor will he be the second." He grinned and looked aside at his companions. "Indeed, I've lost count of how many wizards we've vanquished. They perish like flies when the Warriors Three confront them."

The big Asgardian's boasting was just getting started, as Hogun knew from far too many occasions, but before Volstagg could really warm to his subject, there was a stirring among the fugitives. They parted so that one of the tall, lean-limbed natives could approach them. His skin had a pasty look to it and Hogun could tell that he moved with far less agility than others of his species they'd seen.

The humanoid turned deep-set eyes on the Asgardians. Hogun could feel the intense scrutiny when that gaze fell upon him. "If the intentions you express are true, then I would speak with you."

"You're Terrok?" Hogun asked.

Three Swords   97

"I am Terrok," the fugitive said. "The only slave to escape the Sssthgar's tower." He pointed at each of the Asgardians in turn. "If you seek the Enchanter, I am the only one who can show you the way."

"Then take us there," Volstagg told him. "After we get rid of Magnir, we might even have time to dispose of the Sssthgar too."

Terrok shook his head. "Before you promise anything, you must listen to me." He motioned for them to follow. "I will tell you of the tower and my escape. When you have listened to me, you may not be so eager as you are now. Come, I would not horrify the ears of these others with what I have to tell. For them, the threat of the Sssth is terror enough."

The shelter Terrok led them to was so small that Volstagg had to stand outside in the doorway while the humanoid related his story. He told of the Sssthgar's cruelty and the ferocity of the reptiles while he'd been in the tower. Then he spoke of Magnir and the changes that had come with the Enchanter's arrival. The ghastly experiments Magnir conducted, diabolical studies that were forever demanding more victims. "Knowing that I must soon fall victim to the Enchanter, I seized the only chance that offered me escape." Hogun could almost smell the fear exuding from their host as he paused, nerving himself for what he would relate next.

"Magnir is not the first to enter into an alliance with the Sssth," Terrok stated. "While they enslave most races they encounter, the Sssth were somehow coerced into joining forces with the Vrellnexians, and when they conquered Golden Star, their terrible allies soon followed."

Hogun could see the barely contained horror even thinking about the Vrellnexians caused Terrok. "They must be terrible indeed if the Sssth seem kindly by comparison."

"What are these Vrellnexians like?" inquired Fandral.

Leaning over, Terrok drew a shape in the muck on the floor with a shaking finger. Hogun was uncertain if the image was meant to be a spider or a crab, but whatever it was, its multiple legs tipped with grasping claws and its leering face with sharp mandibles made for an unsavory picture.

Terrok quickly erased the image, shuddering as he did so. He looked uneasily around the shelter, as though afraid to find a Vrellnexian there. "It is a tenuous arrangement that exists between the Sssth and the Vrellnexians. Sometimes it is difficult to tell which is in control of Golden Star. That changed when the Enchanter arrived. The Sssthgar feels strong enough now to defy the Vrellnexians. The Vrellnexians, however, have never trusted the Sssth and they've burrowed secret tunnels all across Golden Star. Even in the Sssthgar's own tower."

"That's how you escaped, by using these tunnels," Hogun commented.

"I discovered the tunnels by accident," Terrok said. "When my fear of what the Enchanter would do to me grew great enough, I used the tunnels to escape." He let his gaze linger on each of the Asgardians. "That is how you can penetrate the fortress and reach the Enchanter. You must use the Vrellnexian tunnels."

"Sounds easy enough," Volstagg declared from the doorway. "So we have to squash a few bugs before we squash

Magnir. If things were too easy, they'd be unfit for inclusion in Volstagg's saga."

"If you meet the Vrellnexians, you'll never defeat the Enchanter." Terrok threw back his cloak and exposed his neck to them. Hogun could see four ugly gashes on the humanoid's throat. "The Vrellnexians found me while I was escaping. They sank their fangs into me and drained my vitality.

"Take a good look at me," Terrok challenged. "What the Vrellnexians take from someone does not come back."

NINE

"Here's something I'd gladly leave out of my saga." Volstagg's deep voice rumbled off into the gloom. Hogun shot him a chastising glower.

"If you'd keep your bellows down to something quiet enough to pass for a dragon's roar, we *might* get through these tunnels without meeting anything," Fandral whispered.

Volstagg knew he was in the wrong, but his mood was too surly to apologize. He knew it was this place agitating him. On his first peep at the hidden tunnels Terrok had led them to, he'd decided they should storm the Sssthgar's front gates, no matter how many guards there were.

The Vrellnexian tunnels were spacious… too spacious to occupy the walls they burrowed into. Terrok made some attempt at explanation before he hurried back to the sewer refuge. Something about the aliens being able to fold dimensions to create gaps between reality. Volstagg was only able to grasp part of what the humanoid told them, but that part didn't comfort him. Instead it only added to his unease. Carving a passage between walls was one thing, driving a tunnel through the molecules of those walls was another.

Each of the Asgardians had a sliver of glowing crystal taken from the meager stores stolen by the fugitive Vanished over the years from their reptilian masters. At every step they were given a distinct view of their surroundings. The tunnels were of a hexagonal shape. Walls, ceiling, and floor were all coated in a resinous material that didn't quite feel solid when Volstagg could bring himself to touch it. It was like a heavy smoke that maintained position and, with the least bit of extra effort, he felt he could push his hand clear through it. He knew that was only a trick of the mind. Hogun had already tested it with his mace and it had rebounded off the side of the tunnel as though he'd struck solid steel.

The appearance was every bit as unnatural as its character. The hexagons had a look that was both fibrous and gloopy, as if the tunnels hadn't so much been constructed as grown. Extruded from some gigantic entity. Gunnhilde had taken Volstagg into an elf's palace once, a structure that existed within the hollowed trunk and limbs of a colossal tree. It was the only thing he could liken the feel of the tunnels to, though where the elfin castle had inspired wonder, the network of the Vrellnexians conjured dread.

"I don't like this place," Volstagg whispered back at Fandral. "It's beneath my dignity to go skulking about like a thief," he added, when he considered how craven the first statement sounded.

"I don't like it either," Hogun hissed, "but if we want to get out of here quick, letting the Vrellnexians know we're here isn't the way to do it."

Volstagg turned the crystal he held towards the walls. The crystals burned with a red light rather than the more pallid hues that were common in Golden Star's great city. Terrok said that the Vrellnexians couldn't see a red light, so they'd be able to navigate without the illumination giving them away. Of course, he also said there were plenty of other ways the spider-insects could find someone. Their bodies were keyed to vibrations to such a degree that they didn't hear sounds, but instead *felt* them. That being the case, Volstagg thought Hogun's test with Hridgandr was far more dangerous than any amount of shouting all three of them could do. He was about to point that out when he noticed a swirling motion on the ceiling. It was like ripples in a pond, but Volstagg didn't think a fish was going to pop its head through the surface.

"Look," he told his friends. "It's like the backside of the entrance we came through. Maybe this is what we're looking for." The hopeful note faded when Volstagg made the suggestion.

"Doubtless another door," Fandral said as he peered up at the shimmering patch. The disturbance was hexagonal in its outlines and some five feet across, positioned so that it was described against two sides of the tunnel. Fandral shook his head. "Terrok said the door into the Sssthgar's tower opened up from the floor, not the roof. Besides, we've not covered nearly the distance he said we'd need to."

Three Swords 103

Volstagg waved his arm just a bit below the disturbance. "Maybe the tunnels rotate," he speculated. "Terrok said they were but loosely anchored to Golden Star. As for how far we've come, Terrok may have been mistaken. He'd just escaped and was being pursued by the Vrellnexians. That kind of experience could wreak havoc on the memory."

"Terrok's been right about everything else," Hogun said. His hands tightened about the heft of his mace. "He also said that when the Vrellnexians chased him, they came out of the walls." He shrugged. "If they can do that, why not drop out of the ceiling or come up through the floor?"

"It's like crawling inside a wasp nest," Volstagg growled. The idea of something springing on him from behind the eerie walls was unsettling enough, he really didn't appreciate Hogun escalating that prospect by including the roof and floor as well.

"More like a spider's web," Fandral mused. His eyes had a hard glint to them as he swept his gaze across the tunnel ahead. "Touch the wrong thread and we'll stir the beast."

"Oh, that's comforting," Volstagg muttered as they continued along the tunnel. He spotted a few other spots where some facet of the place was swirling and shimmering, but to his relief, nothing ever emerged.

"We've come a fair way and have yet to start ascending," Hogun observed. "If we're trying to climb into a tower, this seems a strange way to go about it."

"As level as the walls of Asgard City," Volstagg said. "We might be moving forward, but it's impossible that we're moving upward." He felt anger bubbling up inside him that they'd gone so far, endured the strangeness of the tunnel, only to be misdirected. "We should have insisted Terrok come with us to make sense of this place."

Fandral shook his head. "It took every bit of courage he had just to show us the entrance. His heart would have burst from terror if you'd tried to drag him into the tunnel." He waved the crystal at the passage before them. "There've been no turns or connections, nothing to get us lost. Just a straight line. This has to be the way Terrok came. Perhaps the grade is so gradual it's impossible to notice."

"Or maybe Magnir cast a spell over Terrok," Hogun suggested. "Wizards have many ways of peering into the future. Maybe he laid a trap for us."

"If so, then we've walked right into it," Volstagg said. "Maybe next time you'll..." His words trailed off as he spied a sudden motion near Fandral. A patch of the wall that had been still an instant before suddenly changed into a swirling mass. The dread that had gnawed at him since entering the tunnels now made itself manifest. Something was emerging from the wall itself. Spindly arms, armored in a shiny gray chitin, reached out from the midst of the rippling surface. Clawed hands stretched out for Fandral.

"Watch out!" Volstagg shouted. Concern for Fandral forced him to reject the dread that hammered at his heart. He rushed forward as Fandral dove aside. The shining flash of Brandrheid Undrsigr bit through the darkness. The thin arms dropped to the floor as the sword clove through them. Pungent green ichor burbled from the severed stumps before they swiftly withdrew back into the wall.

"Well, if that was a Vrellnexian, it's no match for a dwarven blade," Volstagg laughed. He turned one of the severed arms over onto its side. The limb twitched, snapping the three curving claws together. "Though I don't think having those clamp down on your skin would be pleasant," he told Fandral.

Fandral probed the severed arms with his sword, turning them over. He fixed his eyes on the spot where the swirling portal had been. The wall was once more a solid mass. "Looks like you changed whatever plans it had."

Volstagg threw out his chest. "Of course. No one wants to contend with Volstagg the Blademaster if they can help it." His bragging brought a smile to his face, but it fell away when he looked over at Hogun.

"That's a good word," Hogun said, gesturing with his mace at the tunnel ahead of them. Volstagg blanched at what he saw. Parts of the walls and ceiling were shimmering with motion. He glanced back the way they'd come and saw more portals forming. "Help," Hogun continued. "That's just what the Vrellnexian you struck is doing: getting help."

"Move, before they surround us," Hogun ordered his companions. He matched action to his words, starting off in a sprint down the tunnel. It appeared it took a little time for the shimmering portals to open. If they could get ahead of the portals, they would at least keep from being surrounded.

"Keep away from the walls," Fandral enjoined them, a bit of a shudder in his tone. Hogun imagined he was thinking how narrowly he'd been saved from those spidery arms.

"Walls. Ceiling. Floor," Volstagg growled. The huge warrior's sword flashed once more, severing a clutch of arms that tried to seize his legs as a portion of the floor swirled open. The Vrellnexian withdrew as its limbs tumbled back into the portal. Volstagg made an awkward jump to cross the rippling doorway. His maneuver ended in a precarious pose just on the cusp of the still-stable floor. Hogun swung around and grabbed the baldrick that crossed Volstagg's chest, using it to pull his friend back before he could tumble into the portal he'd crossed.

"Above you!" Fandral shouted. Hogun turned his head in time to see clawed hands reaching down from a doorway that had appeared directly above them. He shoved Volstagg to one side while twisting away in the other direction. The claws clacked closed just where his head had been a moment before.

The spidery arms flailed about for a moment, then Hogun saw a grotesque head the size of a human's peek out from the portal. It was an utterly inhuman shape, a squat and flattened oval topped by a set of black, multi-faceted eyes and with a massive set of serrated mandibles at its front. Of nose or ears there wasn't the least trace, but he could see a mouth behind the mandibles with four sharp segments clashing against each other in a manner that reminded him of a man grinding his teeth in frustration.

"Here's something you'll find even more annoying," Hogun said, lunging back toward the portal. He brought his mace whipping upward, striking the insectoid head and driving the creature back through the doorway. Green ichor stained his weapon and spattered his clothes.

"At least they're easy to send back to wherever they're coming from," Volstagg grinned.

Fandral pointed at the tunnel behind them. "What about once they're out?"

By Hogun's estimation, there must have been dozens of doorways that had formed in the tunnel. Each was disgorging or had already emitted a Vrellnexian. Seen in the whole, they were more gruesome than their parts. Only their upright posture lent them any similarity to human shape. Their bodies were bulbous and covered in gray fur. Six limbs projected from their sides without any semblance of shoulders or hips. Two of these were thick and ended in a shovel-like foot devoid of toes. The other four constituted two sets of arms. The head seemed to sprout directly from the body without the benefit of a neck.

"We can fight them," Hogun said.

Fandral gestured at the floor. "If we let them pin us, they might just open doors under us and drag us down that way. We've got to keep moving."

Hogun conceded the point. But he was worried they weren't giving the Vrellnexians enough credit. "We can keep moving only until they get ahead of us. One way or another, we'll have to smash our way through."

Volstagg cried out in pain. "Sneaky," he cursed, twisting away from the claws reaching out of the wall beside him. One claw was clamped tight on his arm and maintained its grip. But the Vrellnexian wasn't able to resist Volstagg's mass when he moved. Drawing back from the portal, Volstagg pulled the spidery being through. "This is what happens to sneaks!" he roared as he brought his sword slashing at the creature. The Vrellnexian sagged back, its body cut down the middle. The dead claw maintained its stubborn grip, forcing Volstagg to hack it free as the Asgardians hurried away from the aliens pursuing them.

"If we can find Terrok's door, we might get into the tower before they can catch us," Volstagg shouted.

Fandral thrust his blade into a Vrellnexian as it started to emerge from a doorway. "Even if we were right beside it, how would you tell it apart from all the new ones they're opening?"

As Hogun had worried, the Vrellnexians were creating portals ahead of them. From what he could see, they stretched far enough that there was no way the Warriors Three could avoid being surrounded by the insects.

"By Hela's Crown," Volstagg cursed. "It's like we stirred up a hornet's nest!" He swung at a Vrellnexian as the creature sprang at him. His blade sheared through the creature and the momentum of the blow sent it spinning back into the other aliens.

"Don't let them bite you!" Fandral warned, slashing the mandibles from an attacker as it tried to do just that. "That's how they drain your energy."

"Bugs *and* vampires," Volstagg growled, smashing another of the creatures. "I'd like to know how these things could be worse."

Hogun whipped Hridgandr around, swatting the Vrellnexians rushing at them from behind. "They could be Enchanters like Magnir," he told Volstagg.

Abruptly, the Vrellnexians drew back. As though a switch had been thrown, they stopped their attack. They withdrew only far enough to be out of easy reach of the Asgardians. Their multi-faceted eyes glimmered in the glow of the crystals. The insectoid visages were incapable of expression, revealing nothing of the thoughts and intentions of the creatures.

"Some new trickery?" Hogun wondered.

Volstagg wagged his sword at the Vrellnexians. "Finally come to your senses and decided that battle with the Warriors Three makes for a bad future?"

"They're up to something," Fandral said, uncertainty in his tone. "They've stopped opening new portals."

Hogun noticed that the swirling doors that had already been opened were turning back into fibrous solidity. "Be on your guard. We'll still have to fight our way through these to reach Magnir."

The Enchanter's name provoked a response from the Vrellnexians. The creatures stirred, and he could see claws clacking open and closed in a display of hostility. Suddenly one of the Vrellnexians stepped away from the swarm. It kept its upper arms folded against its body while the others were held out to its sides. Hogun thought the posture looked more appeasing than threatening, but he wasn't taking chances.

"If you can understand me, stop where you are," he challenged the spidery creature, pointing Hridgandr at it.

The Vrellnexian stopped. It tilted its body. "It is strange that you employ vocal vibrations to articulate your thought-impulses," a shrill voice buzzed in Hogun's brain. "Stranger still that you can do so without mechanical aid."

"I can hear it speaking inside my head," Volstagg gasped.

"We speak to all of you," the Vrellnexian said. "To your minds. We can see your thoughts. You would harm us."

Fandral wiped some of the ichor from Fimbuldraugr. "To defend ourselves. What we've heard of Vrellnexians wasn't to your favor."

The insectoid clasped all four arms to its body. "We care nothing for what others think of us. Only that they are of utility to the Vrellnexians." It pointed one claw at the warriors. "You will serve us."

Hogun shook his head. "For a negotiator, you take a haughty tone."

"We don't serve the cause of evil," Fandral said. "Any friends of the Sssth are our enemy."

The Vrellnexian stared at Fandral for a moment. When its thought-impulses came again, Hogun thought there was a confused quality to them. It seemed the spiders had no concept of "friend", only resource and obstacle.

"The Sssth are useful to us. We have advanced their technology, enabled them to range beyond their own planetary system," the Vrellnexian explained. "They provide us with a wide variety of prey-stock."

"You mean the slaves," Hogun bristled.

The Vrellnexian took a step back, aware of the mounting outrage, even if it was unable to comprehend why. "We have controlled the Sssthgar and ensured his decisions brought prosperity to us."

"But now you've lost your hold over the Sssthgar," Fandral said. "Since Magnir arrived, there's been another power behind the throne on Golden Star."

"You have come to destroy Magnir," the Vrellnexian stated. "We can see this too in your thoughts." It gestured at each of the Asgardians. "You seek to use our tunnels to enter the Sssthgar's tower so you may overcome Magnir."

"And you intend to stop us," Volstagg glowered at the alien. "There'll be a lot fewer of you around. That's one thing you can be sure of."

The Vrellnexian's body made a curious shuddering motion. It took Hogun a moment to realize it was trying to mimic a man shaking his head. "No. If your intention is to dispose of Magnir, we would help you. We will open a doorway from this tunnel to where you will find the Enchanter."

"There's a deal too good to be true." Fandral's mouth curled in a thin smile. "And what, my vampiric friend, do you expect in return for this boon you'll grant to us?"

The spindly limbs curled against the bloated body again. "You will remove Magnir for us. He has been an obstacle to our prosperity. In his absence, the Sssthgar will recover his utility to us. We will bring you to the Enchanter, but only if no harm is done to the Sssthgar."

With all they'd heard and seen of the Sssthgar's atrocities, Hogun knew Fandral would never agree to such a deal. Of them all, Fandral was uncompromising in his ideals. He'd let them blind him to the bigger picture. In this case, stopping Magnir, even if the Sssthgar remained, would bring some relief to the denizens of Golden Star. And it would bring the Warriors Three one step closer to ending the Enchanters' threat to Asgard.

"You've my word," Hogun declared before Fandral could reject the Vrellnexians. "Bring us to Magnir and we'll leave the Sssthgar unharmed." It rankled him even worse to leave Golden Star to the Sssth than it had to leave Gunnarsfell to its despot. Still, Onund had brought them to Golden Star once. The seer would do so again, and when he did there'd be an end to all tyrants.

"Then we will help you,' the Vrellnexian said. Its compound eyes glittered malignantly. "At least while you are useful to us."

TEN

Stepping through the Vrellnexian doorway was, in its way, the least unsettling aspect of their weird tunnels. Volstagg considered it little different to walking into another room. One moment there was the tunnel with its fibrous walls and bipedal spiders, the next he was standing in a different place. There wasn't the flash of motion as in the Drop, or the nauseating sensation of being pulled apart by Onund's astral circle. There was simply the seamless transition from one place to another.

That other proved to be as remarkable as his first view of Golden Star's colossal city. Volstagg was poised upon a causeway that ran the circumference of a mammoth hall. Thor could stampede a tribe of giants through the chamber and still there would have been room to spare.

The hall was dominated by rectangular kilns within which molten metal bubbled and steamed. Huge cauldrons suspended by the same variety of levitating lights as the

Sssth sky-sleds flew through the hall, sometimes dipping into one of the kilns to fill themselves. Volstagg saw some kind of shimmering distortion around the cauldrons when they immersed themselves and reasoned they must be protected by a kind of mystical shell. The filled cauldrons then sped across the hall to a battery of strange machines with great funnels above them. The metal was poured into these devices. He watched as the molten metal was stamped into different shapes by presses, then rapidly cooled by a freezing vapor emitted by a hovering, keg-like contraption with a clutch of hoses writhing from its face. Some of the presses shaped the metal into what looked to be swords, others were busy rendering components that resembled enormous pieces of armor.

"The place is a foundry," Volstagg observed.

"An armory to outfit an army," Fandral nodded.

"Big as they are, no Sssth could fit into the armor those machines are making," Hogun said.

Volstagg focused on a vambrace as it left a press and trundled down a sort of sluice to enter a second machine. He saw it pass by a Sssth overseer and saw that Hogun was right. If the vambrace was meant to close around an arm, then that arm was as tall as the Sssth soldier! A sense of horrible foreboding came upon Volstagg.

"By Bifrost's gates!" he cursed. "Magnir's plan must be to arm the giants of Jotunheim and lead them against Asgard!"

Fandral tapped Volstagg's shoulder and turned his attention to another of the machines. "I don't think so. There's some other devilry at work here."

The machine Fandral indicated was at a juncture of two

Three Swords 115

sluices. Volstagg could see pieces of leg armor being brought together and welded into place by a stick-like rod that emitted a searing light. He was wondering how someone would fit into the armor if it was sealed together in such a manner. Then he looked further along the line and saw that each greave was already filled, stuffed with a confusion of wires and gears that he didn't think even a dwarf would be able to make sense of.

"It looks like armor, but it isn't," Fandral stated.

"It won't matter what it is once we've finished Magnir," Hogun growled. He pointed to a space at the center of the hall, a spot where all the sluices finally converged.

Volstagg could see a number of Sssth gathering up the different sections of armor, whether they were legs or arms, pelvis or torso. The reptiles fit them together like squires attending a knight, some of them using light-emitting rods to fuse wires together. The helmets, smooth ovals with only a narrow visor to suggest eyes, were each the size of a Sssth's chest and needed two of the lizards to carry them across to a kind of circular dais.

"The Enchanter," Volstagg whispered when he saw the figure standing to one side of the dais. The shape was that of an Asgardian, his face hidden behind a spike-fringed helm that left only his eyes and mouth exposed. He was encased in a suit of golden armor, but across the chest was the unmistakable outline of a Living Talisman. Volstagg felt his belly churn to see the evil visage within the jewel gibbering to itself and grinning as Magnir went about his labors.

For the Enchanter was at work. Work of a horrible and profane sort. Volstagg could see that the dais was etched with eldritch runes that flickered and flashed with infernal energies. The Sssth positioned the huge helm within this network of runes before quickly scurrying away. Magnir gestured with one of his spiked gauntlets and from the floor beside him a glass globe lifted into the air. Using his magic, he levitated it closer to the helm, then he reached into the sphere. The glass wasn't shattered by his touch, his fingers simply reached through it to grab what was inside and withdraw it.

"A brain," Fandral hissed. "Now we know what he does with the slaves."

Volstagg saw Magnir reverse the process. His hand passed through the metal helm and deposited the disembodied brain within. As he pulled his hand free, his fingers brushed across the forehead. A slithery rune unfamiliar to Volstagg seared itself into the surface, blazing with a volcanic light. Magnir then waved the Sssth over to retrieve the helm and carry it away to where they were assembling the rest of the armor.

"That must be the Sssthgar," Volstagg commented as a tall Sssth who had been standing away from the dais now moved up and joined the Enchanter. The reptile was much bigger than the rest of his kind, an imposing nine feet from his boots to the shock of black hair that grew from the crest of his saurian skull. He wore a long purple tunic and his arms were encased in armor of some dark and lusterless metal. From the belt around the reptile's waist hung a double-edged axe of Asgardian design.

"It looks like Magnir has been making presents as well as threats to keep on friendly terms with the lizards," Fandral said. "Whatever he's promised them makes the Sssth confident that they don't need to stay on good terms with the Vrellnexians anymore."

"We kill the Enchanter, his spells end with him," Hogun said.

"It's a fair distance to cross," Volstagg mused. "We're certain to be spotted before we..."

But even as the big warrior was expressing his concern, the danger was upon them. A Sssth patrolling the causeway saw them when it rounded the edge of a kiln. The reptile blinked at them in shock for a moment, then its clawed hand slapped a badge on its tunic. Immediately a keening alert shrieked through the gigantic hall.

"Slinking wretch!" Volstagg roared. He would have started after the sentry, but Fandral turned him around.

"Too late to worry about that one," Fandral said. "We need to try for Magnir before the Sssth can organize against us!"

Hogun had already leaped down from the causeway to the floor below. Reptiles charged for him, thrusting at him with the electrified poles they used to manipulate the armor components through the sluices. His mace lashed out, swatting one of the lizards across the chamber so that its body dented one of the kilns.

Volstagg followed Fandral in jumping from the causeway. He heard the railing sizzle behind him as the sentry fired at him with its raygun. His mass made him fall faster than Fandral, something his friend had failed to factor when they leaped. A hovering cauldron was just sweeping past. Even a heartbeat's delay would have caused Volstagg to miss colliding with it, but as things stood, he slammed into the flying obstruction.

Instinctively, Volstagg grabbed the sides of the cauldron and arrested his fall. He glanced down to see Fandral hit the floor. The warrior was up in an instant, parrying the attacks of Sssth guards with his sword.

The crackle of the raygun flew past Volstagg's ear. He saw a spot on the side of the cauldron evaporate. From the resultant hole, a spurt of liquid metal bubbled out. So completely insulated was the conveyance that until then he'd imagined it was empty. Now, watching the metal dribble from the hole, an idea formed.

Volstagg could see the Sssth massing for an attack. The workers had only their spear-like poles, but the guards had electro-swords and rayguns at their disposal. Seeing the ferocity with which Hogun and Fandral met their opposition, the guards decided not to try subduing the Asgardians through swordplay. Instead, they formed up into a double file and drew their rayguns.

"Knaves die the death of knaves," Volstagg snarled through gritted teeth. Shifting his grip on the cauldron, he brought his full weight to one side. At the same time, he kicked his boot against one of the lights underneath the conveyance, striking it until he felt a shudder pass through the machine and knew it was out of action.

With Volstagg's weight unbalancing it and with half of its suspensors eliminated, the cauldron tipped over onto its side. The reptilian guards had only a moment to realize their doom as a tide of molten metal poured down on them from above.

Three Swords 119

Volstagg dropped away from the cauldron, leaving it to whizz crazily through the hall. He slammed into the floor only a few feet from the massacred guards. A pair of workers charged at him with their poles, but a flash of Brandrheid Undrsigr cut the tools in half. The Sssth workers were thrown back as the cleft poles sparked and exploded in their hands.

There were no other Sssth near him for the moment. Volstagg could see Magnir and the Sssthgar near the dais, both shouting orders at the reptiles near them. These, however, weren't rushing to attack, but were instead swarming around the giant suit of armor. Volstagg smiled. The lizards must think the Warriors Three were going to steal the oversized mail. Their time would have been better spent trying to stop the Asgardians.

Dismissing the Sssth by the dais, Volstagg turned back to where his friends were surrounded by reptiles. They were holding their own, but it was a precarious stand. Any moment might see the sentry on the causeway land one of its shots and give the advantage to the reptiles.

Volstagg picked up the end of one of the broken poles and hurled it across the hall. It slammed into the sentry, throwing the lizard back and crumpling it against the wall. Firming his grip on his sword, he charged into the melee. "Never fear! Volstagg the Overwhelming will rout these lizards!"

The huge Asgardian crashed into the fray like a typhoon. Sssth were scattered in every direction as he slammed into them. His sword cut down others as they menaced his friends. Soon the floor was strewn with dead and wounded reptiles.

"It'll need better fighters than you to stand against the Warriors Three!" Volstagg roared as he caught one of the Sssth in an overhand grip. Despite the lizard's enormous size, he sent the alien crashing into two of its fellows.

"You should've tried to stop Magnir while you were clear," Fandral complained as he parried a Sssth blade and used the guard of his sword to knock the reptile senseless. As the lizard wilted to the floor, the whole room shook. A pulsing vibration that caused even the massive kilns to shudder and molten metal to slop over their edges.

Volstagg swung around and his eyes widened with shock. "By all the Vanir, what is that?" he gasped as he looked towards the dais. Another vibration shivered through the hall.

"Obviously our enemies took your suggestion," Hogun said as he warded the swing of a Sssth blade. "They built a better fighter."

Fandral slammed Fimbuldraugr against the side of a Sssth skull and sent the lizard senseless to the floor. Dispatching the reptiles was a simple enough chore. What worried him now was dealing with the colossal threat lumbering towards them from the middle of the hall.

The giant armor the Sssth were assembling was now stomping its way across the chamber. Forty feet tall, each time the colossus lowered its foot the impact sent a tremor through the tower. In one armored fist it held a sword with a blade twenty feet in length. Though the visor that stretched across its head was as black and empty as a despot's heart, Fandral could sense an awareness emanating from it. He thought of the disembodied brain Magnir had set into the metal helm and an icy tingle swept down his spine. The mind of a murdered being imprisoned in a monster built by their killer, to serve even after death as a slave to their oppressors.

"Hogun! Volstagg!" Fandral shouted to his companions. "Time to stop playing with the small fry!" He drove the point of Fimbuldraugr into the chest of a Sssth warrior and kicked the alien's body free from his blade. "If we're to stop Magnir, first we've got to stop the abomination he's conjured!"

Another slash of his sword had Fandral free of enemies. He started across the hall, trusting that the other warriors would follow as soon as they were clear too. He didn't know how they were going to stop the metal giant. All he knew was that they had to try.

The giant continued its lumbering advance. When it judged Fandral was near enough, its enormous arm rose. The immense sword shone like a firebrand before the colossus brought it slashing down. Fandral dove from its path, but was struck by debris as the floor exploded under the impact. Slivers of jagged metal slashed into him as the blow gouged a pit in the floor. Even as he regained his feet, a sidewise sweep of the blade slammed into him. The flat of the blade smacked Fandral like a whale's tail. He was flung across the hall, crashing into one of the sluices with such force that it crumpled around him. Gelatinous sludge used to convey the armored pieces splashed across him while his dazed mind tried to regain its senses.

"Pick on someone your own size!" The roar was Volstagg's and when Fandral was able to focus his eyes he saw the big

Asgardian racing to intercept the colossus before it could reach him. Volstagg drove his shoulder against the giant's ankle, a point where its armor appeared thinnest. Instead of caving in the foot, Volstagg glanced off the titan as though he were a fly. He was sent skittering along the floor and ended his slide in a sprawl beneath one of the damaged machines. He was only just able to scramble out of the way as a floating cauldron mindlessly tried to pour molten metal into a funnel that was no longer there. Fiery drops spattered his clothes as he threw himself aside.

The giant turned its attention away from Fandral to Volstagg. It started after him, unaware that Hogun was now moving to the attack. Having seen the futility of Volstagg's charge, he tried a different approach. Waiting until the giant was lowering its foot, Hogun darted into the very shadow of its step. Hridgandr smashed against the descending foot. The armor resisted the impact, but not the momentum. The colossus flailed its arms as it lost its balance and went toppling backwards to slam into one of the kilns. Slag came pouring out, steaming as it struck the giant's titanic frame.

"Well, that didn't work," Hogun growled as he rushed over and helped Fandral. Despite the molten flow around it, the giant was picking itself up from the ground.

"Look at the way the slag just drips off its body," Volstagg grumbled as he joined them. "Whatever spells Magnir has laid on his golem, they're potent. I don't know if Mjolnir would even be able to crack that thing." He grimaced as he rubbed at the shoulder he'd driven into the giant's ankle.

Fandral's gaze fixated on a peculiarity in the way the colossus moved. Ponderous in its motions, anything that even hinted at spryness made for a notable contrast. "I wouldn't be so sure," Fandral told him. "Look at the way it keeps its head away from the slag.

"If we can't beat the body, we need to beat the mind," Fandral stated. An idea was forming. If he was right, it would mean the destruction of Magnir's giant. If he was wrong, he didn't rate their chances for leaving the tower alive.

"It looks like it's decided Hogun is the one it wants now," Fandral said as the colossus started advancing again. He smiled at the grim warrior. "That means you'll have to be bait."

Hogun just glared at the giant. "I knocked it down once, I can do it again."

"Just keep its attention and get it near the other kiln." Fandral pulled Volstagg aside and the two scrambled to put distance between themselves and Hogun. "We're the ones who'll knock it down."

While Fandral led Volstagg away, Hogun brandished his mace and drew the giant after him. "Help me with this vambrace," Fandral told Volstagg. Together they retrieved the immense piece of armor from the crumpled sluice. It had yet to be filled with wires and gears, but even so its weight was considerable. "This should hold," Fandral said approvingly.

Volstagg looked past him to where Hogun was dodging the giant's sword. "Whatever you're going to do, you'd better do it quick."

"What *we're* going to do," Fandral corrected him. "Take that side and follow me." Seizing one end of the vambrace, he dashed towards the giant. Volstagg trotted after him, holding up his side of the armor.

The giant's sword gouged another crater in the floor as it missed Hogun. Fandral ducked behind the vambrace as shrapnel was thrown into the air. Then he was in motion, sprinting for the colossus. "You on one side of its foot, me on the other," he instructed Volstagg.

The Asgardians hurried into position, spreading so that the vambrace was across the giant's foot. "Hold tight!" Fandral shouted as the colossus started to step forward.

The vambrace buckled under the giant's strength, but the combined brawn of Fandral and Volstagg held it fast for an instant before they were lifted into the air and spilled to the floor. The instant, however, was all they needed. The colossus was powerful but ungainly and the slight drag as it raised its foot was just enough to trip it. With a thunderous crash, it fell forwards.

The side of the kiln exploded under the giant's weight. Molten metal surged across the floor, forcing the Warriors Three to leap onto machines to avoid being scalded. The colossus pitched forward, slamming into the fiery pool. It jerked back, as though it was a living thing that had been burned and not an automaton of metal. Fandral smiled when he saw steam billowing from the visor and around the underside of the helm, then his mood became somber. The brain inside had been alive, torn from a slave. It might be a mercy to spare the imprisoned mind such hideous captivity, but it wasn't something to celebrate.

The sword crashed to the floor as it fell from the giant's grasp. The colossus swayed from side to side as molten metal that had entered the head slowly dripped down its chest. The giant remained standing, but that awful sense of awareness Fandral had detected was absent. It was no longer Magnir's horrible creature. The brain had been burned away.

"That's what happens when you challenge Volstagg the Voluminous!" Volstagg shouted at the inert giant.

"No, that's what happens when there are still flaws in the design." The voice echoed through the hall, a savage tone that would have made a wolf's fur bristle. Fandral turned to see the Enchanter stepping away from his dais, the Sssthgar and other lizards close beside him.

"A disappointing test, but an instructive one," the masked sorcerer continued. His lips pulled back in a fearsome sneer. "For that, you have my gratitude. I may even make your deaths painless."

Magnir's sneer curled into something even more hateful. "Of course, I make no promises."

ELEVEN

Magnir's hands gyrated in arcane passes. A bolt of dark energy formed in the palm of his right hand. With a gesture he sent the malefic spell hurtling at his enemies. The Warriors Three were lifted off their feet and sent reeling. Hogun's chest felt like he'd been kicked by a troll and there was a burning sensation throughout his body.

"Filthy wizard," Hogun spat, lunging up from where he'd fallen.

"Wait!" Fandral called after him, reaching out to stop him.

It was much too late for restraint. The fury was upon Hogun now. In casting his spell against Hogun, Magnir had focused all of the warrior's rage onto himself. He wouldn't rest until he saw the wizard vanquished.

Hogun sprinted away from his companions, trying to spare them any further attacks from Magnir. If the wizard was going to conjure, he'd have to fixate on one target.

The Enchanter sent another bolt of searing energy

Three Swords 127

hurtling for Hogun. The warrior brought his mace up to ward off the blast as he had the rays fired at him by the Sssth. Magnir's magic wasn't so easily drawn off and Hridgandr did nothing to blunt the impact. Again he was blown backwards, his body writhing in pain.

"The dogs of Asgard follow my trail," Magnir snarled. He sent another arcane blast into Hogun, battering him across the hall. "Aren't you pleased you found me?" the wizard laughed as his enemy collided with one of the machines.

Hogun felt blood trickling down his chin. Something inside felt broken when he moved, provoking a grinding agony along his left side. It was pride, not prudence, that forced him back to his feet. He hadn't bowed before Mogul, he wouldn't grovel before Magnir.

"Ho, sorcerer! Dare you forget you face Volstagg the Devastating!" Volstagg's shout echoed through the hall. Hogun saw Magnir spin around and redirect the energy bolt he'd conjured. It went speeding toward Volstagg and Fandral.

The two Asgardians had already dipped down. They hefted the immense length of the metal giant's sword onto its side. The spell struck the blade and evaporated into a puff of crimson smoke.

Purpose now restrained Hogun's fury. Strategy tempered the hate that surged through him. Magnir had built the colossus to be impervious to damage. It only made sense that among the things he'd sought to protect it from would be the destructive magic its creator knew so well. Hogun turned and dashed back to the machinery and the sluice winding away from it. He let his mace drop and hang from its tether while he seized one of the immense pauldrons being shifted along by the flowing ooze.

"You think yourselves clever?" Magnir raged. His hands curled into a new weave of gestures. The floor beneath the giant sword heaved and tore itself apart, levitating itself and the blade high into the air. The moment they were exposed, Fandral stood up, a knife in his hand.

"Yes, in fact, we think we are," Fandral mocked the Enchanter as he flung the knife across the hall. Only the strength of an Asgardian could have managed to cover that distance and only the peerless aim of Fandral could have sent the blade to its target. There was a cry of pain and the crack of metal against metal. Magnir staggered back, his cheek gashed by the knife which was now firmly lodged between his bleeding flesh and the edge of his helm.

The Enchanter lost his concentration and the giant sword crashed back to the ground. Fandral and Volstagg scattered to avoid being crushed by the falling blade. Clasping one hand to his bleeding face, Magnir waved his other toward the Asgardians. "Kill them, you witless lizards!" he screamed.

Hogun saw the Sssthgar and his soldiers swarm forward. The robed leader drew the axe from his belt, pointing it at Volstagg. "That one is mine!" the warlord snarled. Hogun wondered if it was Volstagg's size or his bragging that made the Sssthgar single him out for attention. The alien was far from timid, rushing ahead of his troops to enter the fray. Maybe he simply wanted the best fight he could find.

Fandral turned to meet the rush of Sssth that diverted away from Volstagg to charge him. Another clutch of soldiers

Three Swords

advanced toward Hogun, sporting an array of swords and spears. Hogun pulled down the pauldron, gripping it by a handful of the wires inside. The massive piece of armor meant to shape the shoulder of a colossus served the Asgardian like a tower shield, covering him from head to toe. Some of the reptiles, seeing him lift the pauldron, cast their spears in an effort to hit him before he could protect himself, but they were too tardy in their throws and the weapons glanced harmlessly from the golden armor.

Hogun bent down and grabbed one of the fallen spears. The Sssth charge faltered for an instant as the lizards feared which of them would be his target. His aim was far different, however. Deliberately turning and exposing his side to the aliens, Hogun cast the weapon at Magnir.

The Enchanter was still struggling to remove the knife lodged between his cheek and his helm, but he hastily abandoned that task when he saw Hogun turn. He quickly made arcane gestures as the spear came flying towards him. A section of the floor rose up, the metal wrenched away as though by an invisible titan. The levitating floor tipped and placed itself in the path of the spear. Hogun's missile slammed into the improvised shield, its tip punching through but without the momentum to carry the rest of the shaft onward to strike the wizard.

"You will die!" Magnir raged, his eyes blazing. "All of you will die!" In his anger he sent a flurry of arcane blasts toward Hogun. The warrior swung the pauldron about, covering himself with its protection. The Sssth rushing him were afforded no such defense. While many of the bolts sizzled into smoke against the shield, others slammed into the reptiles. The lizards shrieked as their scaly bodies were incinerated by Magnir's spells.

"Only fools trust wizards!" Hogun shouted at the surviving reptiles around him. With the bodies of their comrades strewn around them, the Sssth guards saw wisdom in Hogun's words and scattered through the hall to scurry out hatches and doors.

"I merely require minions who are less fragile," Magnir hissed at Hogun. The Enchanter's eyes closed for just an instant. In that moment the whole hall shook. Hogun noted that sections of the wall beyond Magnir were rolling back, receding into the floor and ceiling. He realized with a start that they were gargantuan doors.

Behind each door, its armored body shining like gold, stood another of the colossal giants. Slowly they stepped away from their vault-like chambers and into the hall.

"You destroyed one of my robots," Magnir cackled. "Let's see how you fare against seven!"

Volstagg felt his bones quiver from the impact of the axe as he blocked the Sssthgar's strike. Resilient as a blade forged by dwarves might be, he half expected Brandrheid Undrsigr to shatter when the reptile swung at him again and he was forced to parry the swing. The warlord was incredibly strong, even by the standards of Asgard.

The Sssthgar, too, appreciated the power of his foe. As they pressed their blades between them, the alien leaned his scaly face closer. "Magnir did not tell me all his people were so strong. Your kind will make good slaves after the Sssth conquer your world."

Three Swords 131

A mental image of Gunnhilde and their children languishing under the Sssth slashed through Volstagg's mind. His body responded with a surge of enraged might. With a great exertion he pushed the Sssthgar back and freed his sword from the pressure of his axe.

"You've not yet tasted a measure of my might, lizard-lord," Volstagg growled at the Sssthgar. "There's a reason Magnir didn't bring your scum to Asgard. He knew my people would thrash you reptiles so badly no one would even call it a fight!"

The Sssthgar's eyes flashed with anger and he started to lunge for Volstagg. The Asgardian made ready to block the warlord's axe, but at the last moment the lizard turned his lunge into a spin. The powerful tail came whipping around, battering Volstagg's knees and spilling him to the floor.

Instantly the Sssthgar sprang at Volstagg, his axe clutched in both hands for a strike that would have split the hero's skull. The cut never landed. Drawing his legs up, Volstagg kicked out, hitting the Sssthgar and hurling him across the hall. The reptile slammed into one of the machines, collapsing it down on himself.

"That's what happens when you have the temerity to tangle with Volstagg the Valiant," Volstagg said. As he rose to his feet and dusted himself off, he saw the pile of wreckage stir. The next moment, tons of mangled machinery were thrown aside and the Sssthgar emerged from the debris. The reptile's robe was ripped, his scales were bloodied, and his tail was broken, but his eyes flamed with a malevolence worthy of Surtur.

"I will make a goblet of your skull!" the Sssthgar roared,

spitting cracked fangs from his mouth. Still gripping his axe, the warlord charged for Volstagg.

"Can't say I like how that sounds," Volstagg muttered. He held his sword in both hands, ready to meet the Sssthgar's strike. The enormous reptile slammed into him with such force that he was nearly knocked off his feet. Dwarven steel crashed against alien metal as the two struggled to overcome one another by main force. Looming over Volstagg, the Sssthgar snapped down with his scaly mouth. Volstagg felt the reptile's remaining fangs scrape against his plumed helm. A heartbeat later he felt pressure against his head as the lizard's jaws began to crumple the helm as a prelude to crushing his skull.

Volstagg's head was forced down by the Sssthgar's attack. Needing both hands around his sword if he was to keep the alien's axe from slashing into his chest, he sought some way by which to escape the warlord's assault. His face turned to the floor, where he saw the now crooked tail. An impish smile worked itself onto Volstagg's face. Quickly he lifted one foot and brought it stomping down on the Sssthgar's broken appendage.

The Sssthgar reeled away, a shriek of pain rasping up from his maw. Volstagg drove after the warlord, slamming his shoulder into the reptile's chest and knocking him back. His foe stumbled and tried to regain his balance, but Volstagg hit him again, the impact pushing the Sssthgar dozens of feet across the hall.

"It'll be a cold day in Muspelheim before I let your scum threaten my home," Volstagg snarled as he barreled into the Sssthgar once more. This time he overestimated his charge and the reptile was able to sidestep his attack. Volstagg hurtled onward, unable to stop himself. His eyes widened when he saw the hole torn open by Magnir's spell looming before him. A cold wind billowed up from the gap and as he staggered toward it he could see the yawning abyss below.

Volstagg dropped to his knees and stabbed his sword into the floor to arrest his motion. His body was whipped around as his momentum was suddenly reversed. Spinning about, he saw the Sssthgar rushing for him. The warlord brought his axe chopping down, narrowly missing Volstagg's shoulder as he continued his spin.

"Missed," Volstagg jeered as he kicked and knocked the Sssthgar's feet out from under him. The next instant he came to regret the move as the lizard slammed down on him and flattened him against the floor.

"I will pick my fangs with your spine!" the Sssthgar hissed, his forked tongue flicking across Volstagg's nose.

"I'll make that easier for you," Volstagg grunted, feeling the Sssthgar's mass pressing his chest. Lurching forward he drove his forehead into the reptile's chin. A spray of broken teeth exploded from the saurian jaws. For a moment the pressure on him lessened and Volstagg wrapped his arms around the lizard, squeezing him in a crushing embrace. With a fierce effort, he used his leverage to roll them both across the floor.

The Sssthgar flailed against Volstagg's grip. Unable to bring the keen edge of his axe to bear, the reptile instead battered the Asgardian with the flat of the blade. Volstagg ground his teeth against the pain and focused himself on maintaining his hold. It was a test of endurance now, trying to see whether Asgardian or Sssth would submit first.

At least that was Volstagg's intention. But their wild grapple across the floor foiled such plans. One instant he felt the cold metal underneath him, the next there was nothing. Frantically he released his grip on the Sssthgar and reached for anything that might keep him from falling. His tussle with the lizard had carried them both over the hole.

Against all hope, Volstagg's fingers clutched a jagged strip of the torn floor. He was just able to stop his fall when his body suddenly lurched downward again. A tremendous weight was dragging at him and trying to pull him down.

Volstagg turned his head and saw the mind-numbing sight of the pit. The hall was somewhere near the top of the Sssthgar's tower, built across a cap that stretched out wider than the levels beneath it. Where the floor had been torn away there was no building below, only a precipitous plunge to the distant depths of Golden Star's great city.

The Sssthgar had failed to find a handhold like Volstagg, but one scaly hand was caught in the warrior's belt. The reptile's eyes were wide with panic... until he saw the Asgardian looking at him. Then they narrowed with hate. One hand gripped Volstagg's belt, but the other still held the axe. Volstagg saw the reptile squirm in a sidewise motion as he tried to raise the axe to strike.

"Don't be an idiot!" Volstagg shouted at the warlord. "You'll kill us both!"

The Sssthgar spat a broken fang up at him. "Death is better than disgrace," he snapped.

The axe came swinging for Volstagg. At the same time,

Three Swords 135

he reached to his belt and undid the clasp. The axehead was diverted as the Sssthgar went hurtling downward, one hand still gripping the Asgardian's belt.

"Those Vrellnexians aren't going to be happy about that," Volstagg sighed as he watched the Sssthgar vanish into the distance. "But there's a lot of people on Golden Star who will be." Mustering his strength, he heaved himself up from the hole. He hoped his friends were having an easier time than he was.

Fandral caught up the sliver of armor from the sluice and pushed his arm into the nest of wires until it was held firmly in place. He'd seen how the components of Magnir's robot had withstood the Enchanter's spells. Now he hoped it would be just as effective against Sssth rayguns. The section he'd taken would have formed one side of a colossal finger, but it was of a perfect size to employ as shield.

"Alright, you scalawags, let's try this again," Fandral yelled at the reptilian warriors pursuing him across the hall. He raised the shield and intercepted the shot from a raygun. The beam's impact against the armor was so slight he barely felt it. The lizard who'd fired the shot snarled and cast aside its weapon to draw its sword. The four alongside it followed suit.

"Five against one? Now it seems to me I've been in this situation recently," Fandral smiled at the Sssth. "It didn't go so well for the five." Without waiting for the reptiles to make their attack, he sprang into their midst. One Sssth fell back, clutching at its slashed throat. Another crumpled to the floor, its skull cracked by a swat from Fandral's improvised shield.

"Then there were three," Fandral said as he parried blows from the Sssth. In the midst of the fray, he felt tremors ripple through the floor. Glancing past the lizardmen, he found a sight that sent a shiver through him. Magnir had called up more of his colossal automatons. It had taken a trick to defeat one of the metal giants. How would they beat an entire column of the monsters?

The answer suggested itself even as Fimbuldraugr cut a Sssth across the shoulder and put the reptile out of the fight. He could see Hogun rushing between the machines, blocking Magnir's spells with his own improvised shield. Foot by foot, he was closing the distance to the sorcerer. But could he get close enough before the robots blocked his path?

"If the warrior can't reach the wizard, maybe we can make the wizard reach the warrior," Fandral mused. His sword ripped into one of the remaining Sssth. As the alien fell, the last lizard turned to run. Before it could move, Fandral slammed into it from behind and knocked it down. He had his blade at its throat before it could rise.

"You can be on your way, friend, if you do me a slight service," Fandral told the Sssth. He pointed up at the levitating cauldrons that continued to zoom through the hall. Throughout the fray, they'd continued to operate as though nothing untoward had occurred. "Tell me how those things are given direction." Fandral thought it over a moment and pulled the lizard onto its feet. "No, better yet, show me how it's done."

Fandral had already seen that when it came to their own lives, the Sssth weren't reckless. His prisoner led him along the hall to a curious bank of levers and lights. He kept his blade at the alien's throat as he told it what he wanted done. "Bring yon cauldron swinging down for the Enchanter."

The Sssth cringed back in horror, an amusing sight, Fandral considered, given its imposing size. "He would kill me," the reptile protested.

"Only if we lose," Fandral stated. He prodded the scaly hide with his sword. "I suggest you do what I tell you so that we don't lose."

The Sssth attacked its task with more eagerness after that threat. Its claws flew about the board and soon the cauldron Fandral wanted was speeding down at Magnir. Intent upon the menace of Hogun, Magnir was unaware of the peril approaching. Fandral waited until the cauldron was almost upon the wizard before he snapped the order to the Sssth.

"Now! Dump it now!" he commanded.

The cauldron tipped, spilling its molten contents across the floor. The fiery splash spattered across Magnir, sizzling against his armor. The wizard sprang back in surprise. His hands curled in complex patterns as he conjured a spell to extinguish the burning metal. While he was occupied, Fandral had the Sssth send a second cauldron hurtling toward the sorcerer. This time Magnir saw the threat and reacted. A bolt of magic struck the cauldron and it disintegrated in a violent explosion.

More cauldrons came swinging down toward the Enchanter, demanding Magnir's focus to destroy them. Empty or full, it didn't matter to Fandral's scheme, only that they maintained the wizard's attention. He could see beyond to where Hogun was. The grim warrior saw his enemy's distraction and dashed out from cover. He threw aside the cumbersome tower shield, relying upon speed to keep him clear of magical reprisal.

"That's it! Come on!" Fandral quietly cheered Hogun. He had a moment of dread when he saw the foremost of the giants raise its sword and bring it crashing down on the warrior. In a burst of speed, Hogun cleared the massive blade and continued his mad dash for the sorcerer.

Fandral couldn't see more of Hogun's progress. After blasting several of the cauldrons, Magnir swung around and glared at the cause of the attacks. At a gesture, the Enchanter sent a bolt of magic slamming into the Sssth. The lizardman wilted across the machinery, smoke rising from its scaly flesh. Fandral brought up his shield just as a second bolt would have struck him. Unlike the rayguns, he felt the force of Magnir's magic and was knocked back.

"Now you die," Magnir howled. He pointed his finger at Fandral. The warrior's arm was jerked to one side as the wires within the improvised shield came to life. They felt like a nest of snakes, writhing against his skin. As they tightened, he felt them bite into his flesh.

Before the wires could constrict enough to break his arm, Fandral watched a triumphant sneer stretch across Magnir's face. The Enchanter lifted his hand to send an arcane blast searing into his body.

The threatened doom was thwarted when Hogun reached the wizard. Hridgandr came sweeping around in a savage arc and crushed Magnir's shoulder. The Enchanter dropped to his knees, stunned by the blow. While he was helpless, Hogun reached down and grabbed the Living Talisman on the wizard's armor. Magnir tried to resist him, clamping his hand on Hogun's wrist. Smoke bubbled off the warrior as the sorcerer's magic scorched his flesh.

Fandral thought no one could withstand such an ordeal, but Hogun refused to relent. The sound of tearing metal sounded from the Enchanter's armor. Hogun stumbled back as he ripped the Living Talisman free.

"You'll die for that!" Magnir shouted. Though one arm hung limp at his side, the wizard gestured with the other at Hogun.

Fandral ignored the pain from the wires and twisted around to the control bank. He shoved aside the dead Sssth and jabbed the array of lights. He'd studied the reptile closely as it operated the machine, and now he only hoped he'd learned enough. "By the mercy of Frigga, let this work," he muttered as he depressed one of the glowing buttons.

Hogun stood helpless before Magnir, but the Enchanter's magic never struck him. Instead, the wizard was engulfed by a shower of molten metal as Fandral sent a cauldron tipping above him. A desperate scream rose from the Enchanter as he vanished behind a veil of steam. When the vapors cleared, Magnir's image stood frozen in place, entirely covered in golden metal.

The robots stopped moving the instant the Enchanter's power was broken. Like colossal toys, they toppled over, crashing down into the same machinery that had been used to construct them, obliterating them utterly. Such Sssth as remained in the hall now fled, scattering in every direction.

Fandral used Fimbuldraugr to cut himself loose from the wires. He dropped his shield to the floor and hurried over to Hogun. His friend was leaning on his mace and breathing heavily. His arm was burned black by Magnir's spell, but his fingers remained locked around the Living Talisman. He gave Fandral a weary smile.

"Next time you take the jewel and I kill the wizard," Hogun told him.

Fandral gave the golden image of Magnir a wary look. "Are you certain he's dead? Wizards are as persistent as roaches."

Hogun stood up and swatted the metal body with his mace. A dull ring echoed through the hall. "If he's not dead, then he certainly isn't happy."

The sound of rushing feet brought both warriors whipping around with weapons raised. Fandral saw a huge shape emerge from the smoke and steam rapidly spill across the hall. He relaxed when he saw it wasn't a Sssth soldier, but merely a battered Volstagg binding his pants with a thick loop of scavenged wire.

"So? Did we win?" Volstagg asked, looking from Hogun to Fandral.

Fandral laughed and shook his head. "We've vanquished the first of the Enchanters and taken his talisman. No thanks to you," he added with a wink to Hogun.

Volstagg threw back his shoulders and puffed out his chest. "I was engaged in a life and death duel with the Sssthgar, I'll have you know. A fight worthy of the greatest sagas ever told!"

"What happened to the Sssthgar?" Fandral asked. He saw from Volstagg's suddenly sheepish expression that their deal with the Vrellnexians hadn't been maintained.

"It was an accident," Volstagg sputtered. "We were

fighting and he fell down a hole. Surely those spiders will understand."

Hogun shook his head. "They didn't strike me as the understanding type."

Fandral found it hard to regret the broken deal. "What's bad for the Vrellnexians will be good for the denizens of Golden Star. I only worry that the spiders will try to revenge themselves on us."

"Which brings up the other question," Volstagg said, nodding at the Living Talisman. "Now that we have the jewel Onund sent us to get, how do we return to Asgard?"

Even as the question was posed, Fandral felt a familiar churning in his stomach. The tower hall, with its toppled robots and crushed machines, began to vanish in a bright light. The feeling of being pulled between worlds rippled through his body.

TWELVE

When his head cleared, Hogun felt the heat of Skornheim envelop him. He didn't need to open his eyes to know they'd returned to Onund's circle.

"You've broken Magnir's power!" the old seer cried. His mismatched eyes gleamed with joy as he danced around the periphery of the astral circle in celebration. "Praise the All-Father! This is a great victory!"

Hogun glanced down at his blackened arm. "Triumph bought with pain," he said. He turned his hand around and stared at the jewel clenched in his fingers. The hideous visage within the Living Talisman snarled back at him, its expression redolent of rage. Whatever power bound it inside the jewel, he was grateful for it. Free to work its will, he knew the force inside would have torn him limb from limb.

"Being separated from the Enchanter doesn't seem to agree with it." Hogun held the talisman away from his body.

"Well that's just too bad." Volstagg wagged his finger at

Three Swords   143

the jewel as though he were scolding a puppy. "Because it certainly isn't going back."

Fandral pulled Volstagg away. "It might not be wise to antagonize it." He fixed his gaze on Onund. "I speak for all of us when I say we'd prefer to see the Living Talisman safely disposed of."

The mystic nodded. "And so it shall be," he said. He beckoned to Hogun. "It is safe now to leave the circle."

The agony pulsing through Hogun's body made him want to collapse, but he wasn't about to show weakness in front of the seer. Hardening his resolve, he marched out from the circle and moved toward the strange chest. The whirlpool design on its lid seemed like any other engraving, but he knew it was much more. He started to reach out, then paused and looked back at Onund.

"What do I do to banish this accursed jewel?" Hogun frowned, a bitter taste on his tongue. "Is there some spell I must invoke?"

"Merely place the Living Talisman in the vortex," Onund told him. "The chest's enchantment will respond."

The jewel refused to leave Hogun's hand. He was forced to pry the talisman free, his charred skin coming away with the leering artifact. The ethereal face glowered at him as he dropped it onto the chest. The image's mouth snapped at him in impotent fury, unable to strike from behind the translucent surface. Hogun locked eyes with the visage, matching its enmity with his own. It was a thing created by evil magic to work villainy across the Nine Worlds. The Realms would be better once it was gone.

After a few moments, the design on the chest began to

stir. The swirling motion began, gyrating faster and faster as it tried to draw the Living Talisman into itself. Hogun could sense the jewel trying to defy the enchantment, to keep from being sucked down into the nothing between worlds. The expression of its visage changed to one of panic. The eyes that had so fiercely glared at Hogun now stared at him in mute appeal, silently pleading for him to save it.

"Not today," Hogun told the Living Talisman. He watched as its defiance of the whirlpool was finally overwhelmed and it was drawn down into the void. "Not ever," he spat as the jewel vanished.

At that moment, the strength that had sustained him reached its limit. Hogun felt his legs go numb and he started to pitch towards the chest. He saw the swirling vortex loom before him.

Onund ran to Hogun, his scrawny arms clasping the warrior as he started to fall. There was a startling degree of strength in the old seer and he was able to wrest Hogun around, turning his fall into a spin. Both men collapsed beside the chest.

"Help me with him!" Onund cried out, shifting Hogun so that his weight was no longer pressing down on the mystic.

"I didn't know he was hurt so badly," Volstagg gasped. The big Asgardian hauled Hogun off the floor and held him upright while Fandral scurried around to inspect his wounds.

"You wouldn't tell somebody if your belly was split open, would you?" Fandral accused, both anger and concern in his tone. "That arm of yours looks more like charcoal than flesh."

Hogun shook his head. "We beat the Enchanter. That's what's important. Not me."

Three Swords 145

"You defeated one of three," Onund corrected him. The mystic hurried to a shelf and pulled down a large alabaster jar. "That still leaves two brothers to be dealt with." He handed the jar over to Fandral.

"What is that?" Fandral asked as he removed the leather covering from the mouth of the jar. A perfumed scent wafted into Hogun's nose and he could see that there was a silvery paste in the lower half of the container.

"A salve used by the wolfhunters of Varinheim to tend their hurts," Onund said. "The wolves of their land are the largest and most hateful in Asgard, so even the least sign of weakness can be ill-afforded." He gestured at Hogun's arm. "Rub it into his wounds and do the same for your own. Your hurts will soon be mended."

Hogun struggled in Volstagg's grip. "I'll not have a magician's unguent slathered over my hide!" he objected.

Fandral scowled at him. "I had a horse once that never wanted to take her medicine. I'd rather not have to wait until you're asleep to do this."

"Nor is there the time to spare," Onund warned. The seer was brushing away the astral circle and gathering up the runestones. "The other Enchanters will know you've vanquished Magnir! The more time we allow them to ponder their brother's defeat, the more they might decide they're also in jeopardy."

"We surprised Magnir," Fandral told Hogun. "Think what would have happened if he'd moved against us the moment we reached Golden Star."

Hogun couldn't deny the logic. Much as it pained him to submit to the magical ointment, he could see that it was necessary. If the other Enchanters escaped because of him, the guilt would be devastating. "Alright, do what needs to be done," he said. He clenched his teeth as Fandral began to administer the salve. Somehow the pain became even worse. Hogun tried to find anything to distract himself from the chilling bite of the paste. He looked over to where Onund was creating a new design across the floor.

"Changing the circle?" Hogun asked.

Onund looked away after setting a runestone at one of the intersecting lines. "The previous pattern was to take you to Magnir. When I am finished, this new circle will send you through time and space to where you'll find Brona." The seer frowned and shook his head. "I will send you as near as I can, but remember that with any magic there's never perfect precision."

"I'll remember," Hogun hissed as the stinging salve sent pain whipping through him. "It's this damned medicine of yours I'd like to forget."

Volstagg laughed, the tremors from his belly shaking the warrior he held. "Maybe next time you'll have sense enough to let me handle the Enchanter for you. One look at me and Brona won't be able to surrender his Living Talisman fast enough."

Hogun closed his eyes as the healing hurt continued to torment him. "One look at you, and the only thing Brona will be thinking is whether he remembered to lock his pantry."

The bewildering sensation of being stretched between realms wasn't any better this time than it was during their passage to Golden Star. Fandral's head felt like a troll was using it for a drum. His ears were ringing with the shrill cacophony of their passage and his eyes burned as if they'd been washed in vinegar. It took the better part of a minute before the white glare that blotted out his vision resolved itself into anything that could be called sight.

When his eyes did adjust, Fandral rubbed them in disbelief. The vast city on Golden Star had been strange beyond anything he'd ever experienced in his journeys. He'd tried to brace himself for anything when Onund sent them back through the portal. A vista of purple suns and trees made of crystal, maybe a sea as red as wine and peppered with obsidian islands. Instead he found a scene that was even more shocking. Not because of its strangeness, but because of its familiarity.

Fandral was looking out across green fields and a blue sky. There were sheep in some of the fields, and dirt roads winding between the fences. Cottages with stone walls and thatch roofs, little streams of smoke rising from their chimneys. These were all common enough things. He'd gazed upon such landscapes before, both in Asgard and Midgard. Although even the stone walls he could see a few miles away, with their towers and crenelations, wouldn't have given proof of precisely where they were.

It was the castle he could see rising some distance behind those walls that sent a thrill through Fandral's heart. There wasn't any mistaking *that* castle! How often he'd spied upon it from a distance, watching the people climbing the hill to its main gate. Several times he'd dared to sneak into its halls to thwart the schemes of enemies. He laughed as he recalled mighty feats and brave friends. A warm feeling pulsed

148 *Marvel: Legends of Asgard*

through his heart as he remembered one who'd been more than friend to him.

"By Garm's collar," Volstagg sputtered, his expression bewildered. "What's got into you?"

"That's a question I'd like answered too," Hogun said. Though his arm was healed, he continued to rub at it as if to assure himself his wounds were really gone.

Fandral looked over at them and smiled. "I know where we are," he stated. "And just now I think we're messing up some yeoman's pasture." He motioned them to follow him over the wooden fence that bordered the field they were in. A pair of cows watched the Asgardians as they climbed out onto the road.

"Alright, so you know where we are," Volstagg said. "Do you mind sharing that information with us?"

Fandral stood in the middle of the road and turned around, taking in the vista in every direction. His brow knotted in concentration. He was certain about that castle, and the landscape itself was familiar. But the architecture of some of the cottages was peculiar and when he saw a shepherd tending his flock, the man's clothes looked far too rich to be those of a mere peasant.

"You don't look certain," Hogun observed.

"I know *where* we are," Fandral insisted. "What I don't know is *when* we are." He scratched his chin as he studied the terrain. "Things have changed. But I know where we can find any answer we need." He started down the road towards the stone walls.

"I hate it when Gunnhilde plays coy with me," Volstagg growled as he trotted after Fandral. "Where are we, blast you!"

Three Swords 149

Fandral stopped and gestured at the fields and cottages. "This, my friends, is England," he told them. He swung about and pointed at the walls. "Over there is the town of Nottingham." He couldn't repress a wistful note as he spoke the name. "More than that you'll have to wait on until I find out a bit more myself."

Volstagg and Hogun dutifully followed Fandral without pressing him further, though he knew they were both bristling with questions. Their curiosity would have to wait. Fandral was too busy studying the people they passed on the road. He was puzzled by the cut and quality of their clothes. He still thought they were too rich for peasants, but neither did they seem luxurious enough for nobles and clergy. It was a perplexing facet that nagged at him. The wagons they passed were of a curious design and he'd never seen the like of the enclosed carriage that hurtled past them on its way to Nottingham.

The puzzled looks Fandral gave the English were returned in kind. The people were obviously curious about the Asgardians, though none were bold enough to do more than look at them. Once he heard a woman whisper to her companion about 'king's men' and again there was a farmer who muttered something about 'Dutch sellswords'.

Fandral was surprised to find a great many buildings outside the town walls. These weren't built of stone, but instead looked to be timber covered in plaster with wooden roofs that slanted at sharp angles. He even saw glass in some of the windows, an extravagance he'd believed exclusive to churches and castles in England. The traffic increased and the Asgardians found themselves pushed to the edges of the road by the many carriages and carts that passed them by.

The puzzled looks continued and now to the common people who'd been giving the warriors curious looks could be added a different category. Fandral noted men dressed in red uniforms wearing steel breastplates and light, open-faced helms marching down the lanes. Some had swords on their belts, others carried halberds over their shoulders and a few had odd devices of metal and polished wood that reminded him somehow of the Sssth rayguns. There was a rough martial aspect to these men, though they bore no heraldry to denote their service to some knight or baron. Fandral wondered if they might be the Dutch mercenaries he'd overheard the farmer mention.

"Busy sort of place, this Nottingham," Volstagg commented.

"All of this out here is new," Fandral said. "When I was here last, the town didn't go outside the walls. Now it's become a veritable city." He stopped when he felt something tug at his leg. He swung around, expecting to see one of the strange soldiers. Instead, there was nothing... at least until he looked down.

A child no more than six was beside him, one of her small hands pulling at his leg. She looked up at him with a face bright with childish innocence and wonder. "Are you Robin Hood?" she asked in a tremulous voice.

Before Fandral could do more than smile, the girl's mother dashed over and pulled the child away. "Don't go bothering no strangers," she scolded her daughter, swatting her backside as she hurried her away.

Three Swords 151

"Now what was that all about?" Volstagg shook his head. He gave Fandral an annoyed look. "And what're you grinning about?"

Fandral nodded, flushed with the joy the little girl's question had evoked. He glanced around, trying to judge precisely where they were. Imagining what their surroundings would look like without nearly so many buildings around. He snapped his fingers as he matched memory to what was around them. "Come along and I'll show you," he told his friends.

Fandral led the Asgardians along the streets until they reached a building much older than its neighbors. An effort had been made to cover its stone walls in plaster so it would match the more recent structures and the roof had been upgraded from thatch to wooden shingles, but the sign that hung over the door was the same. "I give you the Saracen's Head," Fandral announced.

"Looks like a tavern," Volstagg chuckled.

"It is a tavern," Fandral said. He paused and listened as a snatch of song drifted through the door. "I think we'll get the answers we want right in here." Clapping his arms across his friends' shoulders, he led them into the building.

The Saracen's Head was little changed, in Fandral's opinion. There were oil lamps now instead of rushlights, and there were chairs around the tables instead of benches, but the stone hearth was the same, as was the timber counter that ran along one of the walls. He escorted his friends to one of the tables. Within easy earshot of the minstrel plucking away on an oddly shaped lute. Fandral grinned as he listened to the song. The account was wildly out of sorts

Marvel: Legends of Asgard

with what he remembered, but the names were right and it was good to know that they were not forgotten.

"Okay," Hogun said, exasperation in his tone as the minstrel's ballad ended. "Who's this Robin Hood everybody keeps talking about?"

Volstagg suddenly gripped Hogun's arm. He pointed at the wall behind them. Fandral turned to see what they were looking at. It proved to be a woodcut, a scene of battle between a group of bowmen and mounted knights. He couldn't help but laugh when he saw the central figure with its plumed hat and longbow.

"Strike me if that doesn't look like Fandral," Volstagg said.

"Friends, that is Robin Hood and his Merry Men," Fandral explained, running his finger along the letters beneath the woodcut. His eyes sparkled as he glanced at the other Asgardians. "Though you'll find he keeps worse company these days."

The smile broadened as Fandral saw understanding dawn on them. "I told you I'd been here before. I just didn't realize I was so famous."

THIRTEEN

"So you've been here before," Hogun interrupted Fandral's reminiscence. "How does that help us find the Enchanter?" He could sympathize with his friend's nostalgia. For Fandral, returning to Nottingham must have been something like a homecoming, but Hogun was worried that he was letting his memories supersede the matter at hand.

"A blunt way of putting things." Volstagg nudged him with his elbow. "There's no harm hearing about what Fandral was up to when he was calling himself Robin Hood. I've heard some of it before, but not many of the details." He gestured with his thumb at a bowman who was taller than the others. "Who was this, for instance? Looks like he was about my size."

"John Little," Fandral replied absently. "A bit taller and not as stout." Hogun was pleased to see his rebuff had stirred Fandral back to the task they'd come here to perform. His attitude had lost its wistfulness and become more

153

severe. "We could ask around," he said. "The English are a gregarious people and any mistakes in custom or manners we can beg indulgence due to being strangers." He shrugged his shoulders. "They already seem to think we're Dutch."

"Where to start, though? I don't recall England being a small place, or am I mistaken?" Hogun wondered.

Fandral scratched his chin. "Big enough that finding the Enchanter won't be easy."

Hogun's eyes narrowed as he studied the other occupants of the Saracen's Head. They looked to be farmers and tradesmen of one sort or another. A few had shot wary glances at them when Fandral mentioned the Enchanter. Now those same men were whispering among themselves.

"They look interested in what we're talking about," Hogun said.

"Maybe they'd like to join our conversation." Fandral fished a few coins from the pouch on his belt and slammed them down on the table. "Taverner!" he called. "A round of your best mead for my friends... and those likely-looking lads over there." He stood and pointed at a cluster of farmers seated at a nearby table.

A pot-bellied man with a balding pate and a surly face walked over to scoop up the coins. "I've ale, jenever, and beer. Take your pick."

"Ale," Volstagg quickly answered. "And a roasted pig with..."

The taverner jangled the coins in his palm. "Foreign gold only buys you drinks, and be grateful for that much. I don't need the excise men hanging about thinking I'm a smuggler."

Hogun watched the proprietor as he stalked away. The

Three Swords

man paused for a moment to talk to a young boy lounging near the door, then he continued on his way behind the counter. There was a furtive aspect to his actions that set Hogun on the alert.

"Hail, good fellows," Fandral called to the farmers at the other table. "It's been many a long year since I've been in fair Nottinghamshire. How fares the king?"

The farmers whispered among themselves again. A few of the other patrons hurriedly laid coins on their tables and scurried from the tavern like rats from a sinking ship. The proprietor threw up his hands as he was drawing their ale and darted a furious look in Fandral's direction.

"That didn't go over so well," Hogun whispered to Fandral.

"I don't know," Fandral replied. "One of them's coming over, at least."

A burly man with a lantern jaw and thinning hair walked over to their table. He studied them for a moment. "I'd be wary of what you say," he advised. "There's not many King's men in these parts. We support Parliament here, and Cromwell's put enough soldiers in town to make sure we remember that."

Fandral gave Hogun a bewildered stare. "It seems England has changed a good deal since I was last here. Then the argument was who would be king, not whether there was to be a king at all."

"You must've been far from these shores, then," the man declared. "Over in the new colonies, were you? It's been many a year since the crown has rested easy on Charles' head. His Cavaliers hold Oxford and the south, but it's Cromwell's Roundheads who control most of the land."

Hogun guessed that Charles must be the king in question, and from the reverence with which the man said the name, it was obvious to him he was loyal to the monarch, whatever protests to the contrary he made. The turmoil in England between the King's men and those of Cromwell was a conflict the Asgardians couldn't afford to get caught up in. "We're strangers to these lands," Hogun said, "and have no intention of meddling in your affairs."

"We've traveled far to reach Nottingham," Fandral said. Hogun thought it to be a profound understatement. "We'd heard tell of a wise man in these parts. A mystic with peculiar powers."

The burly man drew back, fright in his eyes. The farmers at the table had continued to eavesdrop. Now one of them raised his voice. "That'd be the warlock."

"Aye, that's the one," Volstagg bellowed, slamming his palm against the table and nearly cracking it in two.

"There's tales of a warlock in Sherwood," the burly man stated, his voice lowered.

"Sherwood's not a fit place for man or beast these days," another farmer said. "A sheep wanders in there and it's only the fool who takes in after it."

A third farmer nodded his head. "Strange things seen hanging about the forest now." He took hold of the ale the proprietor brought over. "Ungodly things conjured up by the warlock." He took a long pull from his cup and wiped the residue from his face with the back of his hand.

Hogun could feel the tension mounting inside the room. More of the patrons hurried to leave and he now noticed that the boy the taverner had talked with was gone. He

Three Swords

shot his companions a warning look when the proprietor set cups down on the table before them and backed away. The man's expression wasn't so much surly now as it was anxious. Hogun noted the way his eyes kept drifting toward the entrance.

Volstagg, however, seemed oblivious to the atmosphere in the Saracen's Head. He drained his cup in a single swallow and nodded to the farmers. "So Sherwood is a good place to go looking for this Enchanter?"

"The forest is a place of witchcraft and demons," the burly tradesman declared with a shiver. "Only a madman would go there now." He suddenly turned toward the door, as did the farmers at the other table.

Hogun spun around. Men had entered the tavern, but from their look and attitude, he could tell they weren't patrons. Five soldiers with lowered halberds formed a line across the doorway. Before them was a heavyset man wearing a blue tunic trimmed with sable, a fur-lined cape draped about his shoulders. He had a brimless cap on his head with a long plume pinned to one side. His gloved hand rested casually on the hilt of the sword on his belt. Over the glove he wore a gold ring adorned with a large serpentine that sparkled in the lamplight.

The heavyset man, Hogun judged, was some kind of officer, but he wasn't the one in command. That role the warrior immediately decided belonged to the tall, thin man beside him. He wore a crimson vest striped with gold and a heavy black cape swept down from his shoulders to brush against his knee-high boots. A broad-brimmed hat with a tall crown added to his imposing height and cast much of his face in shadow. What Hogun could see of the man's countenance was unpleasant, evoking the ferocity of a wolf and the foulness of a rat.

The predatory figure's gaze swept the room and the English cringed before his scrutiny. His attention settled on the Asgardians and a cruel, cheerless smile pulled at his face. "Even the mad shun the Devil's works." His words cracked across the room. "It is those who've sworn themselves to the powers of darkness who seek out such places."

"A fine one to speak of powers of darkness," Volstagg grumbled. "You look like something spit out by a devil."

"Far from it," the man's thin voice snapped. He took a step forward, his visage coming into the light. Seldom had Hogun seen a crueler face, but it was the gleam in the man's cold eyes that was unsettling. They were the eyes of a fanatic.

"I am Matthew Hopkins," the man announced. "Witchfinder General for all England." He pointed his finger at the Asgardians. "You stand accused of sorcery and witchcraft!" He glanced back at the officer beside him. "Sheriff, arrest these villains."

Fandral threw back his head and laughed. "Can this be England, then, where a crazed ruffian is free to make such slanderous accusations without evidence?" The sheriff and his men faltered in their advance, surprised by his reaction. "I dare say I'd not expected such a change in this noble land."

Hopkins shifted aside and Fandral saw the boy the taverner had sent away. "I have witnesses," the witch hunter stated. "Those who've heard you condemn yourselves by

Three Swords 159

your own words." His face twisted into a withering sneer. "Or would you deny that you came here seeking the Sorcerer of Sherwood?"

Fandral glared defiantly into those fanatical eyes. "Seeking him? No, I'll not deny that, but for the purpose of stopping him." He matched the witch hunter's sneer with a scornful smile. "Which would appear to be more than you're willing to do."

The retort brought color rushing into the witch hunter's cheeks. His hand dropped to his belt where he had one of the wood-and-steel implements secured in a brief scabbard. "I answer to God and Parliament," Hopkins snarled. "Not to foreign heretics who consort with warlocks." As he spoke, he drew the weapon from its sheath. Fandral saw now that its steel component was hollow at the end like a tube. Reminded more than ever of the Sssth rayguns, he kicked over the table and sent it crashing into the witch hunter. Hopkins' arm was jolted upward and there was a loud report as he pulled the trigger of his weapon. A flare of flame and smoke erupted from the barrel and Fandral saw debris fall from the ceiling as a projectile punched its way through the roof.

"You heard the witchfinder!" the heavyset sheriff bellowed. "Arrest them!" He drew his sword and joined his soldiers as they surged forward.

"Show restraint," Fandral shouted to his companions as Fimbuldraugr left its scabbard. "The people of Midgard aren't built as tough as those of Asgard!"

"Tell that to them!" Volstagg yelled back, blocking the thrust of one halberd while throwing his cup into the face of a second soldier. "Waste of good ale," he grumbled as the vessel broke against the man's nose and sent him crashing back against the bar.

Hogun whipped Hridgandr about, fending off the advance of the other soldiers. The spiked mace warped the axe-blades as it smacked against them and his foes struggled to keep a grip on their weapons.

Fandral was confronted by the heavyset man in the plumed hat. As the officer dashed towards him, he was afforded a clearer look at the ring he wore over his glove. Memories came flooding in and he laughed. He knew that ring and the post that went with it. His opponent wasn't merely a sheriff, but *the* sheriff. However much time had passed in Midgard since he was last here, Fandral was once again crossing swords with the Sheriff of Nottingham.

"We meet again for the first time," he grinned as Fimbuldraugr parried the sheriff's thrust. "I've met a few of your predecessors." Fandral blocked a sweep of his adversary's blade, putting just enough force to swat it aside without breaking the man's arm. The familiar patterns of self-restraint and caution settled over him like an old set of clothes. "They were rascals too. Not caring much who they worked for or what tyrannies they enforced."

Sweat beaded the sheriff's forehead as he struggled to penetrate Fandral's defense. "An innocent man would prove his innocence before a magistrate, not by using a sword."

A clever riposte nearly took Fandral by surprise and he felt the sheriff's blade scrape along his ribs. He chided himself for being incautious. In trying to hold back his Asgardian strength, it was easy to forget that the Midgarders didn't need that kind of strength to hurt him. Midgard steel was every bit as sharp as that of Asgard.

Fandral spun around and cracked Fimbuldraugr's pommel against the sheriff's hand, stunning the fingers and nearly causing the man to drop the blade. "If English justice now appoints men like Hopkins to mete it out then I've little faith that it warrants being called justice at all."

With a flourish, the sheriff tossed his sword into his other hand and resumed his attack. "You may mock English law," he growled, "but by all that's holy, you *will* submit to it!" The fury of his opponent's assault caused Fandral to give ground before him. Yes, things had certainly changed in Nottingham. The sheriffs of old had been either sly or cowardly, but never hearty enough to fight such a duel. This melee reminded him more of his battle with Sir Guy of Gisbourne that ended in the knight's disgrace and losing his spurs.

Thinking of that old enemy put a new fire in Fandral's arm. "I never submit to injustice," he stated. "If you want a devil to fight, there's a good one for you to root out!" His sword crashed against the sheriff's and the two stood locked together for a moment. Fandral's eyes roved across the tavern. Most of the occupants had retreated behind the counter, freeing the rest of the room for the combatants. Volstagg had both of his adversaries by their necks and kept knocking their heads together. One of Hogun's foes lay sprawled on the floor while he continued to fend off the other two with his mace.

Everything appeared to favor the Asgardians until Fandral spotted Hopkins. The witch hunter was rearming his pistol, and as he looked the man's way, he saw him turn and aim the weapon at Hogun.

"My apologies," Fandral told the sheriff. Exerting his full strength, he flung the officer back with such force that the impact made a dent in the wall he collided with. The sheriff slumped to the floor, a dazed look on his face.

Fandral regretted taking advantage of his opponent, but he knew he'd regret letting Hopkins shoot his friend even more. His boot smacked into one of the chairs and sent it flying across the room. It shattered when it hit Hopkins and the witch hunter wilted to the ground. "That's it. Take a seat and have a rest." Fandral laughed at the unconscious fanatic.

The sound of agitated voices in the street outside alerted Fandral to new danger. Whoever Cromwell might be, they'd already seen that he had plenty of soldiers in Nottingham. The tumult in the street was clearly some of them rushing to reinforce the sheriff.

"Time to leave!" Fandral shouted to his friends. Volstagg reluctantly let the two soldiers fall to the floor, their helmets dented by the repeated impacts. Hogun made a final swing with his mace and tore the halberds out of the hands of his remaining enemies. The disarmed soldiers looked at one another and fled toward the door, blocking the path of the reinforcements trying to enter.

"This way," Fandral told the others. He rushed to the far wall near where the dazed sheriff was lying. In the old days there had been a hidden exit at the back of the Saracen's Head. He couldn't remember exactly how to open it, so instead relied upon brawn to clear a path. Slamming into the wall, the masonry buckled outward and crashed into the street.

Three Swords 163

People scattered as the Asgardians ran out across the collapsed wall. Some of the soldiers trying to get into the tavern turned and shouted at the warriors as they emerged. "I think Nottingham is getting a bit too warm for my liking," Fandral said as he led his companions on a circuitous path between the buildings. He could hear the crack and boom as soldiers fired at them with their guns. Fortunately, their aim was imprecise and the only bullet that came close to them merely pelted them with plaster from the wall it struck.

"Where are we going?" Volstagg huffed as he trotted after Fandral.

In his mind Fandral could already see their destination. Enchanter or no, the moment he realized where they were, he knew he'd have to go there. "We'll lose our pursuers and then head for the forest. If Brona has made himself Sorcerer of Sherwood, then it's about time someone told him he's trespassing."

FOURTEEN

"Welcome to Sherwood." There was a boyish exuberance in the way Fandral made the statement. Volstagg could appreciate his excitement. The forest was as lush and green as any he'd seen apart from the sylvan glades of the Norn Forest. Simply walking beneath its leafy boughs provoked a feeling of vitality.

If there had been the least hesitancy when Fandral led them into Nottingham, there was none now. He moved with a confidence that amazed Volstagg. It was as though he knew every rock and bush they came upon. "There is where we robbed the Bishop of Hereford," Fandral told them, pointing to a stand of larch trees just beside what looked like the faintest reminder of a trail through the forest. "We sent his entourage on their way as naked as babes and gave their money and clothes to the poor."

"Seems an odd way for an outlaw to spend his plunder," Volstagg said. "I'd have thought using what you'd stolen to

Three Swords 165

buy arms and armor so these people could rise up and fight would have been better."

Fandral gave him a frank look. "There's no enemy more dire than hunger, and before anyone can fight another enemy, that one must be defeated." He looked off in the direction of Nottingham. "Prince John wanted to dethrone King Richard while he was away. To ensure nobody could oppose him, he levied such hefty taxes that even some barons were turned into beggars. He set Saxon against Norman so that his enemies would be too distrustful of one another to ever unite against him." Volstagg could see the hate boil back up in Fandral's face and voice. "A cruel and cunning man."

Hogun suddenly stopped and bent down to retrieve something from the ground. "Looks like Robin Hood missed this one," he said, holding between his fingers a little oval of metal so corroded that it took Volstagg a moment to realize it was a coin.

Fandral examined Hogun's find. "Even were it not so worn, I wouldn't recognize the royal portrait stamped on this coin." He rubbed away some of the dirt and corrosion and whistled in surprise. "1546," he read. Volstagg could see the emotion shining in Fandral's eyes as he looked out across Sherwood. "It's been over three hundred years as these English calculate things."

"Maybe nearer four hundred," Volstagg suggested. "It's clear that coin's been lying there for quite a while."

"Long enough for Robin Hood to become a legend," Fandral mused. "Long enough for what we fought for to be forgotten." Suddenly he turned to his friends, an air of solemnity clinging to him. "I know this forest like I know the back of my hand. I can't say where Brona has established his lair, but I know where I want to start our search. A place that has hidden outlaws before might be put to such use again."

"Your old hideout?" Volstagg wondered.

Fandral smiled and gestured at the trees to the north. "The Major Oak is that direction. With all the hunters the Sheriff of Nottingham had looking for us, they never found our camp."

The trio hiked onward. A few times Fandral paused when they came upon a scene that was vivid in his memory. "There's where Little John clouted me with a quarterstaff and knocked me into the stream," he related when they came on an old bridge. "Here's where Friar Tuck set his dogs on us ere he became one of my Merry Men," he recalled when they found the overgrown ruin of a stone hut hidden among the trees. Fandral's voice was heavy when they passed through a clearing dominated by a large, moss-covered rock. "After he lost his rank, Sir Guy became a bounty hunter and it was here he caught and killed Will Scarlet." Fandral's hand dropped to Fimbuldraugr's hilt, the fingers clenching around it until his knuckles turned white. "That was the nearest an enemy came to finding our camp, but Sir Guy never left Sherwood to brag about killing Will and collect his blood money."

Soon after leaving the clearing, the trees became incredibly dense. Volstagg stumbled over the many roots that poked up from the ground and struck his head on low-hanging branches. At times the loam under his feet was so thick that it felt like walking over densely packed snow. He kept expecting to break through and find himself hip-deep

Three Swords 167

in old leaves. Vines clutched at his legs and he was plucking fronds from overgrown ferns out of his beard as the hours began to wear away.

"I hope we find your camp before nightfall," Volstagg said, glancing up at the confused canopy above them. "Little enough light peeks through now, I can only imagine how much worse it can get."

"There's something else you haven't mentioned," Hogun commented. "Stop and listen for a moment."

Puzzled, Volstagg did as Hogun asked. "The only thing I hear is the wind groaning through the branches," he confessed.

"Exactly," Hogun said. He turned toward Fandral. "There's no birds singing. No little animals darting about through the underbrush."

"Sherwood looks the same," Fandral nodded, "but it isn't the same. A change has come over it."

"The Enchanter," Volstagg expressed the conclusion they'd all drawn.

Hogun's hands tightened around the heft of his mace. "Animals are wiser than people. They can sense sorcery from miles away. They've sense enough to keep clear of wizards."

"The first proof, if we needed any, that the stories we heard in the Saracen's Head aren't just stories," Fandral agreed. He had an embarrassed flush when he faced his friends. "I should have noticed the change straight away, but I let myself get distracted by my memories." He clasped Hogun's shoulder. "Thank you for being vigilant while I was remiss. It won't happen again."

But it did happen again, and for a reason even Hogun the Grim wouldn't hold against Fandral. It was when they reached the Major Oak and the site of Robin Hood's camp.

Volstagg didn't need to be told they'd found the Major Oak. The tree was of such a size that even in Asgard it would have been remarkable. Compared to what they'd seen in England, it was a leviathan. Fifty men linking arms couldn't have circled its trunk. Its branches stretched away in every direction, forming a canopy unto itself. Peering up through the leaves, Volstagg tried to estimate how high it was to the oak's top. He finally estimated it couldn't be too much shy of a hundred feet from the ground to its summit. The roots that spread out from the massive tree were as thick around as Volstagg's leg and undulated from the earth like so many sea serpents writhing across the ocean. Except for a few clumps of grass and moss, no vegetation had the temerity to plant itself near the mighty tree. It was as though Sherwood had conceded this ground to the Major Oak and the Major Oak alone.

There was little to indicate there'd ever been a human presence here. Volstagg thought he saw a few spots where the ground looked scooped out, where some construction might have once stood. Hogun found the stumps of a timber palisade, time and weather having ground them down to the merest nubs of wood.

Fandral ignored all of this. The moment they were in the vicinity of the Major Oak, his pace quickened. He seemed to Volstagg to be almost in a trance as he hurried toward the gargantuan tree. He almost grabbed him, afraid the former outlaw had been discovered by Brona and put under the

Three Swords 169

Enchanter's spell. Then he saw the purpose behind Fandral's haste.

On the western side of the Major Oak, a stone had been raised. Fandral stopped near to the marker, hands folded before him, his head lowered in a respectful attitude.

Volstagg walked over toward Fandral, careful not to close the distance too quickly. There was that about his friend's manner that warned off any intrusion. When he came near enough to see that there were letters cut into the stone, he understood why. It was a grave marker. The name was that of Marian and the inscription beneath read "beloved wife of Robin".

"It is getting dark," Hogun called out as he walked over to speak with Fandral. Volstagg headed his friend off and steered him away from the grave.

"Leave him be just now," Volstagg said as he led Hogun away. He glanced back, but from what he could see Fandral hadn't stirred so much as a muscle, utterly oblivious to their presence.

"Who is buried in that tomb?" Hogun asked.

"His wife," Volstagg answered. It was all the explanation either of them needed.

"He married a woman of Midgard," Volstagg commented as they circled to the other side of the Major Oak. He shook his head. "He must've known. The Midgarders age and die so much faster than we do."

Volstagg thought of the reputation Fandral had acquired. Fandral the Dashing, the rakish adventurer who took pleasure where it was offered but never lingered overlong in any one place. He couldn't recall a time when Fandral had ever formed a serious connection with someone. Now he thought he understood why. There were some, even among the Asgardians, who were capable of only one great love in their lives. The reverence Fandral showed at Marian's grave made it clear to Volstagg that she'd been unlike anyone else. He frowned at the tragedy of that love, for from its first moment Fandral would have known it was doomed. His wife would age while he remained the same. How great must his feeling have been to invite that inevitable pain onto himself.

"When this is all over, I'm going to see Gunnhilde and the children," Volstagg declared. Hogun gave him a surprised look.

"Feeling guilty about staying away so long?" Hogun asked.

Volstagg smiled and shook his head. "No. Feeling fortunate to have someone waiting for me."

A morning mist filled Sherwood the next day. Hogun wondered if it had been conjured by Brona. Onund's warning that the other Enchanters would sense Magnir's defeat made him think the possibility likely. It only made sense that the wizard would take steps to guard against the same thing happening to him, even if he was unaware of who had vanquished his brother and why.

"No, Sherwood always looks like this in the morning," Fandral assured him. "At least it does unless there's a few inches of snow on the ground."

Hogun wasn't convinced, but he was willing to defer to Fandral's experience. After all, as Robin Hood he'd lived in the forest for years.

"There's still the question of where to look for Brona," Volstagg said. He looked at the handful of berries Fandral had managed to scrounge from the immediate area and frowned. "You might be right about the wizard's pantry," he grumbled.

The theory that Brona would make his lair in the same place where the Merry Men had hidden their camp was disproved. Hogun could see that Fandral was racking his mind over other places the Enchanter could conceal himself.

"If the sorcerer has scared everyone half as much as the locals we met, he could've put himself up almost anywhere in Sherwood," Fandral sighed. "His magic can conjure whatever food and water he needs, so he doesn't have to rely on any pools or streams..."

"Or anything more substantial than berries," Volstagg added, popping one of them into his mouth.

Hogun stared at the sky, just able to make out the glow of the sun through the mist. "A wizard's needs aren't those of normal people," he said. "But that doesn't mean they don't have any. Mogul made his stronghold the Mystic Mountain because magic was drawn to the place. Brona would seek out a similar spot if one was handy. We already know the Enchanters will go to extreme lengths to augment their powers." He couldn't quite repress a shudder as he thought of Magnir's Living Talisman.

Fandral was contemplative for a moment, then he grinned and snapped his fingers. "There might be such a place in Sherwood," he exclaimed as a memory clicked. "Robin Hood and his outlaws weren't the only inhabitants here. We had several run-ins with Maudlin, the Witch of Papplewick.

She moved from Papplewick to a cave in Sherwood. At the time we thought it was because the clergy were making things too difficult for her to remain in Papplewick, but now I wonder. Strange stories were told about that cave and its surroundings well before Maudlin took up residence."

"It's as good a place as any to start our search," Hogun said. There was a weird energy about Sherwood that convinced him that the Enchanter was certainly nearby.

Fandral turned back to the Major Oak. "Wait here for a moment," he said. Hogun and Volstagg watched as he walked into a dark gap in the trunk.

"Now what's he up to?" Volstagg grumbled. He wiped juice stains from his beard. "I'm going to be more than a trifle upset if he comes out of there with victuals after those sour berries he gave us."

Hogun's interest perked up when he saw Fandral emerge carrying an object swathed in what looked like an incredibly old flag. He saw two dragons, one white and one red, on a field of black.

"I didn't think it would still be there," Fandral explained as he undid the bindings. Beneath the folds of the flag was a yew bow and a dozen broad-headed arrows. "This was a gift bestowed on Robin Hood when King Richard reclaimed his throne from Prince John's treacherous stewardship. He claimed it was the finest longbow in England and had been enchanted in the days of Arthur by the wizard Merlin." He grabbed the coil of gut that was around the arrows and began to string the bow.

"A fine weapon," Hogun approved. "You must have been crazy to leave it behind."

Three Swords 173

Fandral looked up from his labor, his eyes piercing. "When Marian was gone, Robin Hood went with her. I took nothing from that life back with me to Asgard."

"String that bow fast!" Volstagg cried abruptly. He pointed at a dark shape flying above the trees several hundred yards away. "There's a meal more substantial than berries."

"A hawk," Fandral proclaimed the soaring bird. "Some poor dining to be had there. If the forest is as empty as it seems, that hawk must be hungrier than we are."

Hogun tensed as something darted up from the trees. It had a long, slithery look to it, with broad wings to either side of its tapering body. The gruesome shape collided with the hawk, throwing its coils around the bird while using its wings to keep them both aloft.

"Shoot!" Hogun told Fandral. There was something repulsive and unnatural about the creature that was attacking the hawk.

The arrow left Fandral's bow faster than the eye could follow. The weird creature was struck in the wing and plummeted from the sky. Immediately the Warriors Three raced through the woods to where it fell.

"Now we know what kind of things Brona is using his magic for," Hogun said when they reached the creature. He'd been right to think of the thing as some kind of winged snake, for it bore more semblance to that than anything else. The thing, however, looked more plant than animal. The broad wings were like giant leaves and the tapering body was more like a vine than a serpent. It had no head, not even a mouth to bite with. Instead, its coils were lined with thorns and it was these that transfixed the hawk it had caught. Blood from the bird was quickly absorbed into the vegetable mass.

"I suspect," Fandral said, "that before we leave Sherwood, we'll find this creature to be the least of Brona's monstrosities."

FIFTEEN

Volstagg didn't need Fandral's expertise to tell him that the forest had changed since he'd walked its paths as Robin Hood. The vine-bat-snake creature he'd shot was merely a fragment of the wrongness that lurked in Sherwood. He saw things that looked like ferns but scuttled off on their roots like hideous spiders. There was something the size of a fox that had peeked out at them from behind a tree, then yawned at them with a face that opened like the petals of a flower. A squirming mass with the texture of a mushroom and the animation of a caterpillar forced the Asgardians to abandon one trail and take a different route into the forest's depths.

"I think I might swap a stroll in Hel for traipsing about these woods," Volstagg commented as he watched a tuber the size of his hand buzz past him on translucent wings.

"Brona will pay for corrupting Sherwood like this," Fandral swore. His tone was so hungry for vengeance that it reminded Volstagg of Hogun's voice when he spoke of his own vanished homeland.

"Settling scores with the Enchanter is why we're here," Hogun agreed.

Volstagg jerked his hand away from a branch he'd started to push aside. The wood felt as though it had a pulse running through it. When he gave it a closer study, he saw that there was some kind of lichen covering much of it, a lichen that stared back at him with thousands of tiny eyes. "If that was all we needed to do, I'd say not to bother looking for the wizard. Just burn the forest down."

"I'll not surrender Sherwood to the Enchanter," Fandral warned Volstagg, clearly upset by this talk.

Hogun crushed a crawling vine beneath his boot and fixed Fandral with an intense gaze. "I know better than you what it means to lose a land you love to sorcery, but you must think of what else stands to be lost." With his mace he picked up the still-writhing plant from the ground. "Think of Asgard being overrun by Brona's monsters. I won't let that happen, and neither will you." He shook his head. "Not for something as selfish as sentiment."

Volstagg shifted uncomfortably. The atmosphere had become filled with hostility. He tried to smooth the tension between his friends. Laughing, he stepped between them and clapped Fandral on the back. "It was a jest. Of course we're not going to burn the forest. We've got to remove Brona's Living Talisman before we slay him."

The attempt at humor failed to impress his companions. Fandral ignored Volstagg and kept his eyes on Hogun. "I made a vow to protect Sherwood."

Three Swords 177

"And you also swore an oath to defend Asgard," Hogun threw back at him. "There are people there who will suffer if Brona realizes his plans." He pivoted and turned a botanical horror that looked like a cabbage with fangs into pulp with his mace. "Anyone who lived in this forest has fled already. Priorities. If it comes to it, Sherwood is a small sacrifice to save Asgard."

Volstagg threw out his arms to keep the two apart. "Don't we have better things to argue about?" he growled at them. "Maybe we should focus on finding the Enchanter."

"That's easy enough," Hogun said, still watching Fandral. "The further we get into the forest, the more abundant this walking vegetation becomes. I'm sure that's because we draw closer to their source."

Fandral's eyes remained chips of steel. "I'll not break my vow," he insisted. There was a bitterness in his smile when he looked at Hogun and added, "I've something to save, not merely avenge."

Volstagg knew the speech was intended to be hurtful. Before Hogun could make a move, he swung around and held the warrior back. Insults now rolled off both their tongues, one more hateful than the last. Volstagg tried to think of anything that might calm them down after provoking such animosity.

"Go ahead and beat each other's brains in," Volstagg finally declared. He released Hogun and stepped away. "I'm sure the Enchanter will be easier to vanquish with fewer blades to fight him." His words slashed at his friends like a whip. They turned as though aware of the big Asgardian's presence for the first time. "I'm sure none of Brona's creatures have heard this racket and slithered away to tell their master."

"They're weeds," Fandral objected. "They don't have ears."

Volstagg tapped Fandral in the chest with his forefinger. "You know that for certain? Somehow that vine-bat-snake found the hawk. Maybe it used its wings to hear as well as fly. Maybe more of them are taking flight even now to find us."

"We can kill a thousand of those things," Hogun stated with an icy confidence.

Volstagg poked his finger in the warrior's chest, pressing Hogun as he had Fandral to make his point. "Then maybe Brona will send something else." He brushed away a bug-like flower that was crawling on his arm. "We don't know what else he's been creating with his magic, but I'm sure his ultimate ambition is going to be a lot worse than any of the pests we've seen so far."

With their attention now focused on him rather than each other, Volstagg drew himself up to his full height and laughed. "If for nothing else, we need to stick together because of the common enemy. Not just victory, but simple survival depends on that." He pointed at Fandral. "Since you know the forest, you take the lead." He waved to Hogun. "You guard the rear in case Fandral misses something and some of Brona's creations start following us."

Hogun and Fandral exchanged a last glare before stepping away and assuming the posts Volstagg had given them. He hoped that separation would cool their tempers, but he knew them well enough to also know how hurtful the things they'd said were. He tried to take some relief from the fact that at least for the moment they were working together.

Three Swords 179

At least that was Volstagg's supposition until Fandral suddenly spun around. He had his longbow raised and an arrow nocked. He was aiming towards Hogun!

"Fandral! No!" Volstagg cried out in shock.

Before Volstagg could move, Fandral let loose the arrow.

The arrow pierced its target's arm. The weapon held by that arm clattered to the ground while its owner screamed in pain. A feeling of euphoria rushed through Fandral. He doubted if anyone in Asgard could have made that shot as quickly as he had.

Hogun stared at him in disbelief. His sleeve was torn from where the arrow had passed and a little rivulet of blood was running down his arm.

Confusion held Hogun only until he registered the screams rising from behind him. He didn't wait to look to see who Fandral had hit, what peril had drawn so close that he was forced to graze his friend's arm to shoot the enemy. Warrior instincts took over from conscious thought and he dove from the path, putting himself behind the trees.

The soldier Fandral had struck was sprawled on the ground, his fingers locked about the arrow transfixing his arm. Nearby lay the musket with its match still smoldering. It had been the hiss of that match which betrayed the soldier's presence to Fandral's keen hearing. But it wasn't the only one he could hear sizzling away in the shadows.

"Get to cover!" Fandral shouted at Volstagg. In a blinding motion he drew another arrow from beneath the band of his belt and sent it speeding into the brush. Again, there rose the scream of a wounded man. A soldier in the red uniform of Cromwell's troops scrambled onto the path, his hand pierced by the shaft. He took one look at Fandral and then fled.

Fandral drew and loosed again, ignoring the advice he'd given Volstagg. The big Asgardian needed a moment to put a tree between himself and their enemies. For that moment, Fandral needed to make himself the more attractive target. The best way he could think of to do that was to be the most immediate threat.

His arrow wounded a third soldier, but he proved to be the last casualty before the forest thundered with the roar of gunpowder. Flares of fire and plumes of smoke erupted from the underbrush. Fandral heard the crash of bullets smacking into the plants around him, a few short shots pelting the ground. The soldiers were hasty when they shifted their aim. Fandral suspected they needed to stay lined up with whatever they were shooting at while the match burned down. A far less versatile weapon than a bow, but he suspected it was something any fool could be taught to use quickly. It would be a grim day for Midgard when its leaders took all the skill and courage out of warfare and reduced it to simple terms of mere numbers.

Fandral's contempt for the guns of his enemy proved premature. One soldier, at least, managed to strike him. He felt a brutal impact against his hip and felt a flash of searing pain. When he looked down, he saw that there was blood running down his leg.

"By God, you hit him!" a familiar voice shouted from among the bushes. The Sheriff of Nottingham stepped onto the path, a sword clenched in his hand. Close beside

Three Swords 181

him, a white bandage visible beneath his hat, was Matthew Hopkins. "Draw swords! The scoundrel's friends have run off and the witchfinder wants this one alive for questioning!"

Fandral chided himself for an oversight he'd never have made in the days of Robin Hood. He hadn't taken steps to confuse any pursuers from Nottingham. The sheriff had chased after them once he gathered both his senses and soldiers. The argument with Hogun had been the perfect opportunity for them to both find the Asgardians and sneak up on them.

Soldiers emerged from the woods. They faltered somewhat when Fandral nocked another arrow. The witch hunter shifted back, putting the sheriff between himself and the Asgardian. To his credit, the sheriff didn't give ground but instead continued his march. "Take him alive," he reminded his men. "He can't take us all down and if he kills me, maybe one of you lads will get my job."

The sheriff's bravado poured fresh courage into his men and the soldiers resumed their advance. Fandral debated whether to put an arrow into the sheriff. It was the only thing that might take the heart out of his troops, but it sat ill with Fandral to do so. He respected courage, even when he found it housed in an enemy.

From behind the advancing ranks, the witch hunter shouted at Fandral. "Don't worry, you won't be alone too long. Once you're on the rack, you'll tell me where your heretic friends are."

"Who says he's alone!" Volstagg's voice boomed from the forest. The huge Asgardian erupted from where he'd been hiding, hurtling into the midst of the soldiers like a great bear. He caught up one man and threw him into the bushes a dozen yards away.

"Make sure your enemy has retreated before you think he's gone," Hogun growled as he swung his mace and spilled one of the soldiers onto the ground.

Fandral could just see Hopkins over the sheriff's shoulder. The witch hunter turned towards Hogun with a raised pistol. There wasn't a chance of striking the weapon from his hand, but he'd seen enough to judge the man's quality. He loosed the arrow still nocked to his bow and put it through the witchfinder's hat, pinning it to a tree. Hopkins shrieked as he felt the shaft graze his scalp and all thought of shooting Hogun was abandoned as he went scurrying for cover.

The sheriff was then upon Fandral. He scowled at the bow the Asgardian held. "You can surrender now or draw your blade. I'll not strike down a good swordsman when he can't defend himself."

"Are you certain you're the Sheriff of Nottingham?" Fandral couldn't hide his surprise. The sheriffs of yore had been villains whose ideas of sportsmanship were weighted dice and marked cards.

"Draw that sword," the sheriff said. "I warn I'll not fall for the trick you pulled in the Saracen's Head."

Fandral was about to drop the longbow and accept the sheriff's challenge when a strange rustling sounded from the forest. He might have thought it was a herd of boars if there had been any sign such animals still lived in Sherwood. There was a grotesque aspect to the galloping, a squamous, squelching sound like a bog expelling gas on a hot summer day.

Instead of dropping his bow, Fandral put an arrow to the string and loosed. Everything was accomplished with such speed that the sheriff didn't have a chance to do more than gasp in amazement. The arrow slammed into the weird creature that charged out from the depths of the forest. Fandral had only a glimpse before the impact sent it rolling into the underbrush, but that glance was enough. It looked like a wolf woven together from peat moss with enormous black thorns for teeth.

"We've other enemies just now," Fandral told the sheriff as he fitted another arrow to his bow. The creature he'd struck was only the vanguard of an entire pack. Dozens of the moss-wolves came rushing out of the arboreal murk, their fungus-like paws sucking at the dirt as they galloped along.

"Saints protect us!" the sheriff exclaimed. "The sorcerer's demons!"

Fandral dropped another of the monsters with an arrow. "Whatever they are, they can die." He whipped around and sent an arrow through the head-stalk of another wolf as it lunged to attack a soldier.

The sheriff's men were screaming in terror, all thought of fighting the Asgardians discarded as several of them turned to run. Fandral saw one man dragged down and torn by thorn-fangs. Volstagg cut another wolf in half before it could bite one of the men. Hogun's mace sent a moss-creature spinning through the air until it impaled itself on an overhanging branch.

"Die with your wounds to the fore!" the sheriff shouted. "You can't outrun these monsters!" He intercepted a wolf that sprang at Fandral, his sword hewing through the fibrous mass that acted as its neck. The decapitated body ran about aimlessly while the head gnashed its fangs in the dirt.

"A truce, then," Fandral laughed. He sent arrows flying as fast as he could draw them. "Though I must confess, I never imagined I'd fight side-by-side with the Sheriff of Nottingham."

The sheriff gave him a puzzled look, but soon had to concentrate on his swordplay when another pack of the monsters came charging out from the trees. When Fandral exhausted his supply of arrows, he drew Fimbuldraugr and joined the Englishman as he slashed the wolves converging on them.

Brona's monsters were mindless but utterly without fear. The Asgardians and their English allies had to slaughter every last one of the plant creatures before the attack was broken. Brief as the fray was, it claimed a grisly toll. Five of the sheriff's men were dead and an equal number had been wounded by the wolves' thorny fangs.

Fandral surveyed the aftermath. "I don't think you've enough soldiers left to arrest us now," he told the sheriff as the man walked beside him.

The sheriff rubbed a hand through his hair. "I've more pressing problems. I think one of these damn things ate my hat."

Fandral smiled at the flippant remark, but his expression grew serious when he saw Hogun and Volstagg watching the soldiers. It would only need the slightest spark to reignite the battle.

"You shouldn't try to stop us," Fandral said. "Believe me when I tell you that we're here to help."

Three Swords 185

"I know that now," the sheriff replied, a strange sparkle in his eye. "Every child in England grows up learning about Robin Hood. The old legends about how, like King Arthur, when times are darkest the hero would return to save the land." He pointed at the witch hunter's hat stuck to the tree. "You don't need to tell me who you are. Your archery speaks for itself. Praise God you've come back to help us."

The unexpected adulation, especially from the Sheriff of Nottingham, caught Fandral by surprise. He'd never imagined his exploits as Robin Hood could have grown into such a widespread legend. A glance at the dead soldiers quickly sobered his mood. "We've come to put an end to the Sorcerer of Sherwood," he confided to the sheriff. "But it's a task we must conduct on our own."

The sheriff nodded in understanding. "I'll take my dead and wounded back to Nottingham." He held out his hand and shook Fandral's. "Forgive a man whose duties caused him to oppose you and believe me when I tell you I'll pray for your victory."

Fandral pointed at the hat pinned to the tree. "What about Hopkins?"

"The witchfinder's probably halfway back to town by now," the sheriff grimaced. "No doubt trying to recruit more men to come after you." Fire entered his eyes as he added, "But he'll not have any of my soldiers in his mob. I'll promise you that. And once people hear about these things that attacked us, he'll not have anyone this side of Scotland willing to follow him into Sherwood."

The sheriff gave Fandral a final salute, then walked off to organize his men for their withdrawal from the forest. Once it was clear that the English weren't going to resume the fight, Hogun and Volstagg moved to join Fandral.

"That went far different than I expected it to," Volstagg said as he dabbed a bandage against his hand. He saw the inquiring look Fandral gave him and showed him his scraped knuckles. "Made the mistake of punching one of those things in the mouth," he said. "I didn't expect their teeth to be so sharp."

Hogun's attitude was more serious and he kept Hridgandr at the ready. "Is it smart letting them go? They might double back or send for more soldiers."

Fandral shook his head. "I've the sheriff's word he'll do neither."

"And you trust him?" Hogun pressed.

"I never imagined I'd say it, but yes, I trust the Sheriff of Nottingham to keep his word," Fandral laughed. He leaned against a tree and pointed at his hip. "Help me bind my wound and we'll be on our way. We've still a wizard to vanquish."

Volstagg kicked one of the dead wolves. "Aye," he said. "Only now he knows we're here."

SIXTEEN

The forest grew more twisted and fearsome the deeper they plunged into its depths. Now Hogun was sorely pressed to find anything they passed that looked natural. The entire landscape had been perverted by magic and the squirming plant-things of before were now commonplace. The trees themselves were viciously distorted, their limbs more like grasping claws than branches and their trunks split to expose jagged recesses like gaping maws.

The more he saw of the magical rot at the heart of Sherwood, the more certain Hogun was that the forest was beyond saving. Fandral's stubborn insistence that there was anything left to protect cut Hogun to the quick. He'd seen how black magic could corrupt a land, he knew how a place could become so polluted by sorcery that it became fit only as a dwelling for demons. Mogul had damned Hogun's home. Brona had done the same to Sherwood, only Fandral refused to accept it.

188 *Marvel: Legends of Asgard*

Hogun had been forced to face the intolerable fate of his land. Now that he was in a similar situation, he expected Fandral to do the same. But his friend remained obstinate, clinging to the past, steadfastly rejecting any overture that suggested Brona's conjuring had already destroyed his adopted home in Midgard.

As he watched Fandral scout ahead of them, Hogun saw him pause to stare at some spot that remained familiar despite the wizard's manipulations. He saw the flicker of pain that showed on Fandral's face when he did so, the agony of seeing his old world consumed by the ugliness of a new one. Hogun recognized that sort of pain. He knew it only too well. That, he supposed, was the reason he was so angry with Fandral. Fandral was his friend, of which Hogun had all too few. He didn't want to see him hurt, and he knew that the longer Fandral tried to resist the reckoning the more dire the agony of losing Sherwood would be. When Hogun had finally accepted that his homeland was gone it had nearly killed him. How he wished he could spare Fandral that kind of pain.

"Either Fandral's finally gotten lost in this wizard's garden, or that witch he knew must've really hated seeing people," Volstagg huffed as they followed Fandral. Even with a bullet in his leg, the rakish Asgardian could still manage a pace Volstagg found taxing to maintain.

"I'd imagine you'd want to keep to yourself if you had to worry about being arrested by thugs like Hopkins," Hogun pointed out.

Volstagg gave Hogun an incredulous look. "It was idle chatter," he said. "My way of expressing a hope that we'll find Maudlin's cave soon."

Hogun shrugged. "Then that's what you should have said. I can't read your mind."

"If you could, you wouldn't like what it's thinking right now," Volstagg said. He pointed to Fandral up ahead of them on the overgrown deer run they were navigating. "I don't think you'd like what he's thinking either."

"No, I wouldn't," Hogun agreed. "Fandral should be focused on watching for any sign that Brona's ready to make another attack." He frowned down at a slithering vegetable that looked equal portions carrot and hare. "Instead he keeps thinking about what the Enchanter has done to Sherwood. He keeps letting himself get distracted by what he's left behind instead of concentrating on what lies ahead."

"He needs to remember the way things looked before if he's going to lead us to the cave," Volstagg said. "So I think he needs to do a bit of both."

Hogun sighed. Worry flashed across his face, but passed too quickly for Volstagg to notice. "Trying to do both is apt to leave him vulnerable when Brona does set his powers against us."

As though summoned by Hogun, Fandral's voice drifted back to him in a surprised cry. "By Sleipnir's saddle!" Hogun rushed forward to see what had shocked the other warrior. When he reached Fandral, he saw that the forest ahead of them had lost its fecundity, instead it withered into a clearing some hundred feet across.

Only one thing grew in that clearing, a lone tree so immense that it made the Major Oak look like a sapling. It was a gnarled and ill-favored giant with black bark and leafless limbs. The trunk was thick and wide, fifty feet and more across and pitted throughout by ragged knots in the wood that stared back at the Asgardians as though they were a multitude of glowering eyes. Such a tree could only rise from a seed taken from Hel, Hogun thought, for surely no other realm could produce such an abomination.

"Its roots are in the witch's cave," Fandral muttered. Hogun let his eyes drift to the base of the towering growth. Indeed, there was a dark opening at the bottom of the tree that suggested a cavern.

"The Enchanter must have decided the cave wasn't good enough, so he grew his own tower," Volstagg commented as he came up to the edge of the clearing. He glanced aside at his companions. "Well, no question about where we have to go now."

All three of the heroes were shocked when a voice spoke to them from nowhere. Its seething tone was like that of an immense serpent. "No question at all," it echoed all around them. "All who trespass in Sherwood belong to Brona. The only question is which of you dies first!"

Before he could move, Hogun saw a figure slowly start to materialize outside the cave. It was a humanoid shape, but far larger than a man. "The Enchanter," he hissed, clenching Hridgandr.

"Shoot before he can materialize," Volstagg told Fandral.

Fandral drew one of the three arrows he'd recovered after the fight with the wolves. His arm tensed as he held the bow taut. He hesitated to loose, however, and Hogun could guess why. It was that irksome sense of fair play that often made him refuse an advantage over an enemy.

"Kill the wizard and maybe you can save your forest,"

Hogun told Fandral, hating to prey upon something he deemed a false hope. The tactic worked, however, and Fandral let the arrow fly. The shaft punched clean through the figure's head and struck the tree behind it.

Any mortal being would have been killed by such a shot, but the shimmering, hazy figure simply advanced towards them with slow, ponderous strides. The ground steamed wherever it stepped and loose leaves were swept up in the whirlwind that swirled around it. With each step, the shape became more distinct, though to Hogun's eyes it gained no greater solidity.

"I don't think that's the wizard," Volstagg said.

The figure's hulking outlines now crackled with energy. A face formed across the head and it was an inhuman visage already familiar to the Warriors Three. It was the same kind of evil countenance that had leered from the depths of Magnir's Living Talisman.

"Wizard or demon, we've got to get past it," Fandral swore. He loosed another arrow at the figure, thinking perhaps it had gained enough substance to be hurt by his shot. Hogun couldn't tell if the elemental had become solid, but certainly it had gained power. This time the shaft didn't pass through the creature's head. Instead the arrow burst into flames before it could strike the monster, reduced to ashes that were swept up in the whirlwind.

"Submit to Brona's mastery and your deaths will be less torturous." The voice billowed from the elemental. As it spoke, the thing's face stretched into a mocking grin, putting the lie to any mercy the Enchanter might show them.

"Save that last arrow," Hogun snarled, fury boiling up

192   *Marvel: Legends of Asgard*

inside him. "We do this the old-fashioned way." Raising his mace, he charged out into the clearing.

The Enchanter might kill him, but Hogun wasn't going to stand idle while Brona's creatures laughed at him.

"Wait!" Fandral shouted as Hogun rushed forward to engage the elemental. He shouldered his bow and drew his sword from its scabbard. Cursing under his breath, he started forward to support his friend's charge. Even if he thought the attack had more of temper than strategy behind it, he wasn't about to leave Hogun to face the elemental alone.

"Fandral, that thing's not the only one of the wizard's creatures lurking about!" Volstagg's shout made him turn. The big Asgardian was slowly backing into the clearing. The trees themselves were stirring, using their roots to drag themselves towards Volstagg. The thin, grasping branches now became in truth so many claws as they raked the air.

"All of you will die in agony," the elemental's voice seethed. The whirlwind intensified, expanding to engulf the Warriors Three. Fandral threw up his arm to shield his eyes as dust and debris billowed around him.

"Taste steel!" Hogun roared. Amazingly, he pushed his way through the raging whirlwind and struck at the elemental. There was a flare of light when Hridgandr struck the entity. The elemental was staggered, but at the same time a stream of fire pulsed from its body and down the mace. Hogun snarled in pain as the flame burned him, but with stubborn tenacity, he reared back and struck the monster again.

"Try to keep them back," Fandral told Volstagg. Of the

Three Swords 193

two, he judged Hogun to most need his help at that moment. Together they might be able to eliminate the elemental. Then they'd only have to worry about the animated trees. He tried not to think about what other horrors might rush at them from the Enchanter's tower.

"Fools charge in where wise men fear to tread," Fandral chided Hogun as he swung Fimbuldraugr at the elemental's body. Again, the monster reeled under the blow. The pulse of fire from its body slithered down his sword and sent a red agony searing through his arm. He staggered back with a new respect for Hogun's resolve. The grim warrior had already invited that near-blinding pain on himself a half dozen times, yet he kept attacking. It was an inspiring show of determination. Clenching his teeth, Fandral threw himself back into the fight.

Inch by inch and foot by foot, the concentrated attack on the elemental was driving the being back toward the tower. Fandral could detect no visible sign of damage to the entity, but the very fact it was conceding ground to them seemed a good indicator that they were inflicting some sort of injury.

At least it was until something erupted from the earth nearby. A pulpy mass, like some immense seed pod, burst from the ground on a thick stalk. Fandral could see it from the corner of his eye while he fought the elemental. A moment after it was clear of the earth, the pod split open and a man stepped out of it.

"Brona," Fandral hissed under his breath. The man could be no one else, for he was encased in crimson armor of Asgardian design and similar in appearance to that adopted by Magnir. If any doubt might have remained, it was dismissed by the jewel set into the breastplate. The evil, inhuman face was a mirror image of the elemental's visage. The stone was another of the Living Talismans.

Brona held a flanged mace in his hand and gestured with the weapon at the elemental. "You can stop toying with them now," he commanded.

A pulsation erupted from the elemental, a wall of force that knocked both Fandral and Hogun off their feet. Fandral saw smoke rising from his clothes as he scrambled up from the ground, yet in his bones there was a chilling cold. The elemental, a manifestation of the Living Talisman itself, pointed one of its arms at him. A spiral of arcane energies spilled from the being's hand and racked Fandral's body. He was thrown back by the blast and his body dug a furrow in the ground as he was driven nearly to the edge of the clearing.

His body shuddering with pain, Fandral saw the elemental focus its attention on Hogun. It tried to throw him back with blasts of force as it had him, but Hridgandr deflected enough of the energy that his friend was able to stay on his feet, even if he was forced to surrender ground while the entity resumed its advance.

Fandral looked aside at Volstagg. The warrior's shining sword flashed across branches as they struck at him with their wooden claws. At least a half dozen of the tree-creatures pressed in on his friend, but he was managing to keep them back. A situation that Fandral knew could change the moment one of those claws got through his defenses.

Both of his friends needed his help, but there was no way to help them both. Or was there? Animated tree or elemental force, the monsters all claimed a single master. If he could bring down Brona, Fandral might break their attack. He turned his head to see where the Enchanter was. Brona stood near the husk of the seed pod, spectating as the elemental fought with Hogun. What little of the wizard's face was exposed by his helm exhibited a sadistic delight in the bloodshed.

"We'll see how you like it when it's your own blood," Fandral whispered. Brona wasn't looking his way. Indeed, Fandral seemed to have been forgotten by all of his enemies. It was an oversight he was determined the wizard would regret. He considered using his last arrow, but after his experience against the elemental, decided to employ Fimbuldraugr instead. Slowly, wary of drawing any attention to himself, he stalked towards Brona.

Ten feet from the wizard, Fandral saw Brona's expression change. Some premonition warned the Enchanter of his peril. Fandral abandoned subtlety and rushed at his enemy. His sword was already swinging for Brona's head when the earth suddenly boiled upward. As Magnir had shielded himself by drawing up the floor of the Sssthgar's tower, so did Brona now conjure a column of earth from the ground to block Fandral's blow.

Before Fandral could strike again, a mass of stalks bubbled up from beneath his feet. Hundreds of leafy tendrils coiled around him, tightening about his body as viciously as the wires animated by Magnir's spells. Only now it wasn't just one arm constrained by sorcery, it was his entire body. Like a swarm of snakes, the stalks began to constrict around him.

"Did you really think you could dispose of me so easily?" Brona sneered as he dismissed the column of earth. Boldly he wrested Fimbuldraugr from Fandral's hand. He studied it for a moment, then tucked it under his belt. His contemptuous gaze returned to the hero. The wizard's eyes gleamed as an idea occurred to him.

"I've experimented much with the fragile creatures of Midgard. It would make a novel change to try my magic on a specimen from Asgard." Brona's sadistic smile returned and glanced over to where Hogun and Volstagg were still fighting his creatures. "But I only need one specimen."

"No!" Fandral managed to shout before a tendril wrapped itself around his mouth and silenced him.

"Yes," Brona sneered. "Very much yes."

The wizard's hands curled in arcane passes. Fandral could only watch helplessly as enormous shells burst up from the ground behind both of his friends. A blast from the elemental sent Hogun stumbling back. The shell snapped closed around him, sealing him inside. The tree creatures surged ahead, heedless of Volstagg's blade as the sword hacked away their limbs. He too was driven back, oblivious of the threat behind him until the shell suddenly encased him.

"An interesting experiment in itself," Brona mused as he looked from one shell to the other. "Those were developed by combining carnivorous plants from Asgard with some of the more intriguing flora of Midgard." An impish grin stretched the Enchanter's face as he warmed to his subject. "The interior slowly fills with digestive acids and whatever is caught within is gradually dissolved. The longest a Midgarder

Three Swords 197

has remained alive inside one of those shells was four days, but I expect an Asgardian to last quite a bit longer."

Fandral strained against the tendrils and even managed to slip a hand free briefly before the stalks re-positioned themselves and regained their grip.

Brona glared at Fandral. "I'm sure you're calling me mad and swearing ten kinds of revenge on me right now. I've heard it all before." He leaned close, eyes only inches from Fandral's face. "Am I not entitled to revenge of my own? I know someone attacked my brother Magnir recently, at least to my perception of time. I expect that was you, or at least some confederate of yours. So, you see, I'm quite justified in exacting my own revenge."

The Enchanter waved at the shells imprisoning Volstagg and Hogun. "My only trouble now," he told Fandral, "is devising a worse death for you than the one your friends will meet."

SEVENTEEN

Volstagg had no idea of what had happened. One moment he was fighting the tree creatures and the next everything went black. Briefly the thought crossed his mind that he was dead and that this must be what it was like while the gods decided whether to send a spirit to Valhalla or to Hel. The reek of almonds and the stifling humidity made him reconsider. When he reached out and his hand touched a wet, fibrous material that stung his fingers, he knew he must still be alive.

"Some trap laid by the sorcerer," Volstagg growled in the pungent darkness. "Well, we'll see how long you can hold Volstagg the Undaunted." He used Brandrheid Undrsigr to probe his surroundings. He couldn't even unbend his sword arm before he struck something solid. The walls of his cell were no more than two feet apart in any direction. An upward thrust revealed he had less than a foot between his head and the ceiling.

"Now that's altogether too cozy," the big Asgardian grumbled. The unpleasant thought came to him that his cell was less like a prison and more like a tomb.

Suddenly Volstagg felt water rising around his feet, only this water burned! It was the same stinging sensation as when he'd touched the damp wall, only this was persistent in its aggression. And growing worse as the liquid continued to slowly rise. He could picture the fibrous walls dripping little beads of venom to feed the growing pool.

"Oh, so the trap's not done with me," Volstagg's voice echoed within the tiny cell. "Brona's going to discover it isn't so easy to kill Volstagg the Indestructible." The confidence in his boasts helped to silence the doubt and fear that tried to gain a hold in his mind. He needed that boost, because of all the things the sorcerer could have inflicted upon him, the close confines of the cell was what had him on the verge of panic. Give him a dragon or a troll to fight and his valor was stalwart, but lock him inside a tight space and his bravery was balanced on a pinhead.

Volstagg had no delusions about this chink in his armor and he knew he had to act before panic made it impossible for him to think clearly. Sheathing his sword, he threw out his arms and pressed his palms against the stinging fibers. Their burn was less torturous than the pool at his feet. He pushed in either direction, and as he stretched, his hands passed through the fibers to touch the sturdy walls of his prison.

"We'll see who's the stronger, Volstagg Giantbreaker or this trap," he snarled through clenched teeth. He strained against the walls, wresting every last speck of strength from his arms. Finally, he felt the walls give way. The material of which they were made split with a loud crack. Light streamed into his prison through a narrow fissure. Volstagg could see that the fibers hanging from the walls were some sort of vegetation. The walls themselves resembled tree bark in their texture. Most alarming of all was the pool at his feet. It had an amber color and he could see its caustic touch already beginning to bleach his boots.

"I'm not sticking around to see whatever that's trying to do to me." Volstagg jerked his gaze away from the acidic puddle. He teased his sword from its sheath and stabbed it into the crack he'd made. Leveraging one foot against the opposite side of the crack, he leaned against the sword and used it to pry the opening wider.

The cell groaned and shuddered around him as Volstagg worked. Finally, with a report that was like the scream of a mountain, the wall split entirely. A great section fell outward and the Asgardian plunged through it and back into the clearing.

Volstagg took a quick survey of his surroundings. There was no trace of Brona or the elemental he'd summoned from his Living Talisman. Nor could he see either of his friends. There was only the shattered cell he'd just extricated himself from. It proved to be something like a giant seed. Another like it, unbroken, stood a short distance away.

So too did the tree creatures he'd been fighting before he was trapped. The monsters shifted around when they became aware of his escape and began dragging themselves towards him with their writhing roots.

Volstagg hacked away a groping branch and dashed towards the other seed. The thought pounded through his mind that his friends might be caught inside it the same way he'd been. A wooden claw slashed his face as he charged past a tree that tried to intercept him. Then he was past the monsters. For a moment, at least, there was nothing between him and the enormous seed.

"Brace yourselves!" Volstagg bellowed, though he didn't know if his shout could reach anyone inside the shell. He was even less aware if his warning would do any good, given what he intended. With the tree creatures chasing after him, there wasn't time to try to cut an opening into the shell. His plan was to crack it with one mighty blow.

Volstagg slammed into the seed, driving his shoulder against its shell. The impact uprooted the thing and sent it crashing onto its side. He staggered back, kneading his bruised flesh. He frowned at the dented side of the shell, then smiled when he heard the sound of someone striking the shell from within. When a section of the damaged shell popped outward, he gripped its sides and pulled with all his strength. A glance over his shoulder showed the tree creatures still advancing. A few more moments and they'd reach him.

A final kick from inside broke a hole in the shell. Volstagg reached down and helped extract Hogun from his prison. "Fandral?" he asked, peering down into the shattered seed.

"Not with me," Hogun said. "Last I saw, he was fighting Brona."

Clawed branches slashed at Volstagg. There was no time to consider Fandral's fate now. He turned to engage the attacking trees, his sword hewing through their clutching limbs.

"Attack the kraken's head, not its tentacles!" Hogun yelled at Volstagg. His hands tight about Hridgandr's heft, he charged the nearest of the tree monsters. The mace crashed against the trunk, cracking it and sending a spray of splinters and sap flying from the creature. The tree swung around to try to catch him when he wheeled away from it, but as the monster moved, its cracked body fragmented under the shifting weight. It broke apart, crashing to the ground like falling timber.

"Oh no you don't!" Volstagg shouted at Hogun. "I've been fighting these things longer than you have!" Swinging Brandrheid Undrsigr as though it were a woodaxe, he attacked the tree creatures with a vengeance. He felt embarrassed that he'd wasted so much effort hewing away branches when common sense should have had him attacking the trunk all along. Visiting ruin upon the monsters helped to restore his equilibrium. It became something of a race to see which of them could destroy more of the beasts. Volstagg laughed heartily when he found his score was six to Hogun's five.

Volstagg's humor sobered when he saw Hogun looking around the clearing. He started towards the broken shell that had held Volstagg. "Fandral wasn't in there," he told Hogun, guessing what the warrior was looking for. He stamped his foot against the ground in frustration. "By the Odinsword, what did that blackguard do with him? Is Fandral still alive, or did Brona kill him?"

Hogun turned and faced the towering tree. "We'll ask

the Enchanter when we get our hands on him," he vowed.

"It'll take hours… days… to search that place," Volstagg cursed. In addition to the height of the hollowed tree there could be layers of dungeons below the old cave.

"You've not paid enough attention to sorcerers," Hogun said. "They always prefer to make their lairs in towers because it affords them a better view of the constellations that influence their magic. They might keep their guards and treasures in the lower levels, but you'll always find the wizard keeps himself in rooms near the summit."

"So we have to fight our way up through the tree." Volstagg's fingers tightened around the grip of his sword and he started toward the dark opening at the tower's base.

Hogun held him back. "The wizard will know we're free if we do that. While Brona believes us trapped, we might still take him by surprise. That's our one advantage."

"How do we manage that?" Volstagg asked him. He suspected he wasn't going to like the answer.

"We climb," Hogun stated, nodding at the tree's craggy trunk.

Fandral knew it was futile to try to break his bindings. The tendrils that gripped him now were even firmer than those the Enchanter had conjured up from the earth. They were wound about his body, pinning him to a flat, table-like slab of wood. Only his head was allowed any degree of motion. Given Brona's sadistic streak, he knew that courtesy was because the sorcerer enjoyed the fear the sights within his laboratory caused his captives.

Certainly, it had succeeded with him. It was why Fandral

struggled even when he knew there was no hope. He couldn't submit to the Enchanter's experiment without fighting to the very last.

The arcane laboratory was situated near the summit of the hollow tree that was Brona's tower. Much of the equipment appeared to have been *grown* rather than constructed. Vessels of translucent amber rested on shelves that grew out from the walls themselves. Some held preserved examples of Brona's labors, horrid things that fused animal and vegetable life in hideous combinations. The smallest of these was no bigger than a mouse while the largest looked like it might once have been a horse. Several had clearly been human, their skin changed into bark and their hair into leaves. Even dead and pickled in a jar, the agony they'd endured was apparent on their faces.

Racks of preserved herbs and strange roots dominated one corner of the laboratory. The mummified remains of animals and people were ensconced in another. A niche held several long tables with root-like chains dangling from each corner. Arrayed about each table were implements that hadn't been grown to suit Brona's whims. Fandral saw a cruel selection of knives and hooks laid out and ready for use.

"Yes, you'll find out what those are for soon enough," Brona taunted him as he noticed where Fandral's gaze had turned. The Enchanter was seated at a desk, studying Robin Hood's bow and scribbling notes on a sheet of parchment. "I have to be wary of how much change in one session that I induce in a Midgarder." The evil grin flashed across his lips. "They are such fragile things. But I expect I can work on

Three Swords 205

you from start to finish. At least it is a hypothesis worth investigating."

Defiance filled Fandral's voice. "Do your worst," he spat. He heard something stir above him, roused by the anger in his voice. He watched in shock as what he'd taken to be part of the ceiling began to undulate. As it moved, he was able to differentiate it from the beams it was wound around. The thing was a gigantic snake, a serpent big enough to swallow a bull whole. Its body retained a scaly texture, though its coloring almost perfectly matched that of the black tree. He was surprised to see leathery wings folded against the sides of its body as it dropped down from its overhead perch and wound itself into a coil nearby on the floor.

"You're interested in my pet?" Brona stepped away from the desk and laid his hand on the serpent's wedge-shaped head as though he were patting a dog. "I believe she is the last of her kind in Midgard, though I understand they were once quite common in the realm the Midgarders call Wales." The Enchanter's voice seemed to soothe the snake and it slipped into a more restful pose. "I used my magic to develop her to her current size. Once every summer she produces a clutch of eggs and I use them in my experiments." A note of mockery entered his voice. "You shot one of the results with an arrow. It might amuse you to know that was when I knew you were in my forest. So you see, you really never had a chance. Magnir must have become feeble-minded if he allowed buffoons like you and your friends to overcome him." The Enchanter stroked his fingers along the serpent's head, scratching it between its lidless eyes.

"This one isn't for you to eat," he chided the snake.

Brona looked back at Fandral. "Sometimes it's helpful to tell her these things. She's completely enthralled by my enchantments, but you can only expect a limited comprehension from such a tiny brain. She's more instinct than intuition, even after I tried to expand her intelligence with my spells." He leaned down and followed the direction of the serpent's unblinking gaze. "Right now, she's watching you. She's convinced you're dangerous to me." Brona's laugh was like the lash of a whip. "Of course, that time is past. All you can do is disappoint me if my experiment fails. The threat you posed me is quite finished."

"What about the threat *I* pose!" Volstagg's bellow suddenly roared through the laboratory. Fandral tilted his head and saw the big Asgardian standing just inside one of the windows. From the heroic attitude he struck and the arrogance in his manner, Fandral knew he was trying to draw and hold the Enchanter's attention. He could readily guess why. He could just see a shadow outside the window on the opposite side of the laboratory. He knew it was Hogun preparing to ambush the wizard.

"So you escaped," Brona snarled. "How tedious." The wizard's hand reached to the Living Talisman on his chest. A tempest suddenly swirled through the laboratory, hurtling towards Volstagg and trying to fling the big Asgardian back through the window.

"You'll have to do better than that to stir Volstagg the Unmovable!" Volstagg bragged.

"I intend to," Brona snarled. A litany of eldritch tones rasped across his lips. The tempest seemed to collapse in upon itself, concentrating until it formed a huge figure.

Three Swords 207

With far more rapidity than its previous appearance, the elemental took form and charged at Volstagg.

While Brona was occupied with Volstagg, Fandral felt something strike the table near his wrist. He glanced aside and saw Hogun's dagger embedded in the wood, partly severing the tendrils that were wound about his hand. He hesitated to rake the remaining strands across the bladed edge, for at that instant, Brona swung around.

The Enchanter, however, was too busy to notice his prisoner. At that moment Hogun charged at him from the gloom. Brona's mace parried Hridgandr and the two combatants squared off.

"I knew if that bloated idiot escaped, you did too," Brona snarled. "When this is over, I'll try to improve your minds by replacing your brains with radishes."

"When this is over," Hogun snarled back, "the only thing you'll do is feed worms."

While the Enchanter was embattled, Fandral sawed through the remaining strands binding his arm and pulled the dagger free. The motion instantly roused the winged serpent. The snake slithered over to the table. He felt its fetid breath as it reared up and its jaws stretched wide. The reptile knew he was escaping and was trying to prevent it. But it froze instead of striking at him. He could almost see the frustration in the snake's eyes as it watched him slash through his restraints. Brona had spoken truly of the limited scope of the snake's mentality. It wanted to defend its master, but it didn't know how to do that without eating the enemy he'd forbidden it to devour.

Fandral scrambled free from the table as the serpent

remained where it was, immobilized by its confusion. He turned towards Brona's desk where the Enchanter had been studying both his sword and his bow. Without weapons, he knew there was little he could do to help his friends.

As Fandral dashed towards the desk, he saw Volstagg being battered by the arcane blasts from the elemental's hands. Hogun, however, looked to be gaining the advantage over Brona. A solid hit from Hridgandr sent the Enchanter stumbling back, his breastplate crumpled so that one side of his Living Talisman projected away from the wizard's armor.

The strike infuriated Brona. A mighty bolt of energy leaped from his fingers and struck Hogun, flinging him across the room. The conjuration left the Enchanter winded, but not so exhausted that he couldn't snarl an order to his pet. "Destroy that vermin!"

The snake snapped into animation, surging across the laboratory to where Hogun had fallen. Fandral shouted to his friend, but Brona's spell had left him dazed. The distance was too great to cover before the serpent reached him. Beyond, he could see Volstagg being pushed by the elemental towards the open window. Desperately, Fandral took up the bow and nocked the last arrow.

The shaft went speeding away, striking with the unerring aim and incredible power only Robin Hood could have shown. There was a shrieking clamor as he hit his target. Already partly dislodged from Brona's armor, the Living Talisman was sent rolling across the floor when the arrow hit it. The Enchanter screamed in horror as he watched it clatter off into one of the niches.

The elemental conjured by Brona's magic vanished the instant the Living Talisman left his possession. So near to the window was Volstagg that the abrupt disappearance of his foe almost sent him falling anyway. Only a hurried grasp at the ledge kept him from plummeting down the tower.

Hogun was looking up into the gaping jaws of the serpent when he realized his peril – too late to stop its strike. Instead of attacking, however, the snake quickly turned aside. Swiftly it undulated across the laboratory. Fandral thought there was a greater awareness in the reptile's eyes. Certainly, there was an impression of vindictiveness when it struck Brona with its blunt snout and spilled him to the floor. Just as the elemental had been banished, with the loss of the Living Talisman, Brona's control of the reptile had vanished. In a single motion, the snake seized its former master in its jaws. Throwing back its head, it swallowed him whole before slithering out of one of the windows. Fandral had a momentary view of its great wings spreading wide as the snake soared across Sherwood's canopy, intent perhaps on returning to the Welsh countryside it had been taken from.

"That makes two," Hogun declared. He moved stiffly across the laboratory to where the Living Talisman had fallen. He scowled down at it for a moment. Volstagg came over and relieved him of the loathsome burden.

"I'll take this one back to Onund," Volstagg said.

Fandral returned Fimbuldraugr to its sheath and walked over to his friends. He ran his hand along one of the shelves. His fingers came away with a layer of wood dust. "With the Enchanter gone, his creations begin to rot." His statement was punctuated by the sound of amber vessels shattering as they lost their integrity.

Hogun nodded. "You were right and I was wrong. Sherwood wasn't beyond saving."

He clasped his friend's shoulder. "We were both wrong. I let my memories of this place cloud my judgment. You were right to question me for allowing that to happen." He looked at the bow he still held. "But a vow isn't lightly made or easily broken." Reverently he set the bow aside and leaned it against one of the decaying walls.

"We've still one Enchanter to face," Volstagg protested. "That would be very handy when we face him."

Fandral shook his head. "I promised Marian that Robin Hood would always remain in Sherwood. That bow belongs to Robin Hood, not me." He turned and brushed the tears that were forming in his eyes. "It belongs here. With her."

The transition across time and space brought them again into Onund's hut. Like Hogun, Volstagg couldn't send the Living Talisman into the maelstrom chest quickly enough. Hogun took a strange reassurance that it was an aspect of the Living Talismans themselves that evoked such disgust rather than some failing in his own character.

Hogun found less reassurance in the seer's words as he used his salve to tend their wounds. "You've defeated two of the Enchanters, but do not become overconfident. There remains Forsung, the eldest of the brothers. The most fearsome of them all." The mystic wagged his finger in warning. "His powers are augmented by a devious intellect cunning enough to defy Odin himself.

"More, you will have no advantage of surprise when you move against Forsung. Magnir you were able to take unaware, while Brona merely suspected your intentions. With two Enchanters defeated, there will be no deceiving Forsung. He will *know* there is a danger to himself. He'll be certain that you're coming for him."

Hogun shook his head. "It can't be helped." He looked aside at his friends. "We may lose the ability to surprise him, but now we know more than we did about the Enchanters and their Living Talismans." His fingers tightened around Hridgandr. "We know how to fight them."

"Good," Onund approved. "I knew the Warriors Three had the heart for this quest." He moved to the astral circle and began drawing a new design and rearranging the runestones. "Forsung has established himself in another dimension of existence, a parallel reflection of Midgard as it was many eons ago." He looked up from his work and fixed the heroes with an anxious gaze. "The moment you are drawn through the portal, Forsung will know you're there. You must try to find him, before he finds you."

"It might be better if he does find us first," Volstagg laughed. "Then we can put a finish to this whole thing then and there." He slapped his hand against his stomach. "We've been bouncing around realms so much, it's been days since I had a decent meal."

In spite of his dour nature, Hogun found himself smiling at Volstagg's joke. He only wished he could believe it would be that easy. The only constant he'd ever found in fighting wizards was that nothing was too incredible to discount.

Unfortunately, the incredible was rarely beneficial. More often the caprices of fate sided with sorcerers instead of those who strove against them. It was Hogun's experience that the only luck he could depend on was the luck he made for himself.

EIGHTEEN

The transition from Skornheim to the world to which Forsung had withdrawn was accomplished in a matter of heartbeats. When his senses recovered, Fandral wondered what sort of place it was that they'd entered. He was at once struck by a heat as intense as that of the desert, but so humid that he seemed to drink rather than breathe the air. All around them was lush growth as strange as some of the things they'd seen on their way to Brona's tower. Ferns as tall as trees. Weird plants with scaly trunks and frond-like branches. Clumps of weeds taller than a man. Scraggly bushes with thorns as long as daggers. Bizarre plants with rings of spikes projecting from their pulpy stalks. An absence impressed Fandral as keenly as the curious plants themselves. Nowhere did he detect the bright bloom of a flower, everything was hued in drab greens and browns.

"Smells like a midden heap that's been left too long," Volstagg commented. He took a step and his boot sank down into mud up to the knee. With some difficulty he managed to extract his foot. Black slime encrusted much of his boot. "Are we supposed to march through this or swim it?"

Hogun looked up at the sky and brought Hridgandr to the ready. "Forsung's already found us!" he warned the others. He pointed to a flock of creatures gliding through the air. Fandral thought they were some sort of dragon, for they were clearly neither bird nor bat. Their bodies were scaly and their wings devoid of feathers. Long tails with a broad tip stretched behind them as they arced through the sky. Their heads were lizard-like with rows of sharp teeth visible in their gaping mouths. They had a mottled coloration, alternating splotches of black and brown. Small feet dangled beneath their bodies, each toe tipped in a curved claw.

Fandral tensed as the creatures dove closer, but the nearer they came the more he relaxed. It was often difficult to judge the distance of an unfamiliar bird soaring through the sky. So it was with these weird animals. Hogun had taken them to still be quite distant, and therefore much larger than they really were. The flock lighted into the tree-like ferns, gripping their stalks with their feet and the clawed finger in the middle of each wing.

"Awful small for dragons," Fandral quipped. The creatures were perhaps a little bigger than a hen in size. They peered down at the Asgardians with a wary caution. Sometimes one would slowly close its eye only to quickly open it again, as if to convince itself that the warriors were still there.

"Flying lizards," Volstagg shrugged. He blinked in disbelief as a centipede as long as his arm skittered around the periphery of the mud hole in front of him, its long antennae wagging in perplexity as the arthropod tried to make sense of these intruders in its domain. He kicked a stone at it and the creature scurried away. "Why can't wizards ever live someplace nice and normal? If it isn't already strange, they have to make it so. If it is already strange, they have to make it worse."

"If they were normal people, they wouldn't be wizards," Hogun said, fire in his tone. He studied the mud pit Volstagg was frowning at. With a lunge he brought himself across it and onto the firmer ground the centipede had just surrendered to them.

Fandral jumped over to join Hogun, quitting the rocky shelf they'd been on. He looked back at the flock of reptiles. "They could just be some of the local wildlife," he said, though not without a note of doubt. He was thinking of Brona's flying spies in Sherwood. "Even if they aren't, we'd never be able to catch all of them. Not with how they're spread out."

Volstagg started swinging his body back and forth, readying himself to follow his friends. At the last moment he reconsidered the idea. "I'll wade across," he told them. "If I try to jump, I'll wind up with either my face or my backside stuck in the mud."

Volstagg began to cross the mud pit, but at once Fandral noticed it was proving to be a rough slog for the warrior. He spotted black sludge bubbling up whenever he took a step, displacing the brown muck on the surface. The mud, it seemed, was only a thin skin across the gunk underneath. A strong, yet faintly familiar odor hit Fandral as Volstagg kept advancing and stirring up the pool.

"Smells like a shipyard," Hogun said, detecting the same smell.

"Tar!" Fandral exclaimed. He'd once seen a rat fall into a barrel of tar being used to treat the hull of a longship. The more the animal had struggled to extricate itself from the muck, the faster it was sucked down into it.

Volstagg appeared to be under the same threat. He'd covered only half the pit and already the tar was up to his waist. Each step was more of an effort than the last and the strain of moving his legs was visible on his face.

"Stop there! Don't keep going!" Fandral cried out.

"Easy for you to say, this gunk is trying to pull me down!" Volstagg snapped at him.

"And it'll do that even faster if you keep trying to move," Fandral snarled back.

Hogun started down into the pit but Fandral pulled him back. "We can't get him out that way. We'll have to get a line around him and pull him out."

"Then we'd better hurry," Hogun said. "It's up to his belly now."

Fandral nodded and the two of them fanned out to search the terrain around them for something they could use as a pole or a rope to extricate Volstagg. They could hear him calling after them with mounting agitation. Fandral hoped he would stay calm and not start trying to move again. It would be bad enough getting him out already.

Hogun found a toppled fern that looked long enough

and thick enough to serve their needs. Fandral helped him carry it back to the tar pit. Volstagg had his sword raised up above his head while the other hand lifted his beard and tried to keep it away from the tar. The sludge was up to his chest now.

"That took five inches too long," Volstagg complained.

"Maybe we should leave him," Hogun said.

Fandral shook his head. "You know Gunnhilde would track us down if we lost her husband," he joked. Volstagg glared at them from the pit but didn't say anything.

The fern stalk was long enough to stretch over to the rocky shelf to create a kind of bridge across the tar pit. Fandral jumped back over to secure the opposite end while Hogun anchored the portion on the shore. They shifted it until it was in easy reach of Volstagg.

"Don't try to pull yourself up, just use it to support you while you pull your way to shore." Fandral watched Volstagg throw Brandrheid Undrsigr to Hogun. Volstagg scowled down at his beard and reluctantly let it drop into the gunk.

"The sacrifices a hero makes," Volstagg groaned as he pulled himself along the bridge. It was an arduous process, but with the stalk to bolster him, he was able to keep from being drawn deeper into the tar pit. After what felt like hours, Volstagg finally reached the other side and drew himself onto firmer ground. His body was caked in clumps of tar and his beard was stained for a quarter of its length.

Fandral jumped back across the pit and rejoined his friends. Volstagg snatched his sword back from Hogun and glared at both of them. "If I can't wash this out and I have to cut my beard, I'm not speaking to either of you until it grows back."

Fandral smiled at the huge warrior. "If I thought you meant that, I'd dunk you in there again."

Volstagg sighed. "When they compose my saga, the bards will marvel that I suffered such insubordinate sidekicks on my adventures."

"*Sidekick*?" Hogun bristled.

"Well clearly I'm the hero in my own saga," Volstagg said, making it sound like the most obvious thing in the world.

Fandral broke out into laughter. "If you keep that up, Volstagg, you'll be dead before Forsung can get a chance to murder you." He pointed up at the winged lizards. "I think it's safe now to say those aren't the Enchanter's spies. We've been here long enough for Forsung to send something to try and kill us. I doubt there would be a better time than while we were getting you out of the tar pit."

"Then we've still a chance to find the wizard before he finds us, as Onund would say," Volstagg said. He looked at Brandrheid Undrsigr's tar-choked scabbard and tucked the blade underneath the band of his wire belt instead.

"We've a chance," Fandral agreed, scratching his chin. "The only problem is where to start looking."

Hogun gestured at the heavy plant growth all around them. "Maybe once we're clear of this swamp, we can get a better look at this land."

"I don't have a better idea," Fandral confessed. He spat in his palm and held it up. "There's a slight wind from that direction, so let's go that way."

"Why?" Volstagg asked.

Three Swords 219

Fandral grinned at him. "Because it makes more sense than just picking a direction completely at random."

When they left the tar pit, the plan had been to march until they were clear of the swamp. In Volstagg's opinion, this entire world, dimension, whatever it was, must be just one big swamp. They'd been walking for hours with no end in sight. Sometimes the ground would be firm, at others it was soaked to the consistency of soup.

The distant roars of what sounded like colossal beasts rumbled through the steaming jungle. Insects so large that they'd grown past all belief, scurried and flittered among the fronds and branches of the trees, or at least the tall, weedlike things that posed as trees in this primordial world. Volstagg saw lizards, both winged and terrestrial, of astounding variety racing through the vegetation. A toad big enough to swallow a goat stared blankly at them from a puddle, its throat bobbing as it watched them.

For all the strangeness, nothing showed overt signs of hostility until they finally came into a region of ground where it wasn't utterly overgrown with cycads and ferns. There was enough open space that Volstagg could actually get a glimpse of the rich black soil. He knew enough about farming to be surprised that this area wasn't as fecund as the rest. Then Fandral pointed out the tracks to him.

"Something big has been lumbering through here," he said. "Often enough that it's crushed anything that tries to grow." He gestured with his finger to indicate the outlines of one track that hadn't been quite obliterated by others stamping across it.

Volstagg whistled, impressed by the size of the track. It was as wide as a shield and sunk to a depth of several inches, testament to the creature's great weight as well as size. From what he could make out, the foot seemed midway between that of an elephant and a crocodile. "I'd hate to run into whatever made that track," he told his friends.

One day, Volstagg promised himself, he was going to learn to stop tempting fate. The moment he spoke, a deafening bark that felt equal parts bull's bellow and lion's roar crashed down on them. The Asgardians spun around, their weapons at the ready. Only a few dozen yards away, rearing up from where it had been lying on the ground, was the tremendous beast in question.

The nearest thing Volstagg could liken the beast to was a rhinoceros, for its skin had a similar pebbly texture and its face sported a horn at the end of its snout. There the resemblance ended, for there were two more, even longer horns, pushing out from above its eyes. A wide collar of bone encircled its neck and its upper lip formed a sharp beak at the front of its mouth. Its forelegs were shorter than its hind legs, giving the beast an arched back. Behind it stretched a long, scaly tail he could compare only to that of a dragon.

Volstagg wasn't the only one to make that comparison. "So Forsung sends a dragon to ambush us," Hogun growled, tightening his grip on Hridgandr.

"Spread out so if it breathes fire, it can't strike all of us," Fandral advised.

But the beast didn't intend to send a sheet of flame at them. Before Volstagg could move, the creature barked a second time and charged forward. The attack was so

Three Swords

221

sudden, the warrior was caught utterly off guard. He felt the beast slam into him. It tilted its head down and caught him with its nasal horn. Twisting its head back, the beast tossed him through the air. Cycads cracked as he struck them, but each painful impact lessened his momentum. He came to rest against the broad stalk of a giant fern. His hand flew to where the animal had caught him. Relief rushed through him. The beast had merely hooked him with its horn, it hadn't pierced his body.

Volstagg painfully regained his feet and drew his sword. "Dragon or devil, nothing does that to Volstagg the Profound and gets away with it." He strode back towards the sounds of the fray, bristling with anger.

Fandral and Hogun strove to keep the thunder horn from throwing them the way it had Volstagg. Fimbuldraugr slashed at the thick hide, but managed only a few shallow cuts. Hridgandr cracked a portion of the bony shield around its neck, but when Hogun tried to circle around the animal and come at it from behind, the scaly tail lashed at him and forced him back. There was awful power in that tail, snapping tall cycads like they were twigs when its swings failed to find Hogun.

"Take heart!" Volstagg shouted to his friends. "I'll be with you in a moment!"

Rushing towards the fight, Volstagg almost stumbled into another pit. This one, however, was shallow and sandy, its bottom lined with a cluster of white oval objects roughly the size of his hand. His brow knitted in confusion when he spotted them, wondering what they were.

The thunder horn barked again and swung around.

Ignoring any threat posed by Fandral or Hogun, the beast came charging back for Volstagg.

This time the big Asgardian was able to dodge the beast's rush, letting its horned face slam into a fern-tree instead of himself. As Volstagg scrambled away, the snorting thunder horn turned about. Its feet pawed the ground and then it came bellowing towards him for a third attack.

In angling itself for its drive, Volstagg noticed the thunder horn do something peculiar. It circled around the shallow pit he'd stumbled on. He realized now that the hole was where the beast had been lying when they first saw it.

"Eggs!" Volstagg shouted to his companions. "It's trying to protect its eggs!" He dove away as the thunder horn charged him. He collided with a cycad and nearly fell under the heavy tread of the animal as it rushed past.

"We'll try to withdraw," Fandral called back. "If it'll let us."

Volstagg turned as the huge beast poised itself for another run. The thunder horn was fast, but hardly agile. It had to stop to turn itself and once it was committed to an angle of attack it couldn't deviate. Volstagg had learned that much from its previous charges. Now he put it to use.

"It'll let us go," Volstagg declared. The thunder horn ran towards him, its head lowered so it could toss him again with its horns. The warrior shifted aside, but this time with a purpose beyond merely avoiding the animal. As it stormed towards him, he slammed its face with Brandrheid Undrsigr's pommel. The beast's momentum struck the unyielding dwarven metal with a thunderous crash. Volstagg himself was thrown back by the collision. Fandral and Hogun helped him up from where he landed.

The thunder horn glowered at them and took a few staggering steps in their direction. Then it slumped against the ground, its nose pressing into the dirt.

"I convinced it to take a nap," Volstagg bragged. "You may now call me Volstagg the Beast-tamer."

"Clouting an animal isn't exactly taming it," Fandral pointed out.

Volstagg chuckled. "Alright, I'll go wake it up and we can see if you do any better."

Fandral and Hogun pulled him back. "Have it your way, Volstagg the Beast-tamer, and let sleeping behemoths stay asleep."

"I thought you'd see it that way," Volstagg laughed as they continued their march through the primordial swamp.

NINETEEN

The farther they trudged through the swamps, the more often the Asgardians came across the world's mammoth reptiles. Fandral saw creatures with small heads and long necks wading through rivers while they pulled leaves from the treetops. He saw a beast that looked like a great spiked turtle dragging an armored tail behind it, a clublike knob of bone at its end. There were bipedal lizards with beaked faces that lumbered through the fens, grazing in the tall reeds.

Strange as the reptilian beasts were, they lacked that impression of corruption that Fandral had sensed with Brona's monstrosities. These, he felt, were simply the creatures that belonged to this land rather than products of Forsung's sorcery. Indeed, as yet they'd seen no trace of the Enchanter. He was beginning to wonder if Onund had made a mistake and his astral circle had sent them to the wrong place.

Three Swords 225

When proof of the Enchanter's presence did manifest, it did so in a demonstration that was unmistakable. A tremor passed through the earth, making Fandral think that one of the enormous reptiles was somewhere near them just beyond the cycads. The beasts had done so a few times before but usually deviated when they detected the Asgardians. It was only when the heavy footfalls continued to come closer that the warriors made ready to defend themselves.

"What we've seen so far have been the elk and boar of this world," Fandral cautioned his companions as he tried to get a glimpse at whatever was moving through the overgrown swamp. "It stands to reason that this world will have wolves and lions of its own."

Hogun nodded, hefting his mace. "The beast that thinks it will make a meal of me is going to regret that idea."

Volstagg gave him a wry look. "I expect it'll get sick to its stomach if it tries."

Before Hogun could offer any retort, the heavy steps broke into a run. Fandral knew there was no mistake now. Whatever was out there had discovered the Asgardians and was charging straight towards them.

The wall of towering ferns and cycads burst apart as the creature broke through. Splinters pelted Fandral and forced him to shield his face. He had only a brief glance at the thing that had rushed them, an impression of something a dozen feet tall with green skin. He lashed out blindly when he sensed the attacker spring towards him. Fimbuldraugr struck something, but whatever he hit felt like granite. Before he could bring back his arm to strike again, he felt a powerful grip close around the blade.

Lowering the arm shielding his eyes, Fandral found that his blade was clenched in a massive three-fingered hand. The creature the hand belonged to leered at him with pitiless hate. It wasn't one of the huge reptiles, though it was on a scale to match many of them. It was a humanoid being, though a long tail snaked away from its back. Its body was covered in a rough, craggy hide, dark green in color. The head rested on two broad shoulders with only the merest suggestion of a neck. The face that stretched across that head, however, betrayed what the being was… and who had sent it. It was the same face as the elemental Brona had conjured, the same inhuman visage that filled the Living Talismans the Enchanters each wore.

"You think to kill the master," the manifestation rumbled, its voice as deep as the mines of Svartalfheim. "But here you will find only your own death." As effortless as if it were taking candy from a child, the creature plucked Fimbuldraugr from Fandral's grasp and tossed it into the brush.

Fandral jumped back as the green humanoid glowered down at him, its expression scornful. Before the monster could attack the weaponless warrior, it was itself attacked.

"At least this one's solid!" Hogun exclaimed as he smacked the brute's leg with Hridgandr. Volstagg lunged at it from the opposite side, raking his sword down the manifestation's side. As with Fandral's assault, their blows didn't appear to inflict the least damage on the creature. Its long tail whipped around and slapped Volstagg, throwing him a dozen feet, his body smashing through the vegetation in his path. It kicked at Hogun with the leg he'd tried to crush with his mace. Narrowly was the warrior able to dodge aside and the

Three Swords

stamping foot gouged a hole several feet deep in the spot where he'd been standing.

"We can't fight it that way!" Fandral shouted. He was thinking of Brona's elemental and how futile their attacks had been against it. To destroy it they'd need to get the Living Talisman away from Forsung. Unfortunately, the Enchanter hadn't been so obliging as to accompany the monster he'd sent to destroy them.

Fandral darted to one side as the brute swung at him with its fist. The blow struck a cycad instead, shattering its thick trunk as though it were made of glass. The monster glared at him and opened its mouth wide. A sheet of crimson flame erupted from its jaws, barely missing Fandral as he threw himself to the ground. The vegetation caught by the blast shriveled in its intensity. Charred ashes spilled down over Fandral as he scrambled away.

Hogun swung back to the attack, swatting the monster in its shoulder as it leaned down to find Fandral. Without even looking at him, the manifestation swung its arm backwards and shoved him away. Hogun spilled to the ground and had to roll aside when the long tail tried to pound him into the dirt.

"Our weapons can't hurt it!" Fandral yelled at Hogun. It was obvious the monster was already aware of its immunity. "We have to get away."

The monster lunged at the sound of his voice. Fandral dove away as both of its fists slammed into the earth. The creature spun around and sent another blast of fiery breath chasing after him. "There is no escape," the rumbling voice bellowed. "There is only what the master demands: death!"

"Nice to know it's open to negotiations," Fandral

muttered as he leaped away from the brute's driving fists. The talisman's avatar was unimaginative in its methods, falling into a pattern of trying to smash him under its blows and when that failed sending a sheet of flame crackling at him. It single-mindedly kept pursuing him, treating Hogun's attacks as a mere nuisance.

And why wouldn't it? Fandral reflected. Hridgandr wasn't able to so much as scratch the brute and all it needed to do was land one hit to put an end to Fandral's life. The manifestation didn't need sophistication when there was such power at its command. For the first time, Fandral began to appreciate the strength of these Living Talismans and the terrible reserves of magical energy they must provide the Enchanters who wore them.

"Over here, you slack-witted ogre!" Volstagg returned to the fray, slashing his sword against the manifestation's tail. "You've not finished with Volstagg the Grandiose!" He stumbled back as the tail swung for him. "You need to do better than that, oaf!" he shouted. "I've seen drunken goblins who were more threatening!"

The monster ignored Volstagg's insults, refusing to deviate from the warrior it had marked as the first it would destroy. Fandral scrambled as a green fist crunched through the cycad he was crouched behind.

"It's not listening!" There was frustration in Volstagg's voice. "Fandral, you'll have to lead that thing this way." The big Asgardian waved his arm and beckoned to him. Hogun drew away from the green humanoid and followed Volstagg through the vegetation he'd broken when the creature threw him.

Three Swords 229

Fandral avoided a gout of crimson fire and sprinted after his friends. The brute charged after him, gaining on him with every stride. "There is no escape," it growled.

Fandral couldn't see any purpose to Volstagg's design. There didn't seem to be any way to hide from the talisman's avatar and it looked fruitless to try and flee. They couldn't fight the monster, and the only way to destroy it was through a mystical artifact held by a villain who was probably miles away.

Still, as hopeless as it seemed, Fandral trusted there was something to Volstagg's plan. Twice he felt the creature's fingers brush against him as he ran. Once a blast of flame passed so near his head that it singed his hair. His ears were filled with the sound of cycads and ferns being crushed by the monster as it plunged through the jungle after him.

"Jump!" Volstagg and Hogun suddenly cried out in unison. Fandral couldn't see any cause for their shout, but he did as they said and flung himself forward in a great leap. Vines and fronds whipped past him as he hurtled forward. He landed hard on a spit of marshy ground. Hogun grabbed his arm and pulled him to his feet.

"There is no..." The monster's rumbling voice broke away in a confused warble. A loud squelching sound rolled through the swamp.

Fandral turned to see the green humanoid sunk up to its chest in a bubbling tar pit, a pit that his jump had carried him safely across. The monster flailed and thrashed in the mire, still intent upon seizing its prey. It opened its mouth to send a blast of fire at him, but the gases rising from the tar were ignited the moment the flame appeared. A huge ball of fire flashed above the pit, momentarily obscuring the trapped creature.

The flash subsided and Fandral could see that the monster was now up to its shoulders in the muck. It stubbornly tried to slog its way through the sludge.

"If it would listen to me, I could tell it that won't work," Volstagg laughed as he stepped around the pit and joined his companions. He handed Fandral Fimbuldraugr. "I saw that you dropped this. Thought you might need it."

Fandral took his sword and clapped Volstagg on the back. "An inspired plan!" he applauded. "We couldn't fight the thing with weapons, so we lure it into the tar!"

The monster continued to struggle in the pit, but the sludge held it fast. The greater the weight, the more firmly the tar clutched its victim. The more the trapped brute fought, the faster it was drawn down.

"So much for Forsung's assassin," Fandral smiled. "We might even be able to follow its trail back to the wizard's lair."

"About time we caught a break," Volstagg chuckled.

The big Asgardian's laughter evaporated when a chorus of chirping howls rang out across the swamp. Whatever made those sounds, there were a lot of them.

And they had the Warriors Three surrounded.

Hogun braced himself for battle. He didn't know what sort of beasts were making those howls, but there was no mistaking the meaning. They were hunting cries. Now, he felt, they would indeed meet the wolves of this primordial world.

The rustle of creatures moving through the foliage came

Three Swords 231

from every direction. Hogun guessed there must be at least a dozen rushing through the swamps toward the tar pit. A blur of motion drew his gaze to one spot in particular and he saw the moment when a grotesque reptile hopped into view.

It was only a little shorter than a human, with a lean build that nevertheless suggested a pantherine strength. It stood on two legs, with feet tipped in hawk-like talons. Short arms were folded against its breast, each finger tipped with a sharp claw. Its head, as much like a weasel's as it was a crocodile's, was poised upon an upthrust neck. The scaly jaws contained dozens of long fangs. A slender tail lashed the earth behind it as it trained its keen eyes on the tar pit.

The reptile sprang at the trapped monster, reaching it in a single hop. Hogun was impressed by the animal's accuracy, for it put its feet squarely on the creature's sinking shoulders. Hissing, the saurian tried to bite the manifestation's head. The sharp fangs had as little luck penetrating the monster's hide as their swords had.

With reckless persistence, the hopper kept trying to find a way to bite the trapped monster. It ignored the tar bubbling up over its feet as the creature sank still lower.

"Sometimes you have to miss a meal," Volstagg commented as the reptile sank deeper.

Hogun wasn't watching the scene in the tar pit. His eyes were turned now to the jungle. "There's more of them," he warned. He imagined the reptiles hunted in some kind of pack and that they were waiting for the first one to call them in to eat. But from the increasing agitation of the foliage, he was getting the impression the hoppers were growing impatient.

A shriek-growl sounded almost at Hogun's ear. He spun around just as one of the brown-scaled reptiles leaped out at him from behind the cycads. He swung his mace, hitting it in mid-jump and sending it crashing into the vegetation.

Other hoppers now erupted from the jungle, lunging at the Asgardians. Volstagg struck one with his shining sword, hewing it from shoulder to hip. The slaughtered beast crashed into him and rolled off into the mud. Another lizard made a dive for Fandral but found itself spitted by his blade. It slashed at him with its clawed feet until he ripped Fimbuldraugr free and let the reptile collapse to the ground.

Panicked hoots now rose from the tar pit, the pack leader having finally noticed its peril. It struggled to spring away from the sinking monster, but already it was firmly embedded in the sludge. It weighed less than the creature it had thought to feed on, but its mass was still too great to avoid being sucked down.

The hoots sowed confusion among the other hoppers. Hogun guessed it was some sort of an alarm, a cry of warning to the pack. Hunger and self-preservation fought for control of their reptilian minds.

"Run away," Hogun snarled at the saurians, but as soon as he moved the nearest of the hoppers decided it was more hungry than afraid. The lizard lunged at him, claws ready to shred his flesh. The spiked mace slammed into it, flinging it away to crash into the pit. For a moment the hopper looked like it was swimming through the tar, but then the drag of the sludge started to suck it under.

"You'll not have Asgardian for supper!" Fandral shouted, brandishing his sword until one hopper finally tried to get

Three Swords 233

too close. His blade cut across its breast and sent it stumbling back, blood pumping from its wound.

Hogun had seen the wolves of Varinheim, the most vicious of their breed, but what followed made those terrifying canines seem but tame lapdogs. The hopper Fandral wounded tripped and fell. Instantly the others of its pack leaped upon it, tearing into it with fangs and claws. Even the hungriest wolf would starve before turning cannibal and devouring a member of its own pack.

The hoppers lost interest in the Asgardians, converging upon the helpless saurian. Volstagg turned away from the gruesome spectacle, one hand covering his mouth.

Fandral glanced around, expecting at least a few of the hoppers to remember their presence.

"I think we can just leave," Hogun said. He nodded at the cannibal pack. "And we'd better do it fast, because I don't want to be around when they're finished.

"They'll probably still be hungry," he added as he cautiously made his way around the tar pit and away from the feasting reptiles.

TWENTY

The warriors finally reached the end of the swamp after trudging through it for many hours. The sun was sinking towards the horizon and dusk turned the sky a dull orange when they emerged onto a grassy veldt. Fandral could see mountains in the distance. Not a range, but individual peaks that defiantly thrust themselves up from the earth to rebellious heights. Many of them had smoke billowing from their summits, others glowed a fiery yellow as lava spilled down their slopes. Like distant thunder, the roar of the volcanoes reached his ears.

Nearer to hand was the jungle that loomed like a dark shadow along the periphery of the veldt. A wall of trees and bushes stretched away into the west. East and north there was only the grassland, spreading as far as Fandral's gaze could follow.

"At least that's an end to the swamps," Volstagg said. For

hours he'd been looking over his shoulder, wary lest the hoppers should decide to follow them.

Hogun waved his mace at the trampled path through the tall grass. It was a continuation of the track they'd been following out of the swamp, the trail left by the Living Talisman's avatar. "No doubt which way to go."

Fandral felt uneasy. "That's what's worrying me," he told his companions. "Onund warned that Forsung is the craftiest of the Enchanters. More than that, he knows we've beaten his brothers. He knows someone is moving against the Enchanters."

"What are you suggesting?" Volstagg asked.

"What if Forsung made a contingency plan for what to do if we defeated the talisman's monster?" Fandral stared at the trail through the grass. "The thing might have been told to leave a trail for us to follow. Just like how we lured it into the tar pit, the monster's path could be bait to draw us out."

Hogun nodded. "A good strategy. But what do we do if we don't follow?" His gaze roved from Fandral to Volstagg. "If we don't follow the trail, we might never find Forsung's lair."

"Part of avoiding a trap is knowing that it's there," Fandral said. "Our best chance to find the wizard is to accept his challenge."

Volstagg had a worried look. "What if Forsung proves to be smarter than we are?"

"He probably is," Fandral said. "We'll just have to hope luck is on our side."

"That's not much of a plan," Volstagg objected.

"We've already beaten two of the Enchanters," Fandral returned. "Defeating Forsung might be harder, but I'm not ready to call it impossible." He sighed and started out into the veldt. "Before we do anything, we have to find the sorcerer."

The Asgardians marched parallel to the track left by the green monster. Fandral was too wary to walk the track itself. The ground might conceal any number of traps left by the wizard. It was tempting luck just a bit too much to invite some hidden danger to spring up from the earth to ensnare them.

The trap, however, wasn't focused on the ground.

The final rays of the sun as it vanished over the horizon drew Fandral's attention to the sky. It yet retained something of dusk's orange hue, but now he could clearly make out the stars and the gibbous moon peeking over the volcanoes. He could find no constellation that he recognized, not those of Asgard or Midgard. It was because his eyes lingered on the sky trying to find any star that seemed familiar that Fandral spotted the creatures soaring upon the night winds.

They were similar to the winged lizards they'd spotted when they first entered the primordial land, but without tails. Their heads had long beaks and a crest projecting from the back of their skulls as a kind of counterbalance to their elongated jaws. Fandral was more confident declaring these fliers to be enormous, for they had on their backs something to give them scale. Each of the winged reptiles had a man riding it!

"Above us!" Fandral called to his companions. At once the Asgardians closed ranks and turned their faces toward the sky.

"Kill the outworlders!" they heard one of the riders shout.

Three Swords 237

The others took up his cry, turning it into a chant. The men prodded their winged steeds with the butts of spears and goaded the reptiles into a sharp dive.

"Just get close enough," Hogun hissed through clenched teeth.

The riders closed the distance faster than any of them had expected. The enormous weight of the flying reptiles and the men who rode them made their dives less of a swoop and more of a controlled fall. Their enemies hurtled down toward them. As they did, the riders thrust at the Asgardians with primitive spears.

Primitive in design, at least, but as Fandral ducked one thrust he saw that the spearhead was made from obsidian, a material that could hew through bone if even a modicum of force was behind the blow. The riders looked like they could put more than enough strength into an attack. They were an ill-looking sort, extremely hairy with long arms and short legs. Their features were heavy, with a low brow and almost no forehead. Such raiment as they wore was crudely fashioned from saurian hides. Some of the riders affected helmets crafted from the same material and a few even bore small shields of reptilian hide.

Fimbuldraugr slashed at a second rider as the man urged his mount towards him. Fandral's sword bit into the enemy's arm and caused him to drop his spear. Then the reptile's massive wing struck him and he went tumbling through the grass.

Fandral started to rise when a leathery canopy crashed down on him, pressing him into the dirt with smothering force. The canopy rose and fell, slapping him prone each time it descended. Fandral quivered under the repeated blows. He knew that soon he'd be overwhelmed.

Instead of trying to rise or crawl away, Fandral twisted around and drove his sword into the smothering canopy. An agonized shriek blared through his ears as the leathery substance split apart. He scrambled out from the torn mess to see one of the huge reptiles lying on the ground, warbling in pain as it continued to beat its ripped wing against the ground.

The rider jumped off the back of his steed and lunged at Fandral with his spear, his gashed arm hanging limp against his side. The Asgardian met the attack with a slashing sweep that slid down the length of the spear to cut the enemy's hairy throat.

Volstagg and Hogun were beset by more of the riders, but were managing to hold their own. Two of the hairy men were sprawled on the ground and one of the winged reptiles was stretched out in the grass, its skull cracked by what Fandral thought could only be a blow from Hridgandr.

The initial wave of the attack was broken and the riders urged their mounts back into the sky. As swift as their descent had been, the climb was clumsy as the reptiles seemed to lurch upward with great buffets of their leathery wings. So lethargic was their climb that Hogun was able to run after the riders and fell one of their steeds before it could get away. His mace smacked down on the reptile's wing, dashing it to the earth. He wasted no time braining that shrieking beast, then fixed his attention on the hairy man who rode it. The rider tried to stab him with his spear, but Hogun swatted the weapon from his opponent's hands. The next instant he knocked the rider senseless with Hridgandr's heft.

"They're coming back for a second run!" Fandral warned his companions as he watched the riders wheel about in the sky.

"Come down to your deaths, wretches, for it is the Warriors Three you fight!" Volstagg shouted his defiance at the riders.

The riders, however, had changed tactics. They weren't as bold as they had been before. Instead of charging straight for the Asgardians, they spurred the winged reptiles into a slow glide. Fandral discovered the reason for the maneuver when the lizard's beaks opened and crackling bolts of arcane fire rained down upon the warriors.

"Forsung's sorcery!" Hogun cursed, blocking one of the bolts with Hridgandr.

Fandral knew the accusation was true. The riders' steeds might once have been normal creatures of this savage world, but the Enchanter's magic had transformed them. As the flight of reptiles spewed their arcane venom and seared the veldt, Fandral feared they'd made the discovery too late. Forsung's minions had them out in the open. There was nowhere for them to take cover. Sooner rather than later, the magic fire would fell them.

"Make for the jungle!" Fandral shouted, turning to the shadowy expanse that bordered the grasslands. It was too much to hope that they could reach shelter before the barrage from the mutated reptiles brought them down, but it was the only hope they had.

•••

The ground exploded off to Volstagg's side, spattering him with dirt and charred grass. With every bolt that the winged reptiles spat at them, the creatures were getting nearer to hitting their mark. Even after losing some of their number in the initial assault, there was still a score of enemies chasing them. The Asgardians still had a hundred yards to cover before they would gain the shelter of the jungle. Volstagg thought maybe one of them, possibly two, might reach safety. The chances of all three of them escaping Forsung's trap, however, looked slim.

Then Volstagg saw some of the riders swoop past them. The hairy men wheeled their steeds around, putting them between the warriors and the cover they were trying to reach. The reptiles dove back to the attack, pelting the Asgardians with bolts striking at them from before and behind. Volstagg reconsidered their chances. He didn't think any of them would reach the jungle now.

Suddenly the jungle thrashed into motion. From its edge a huge saurian burst into view. It was a creature unlike any Volstagg had yet seen in this savage world. The beast stood twenty feet high on two enormous legs, the clawed feet by themselves were the size of a human. The tail that whipped the ground behind it was thick and muscular. It had a set of arms hanging from its chest, but they were short and thin, almost vestigial, and only two short fingers protruded from its hands. The head, however, was massive, with jaws mightier than even a dragon's, the glistening fangs as long and sharp as daggers. Red eyes gleamed beneath the heavy ridges that ran along the sides of the creature's skull. Indeed, the entirety of the reptile was covered in flame-red scales.

Three Swords   241

The warriors paused in their rush for the jungle when the giant red saurian appeared. There was certainly no way to reach cover with the enormous devil in their way.

Then the incredible happened. Instead of attacking the Asgardians, the huge lizard sprang at the riders! Its mighty jaws caught the wing of a reptile and dashed it to the ground. The other riders tried to climb beyond the saurian's reach, but their ascent remained slow and clumsy. Discarding the enemy it had already claimed, the red giant made another lunge and brought down a second of the fleeing reptiles.

The riders pursuing the warriors across the veldt now changed targets. Arcane bolts pelted the grass around the red saurian as the squadron dove to attack. Several slammed into the lizard, steaming against its scales and knocking it back.

In shifting their attention to the red beast, the riders made the mistake of forgetting about their other foes. "They dive low enough to strike!" Hogun shouted. He jumped from the ground and swung his mace with both hands. The blow cracked the neck of a flying reptile and sent it and the man riding it slamming into the ground.

"That toothy dragon has done us a good turn, we'd be remiss not to return the favor," Fandral laughed. Fimbuldraugr slashed through the leathery folds of a wing and another of their adversaries was brought to earth, crashing with such momentum that the reptile careened dozens of yards through the grass, each brutal roll breaking a few more of its bones and crushing the hairy man on its back.

It was as well for Volstagg that he didn't need to jump to

strike one of the riders. He knew better than to try and match the agility of his friends, loath as he was to admit the fact. With his height, however, he was able to swirl Brandrheid Undrsigr's shining blade in the air. The effect created a blur of gleaming steel that frightened the diving reptiles. They broke away from the attack, clumsily climbing into the air against the protests of the riders – at least those men who managed to remain mounted. A few were jarred from their steeds and hurtled to the ground with impacts that snapped their bones and shattered their skulls.

The red saurian continued its campaign against the winged reptiles. It caught another of the creatures in its mighty jaws and shook it as a lion would shake a jackal trapped between its fangs. The rider was thrown, screaming as he slammed into one of the jungle trees with such force that his body folded around the trunk. The giant lizard dropped its prey once it sensed the creature in its jaws was dead.

"Now we come to it," Volstagg whispered. The bipedal saurian had displayed its awesome strength fighting the riders. So much so that they now broke off their attack and were in complete retreat. There weren't any more of them low enough for the lizard to catch.

The red beast turned toward the Asgardians. It huffed as it drew their scent into its nostrils. Though the riders were gone, the huge saurian remained standing between them and the jungle.

"Looks like this brief alliance is over," Fandral said, shaking his head. "I'm not looking forward to fighting that dragon."

The saurian threw back its head and issued a deafening roar. But instead of charging at them, the beast turned and picked one of the winged reptiles off the ground. Holding it in its jaws, the red lizard returned to the jungle.

"If I didn't know better," Volstagg muttered to Fandral, "I'd swear it understood you."

"Whether it did or not, let's just be grateful it decided to make a meal of that winged horror instead of us," Fandral replied.

Volstagg started to say something more on the subject, but suddenly the grass around them was alive with enemies. He spun around and deflected an obsidian-tipped spear with his sword. The hairy spearman danced back a pace and made another thrust, stabbing at Volstagg's gut. A slash of his shining sword dropped the attacker, his scaly helm and the thick skull inside it cleft by the dwarven blade.

Fandral was beset by two attackers. A riposte turned the out-thrust spear of one adversary into the face of his other opponent. The point pierced the other man's eye and he collapsed to the ground, dragging the spear with him. "You should run," Fandral advised the survivor.

Instead, the hairy man snatched an obsidian knife from his belt and flung himself at Fandral. The Asgardian had no choice but to cut him down with a sweep of his sword.

Hogun too was beset by enemies. A swat from Hridgandr sent a hairy fighter spinning through the air a dozen feet. He spun around to meet his other enemy as a spear was thrust at his back. He smacked the side of the man's head with the heft of the mace. It took a second blow to drop him senseless at the warrior's feet.

"These ones must've survived the fall of their steeds." Hogun nodded at the fighter sprawled on the ground.

"Tough little rascals," Volstagg commented. "I don't think I'd be so spry after that kind of fall."

"Tenacious as well," Fandral mused. "They could have slipped away, but instead these decided to keep attacking." He gestured at one of the pair he'd fought. "Even with broken bones, their only thought was to kill us."

"Maybe they're more afraid of the Enchanter than they are of dying," Volstagg suggested.

Hogun let Hridgandr dangle from its thong and picked up the unconscious rider. "We can ask this one when he wakes up," he said.

Fandral nodded, then turned a worried glance at the sky. "We'd better do that in the jungle," he stated. "Once they regain control of their steeds, it's a certainty they'll be back here looking for us. I'd rather be under cover when they do."

"That," Volstagg declared, "is the best idea I've heard all day."

TWENTY-ONE

The prisoner was trussed with vines, binding him to the timber-like stalk of a giant fern. Hogun thought the man would burst his heart, so fiercely did he struggle against his bonds, but at last he resigned himself to the reality of his capture and lapsed into a sullen lethargy.

"Do you really expect to get anything out of him?" Volstagg asked.

"The Allspeak will make him understand us," Hogun answered, his eyes never leaving their hairy captive.

"Because he understands doesn't mean he'll speak," Fandral said. "I saw simple peasants endure unspeakable tortures rather than inform on my Merry Men." His face darkened. "I expect whatever hold Forsung has on these people, it is stronger than gratitude and loyalty. Aye, and much more fearsome."

Hogun turned to Fandral. "Then what we have to do is find out what he's more afraid of than the Enchanter."

Volstagg drew a deep breath. "That won't be easy," he grumbled. "These people are as fanatical as berserkers. You saw how they kept rushing to the attack, whatever their losses. Even when that big lizard surprised them, they..."

Hogun didn't hear the rest of what Volstagg was saying. He was too intent on the change that had briefly shown on the rider's savage face. At the mention of the red saurian, fear had flickered across his features. There, he knew, must lie the key to breaking the man's resolve.

"If he won't talk, then we have no use for him," Hogun stated. He turned his back on the prisoner and made furtive gestures to his friends. He needed them to support the ploy he had in mind. "We'll just have to call the red monster back."

Volstagg stared at him in bewilderment. Before he could ask anything, Fandral kicked him in the shin. "Yes," Fandral said. "I'm sure it must be hungry again. Those flying reptiles didn't have nearly enough meat on them."

The change that came over their prisoner was as abrupt as it was profound. From sullen defiance the man descended into voluble submission. "No! Do not feed me to the devil-beast!" he pleaded.

Hogun spun around and glared at the man. "You've refused to tell me what I want to know," he accused. "If I have no use for you, then the devil-beast is always hungry."

"No! No!" the rider implored. "I will speak! I did not know you were such powerful witchmen that you could command the devil-beast. Even the Chief of the Sky-Stone can't do that. He has promised many times to kill the red devil-beast, but never has he succeeded."

"The Chief of the Sky-Stone is a liar," Hogun told the

rider, guessing that the primitive title referred to Forsung. "He claims magic he does not possess."

Fandral stepped forward, adopting a sympathetic manner to counter Hogun's domineering one. "We've come here to punish the sorcerer for his lies. It was he who told you to attack us, wasn't it?"

"Yes," the rider confirmed. "He told us that enemies of our tribe would appear in the Lake of the Waving Grass and that we must destroy them before they could curse our villages and bring famine to our people."

"More of his lies," Fandral assured the captive. "We mean no harm to your tribe. Forsung is our only enemy in this land. He is the only one we've come here to fight."

The rider looked at them uncertainly. "His power is great. He is strong."

The hairy man's attitude was something Hogun had seen before. It confirmed for him that there was no true loyalty between the riders and Forsung. Only fear of the Enchanter kept his minions obedient. "Have we not commanded the red devil-beast?" Hogun saw the rider's heavy brow knot as he pondered that point.

It was Volstagg who expressed things in such a simple way as to finally sway the rider. "There's only one of him. There are three of us," he stated flatly.

Their captive grinned. "What you say is true," he admitted.

"Then you'll show us where Forsung's lair is?" Fandral questioned the man.

Their prisoner peered up at him. "I can show you," he said. "But how will you reach the Sky-Stone?"

Now it was the Warriors Three who were feeling uncertain. Their prisoner was certain they had no way to reach the Enchanter. Patiently, they teased the details from the rider. From what he said, Hogun was able to piece together the image the captive was trying to convey.

"The Enchanter has used his magic to not only build a tower here, but to suspend it in the sky." Hogun despised all feats of wizardry, but even he was awed by the power Forsung must possess to accomplish such a deed.

Volstagg pulled a tar-stained strand of hair from his beard. "That's one way to keep from having any of these giant lizards knocking at your door."

Fandral paced around the fern their prisoner was tied to. "There must be a way of reaching the tower," he insisted. "We haven't come across dimensions simply to give up."

Hogun turned his gaze on the rider. "When your tribe offers tribute to Forsung, what do you do?"

The prisoner actually laughed at the question. "We use the terror-wings to fly to him. The terror-wings that haven't been changed by his magic will still fly there." He shrugged his shoulders as much as his bindings would allow. "The other terror-wings will not go back and will sometimes throw the rider they carry if he tries to make them do so."

"Terror-wings are those winged lizards," Fandral mused. "If we could use them, we'd be able to reach the wizard's tower."

"I don't think we've time enough to catch and train a bunch of flying lizards," Volstagg quickly interjected. From his look, Hogun could tell his friend was more disturbed by the idea of flying than he was the logistics of securing winged steeds.

"Maybe we only need to catch them," Hogun suggested.

He turned back to their prisoner and began asking for more particulars about the terror-wings his people rode.

Fandral crawled through the tall grass and helped Hogun secure the trap. It was a sultry day, with a cloudy sky conspiring to maintain the humidity. It wasn't so overcast that he couldn't pick out the shapes soaring above the veldt. A half dozen of the riders maintained a patrol, looking for any sign of the warriors Forsung had sent them to destroy.

"We'll have to hope at least three of them haven't been changed by Forsung's magic," Hogun reminded Fandral as they secured the trap with wooden stakes. "Otherwise, all of this is wasted effort."

"We won't be able to tell until they try to spit fire at us," Fandral said. "Unless you can figure out a way to see if they're too smart to be just a lizard."

Hogun cast a wary glance at the sky. "Even if we catch them, we might not find that out before it's too late."

Fandral felt a chill rush through him. Interrogating their prisoner, they'd learned something about what Forsung had done to many of the terror-wings. The reptiles were flown to the wizard's floating tower. There he had the creatures chained within circles drawn in blood. A monstrous ritual followed, after which the terror-wing became stronger and could spit blasts of energy from its mouth. They also exhibited an increased intelligence and a malicious tendency that was sometimes turned against the men who rode them. From everything the rider described, it sounded to the Asgardians like Forsung was summoning demons and ordering them to possess the flying lizards.

"You're the one who's always sharp to sniff out anything that smacks of magic," Fandral said. "At worst, we'll have to trust your nose to tell us if any of the reptiles aren't natural." He gestured at the grassland where a dozen other traps were hidden. "If we're able to catch them at all, that means they can't be too smart."

"Or they are too smart," Hogun rejoined. "Never underestimate the cunning of demons. One might feign innocence, waiting for the perfect time to reveal itself." He glanced again at the sky. "Like when one of us is on its back and we're a thousand feet off the ground."

Fandral started crawling back for the jungle, playing out the cord of vines that was fitted to the trap's trigger. "If that's to be our doom, then so be it. We've got to try and stop Forsung and this is the only way I see of doing it."

They slipped through the grass, careful not to disturb it enough to draw the attention of the riders above. Soon enough it would be time to provoke them, but if the Enchanter's minions attacked too early it would ruin their plans.

Fandral and Hogun spread out, each of them grabbing vines attached to some of the traps. Fandral looked back at the captive tied to the fern. Though he'd become more passive, the Asgardians took the precaution of gagging him lest he have a change of heart and try to shout a warning to the riders. "If this works," Fandral told the man, "we'll let you go."

"And if it doesn't work, I'm the one who gets to find out first," Volstagg grumbled. He carried a set of long poles that Hogun had cut from oversized ferns. Between the poles a

Three Swords 251

mat of reeds was tied. The reeds were dyed red with the juice of berries Volstagg had gathered. The color wasn't as vibrant as Fandral had hoped, but he was depending on the hue being close enough to draw down the terror-wings.

The key to the trap they'd set was the bait. Fandral had asked the prisoner many questions about their steeds. One thing that was revealed was the great enmity that existed between the terror-wings and the red devil-beast. The savage hate was such that the reptiles would instinctively dive on the saurian if they spotted it, refusing the commands of the riders to turn away. Such attacks invariably led to misfortune for the riders and the only way for them to regain control was when enough terror-wings had been injured or killed that self-preservation caused the rest to retreat.

"Just get out there and wave your banner high," Hogun told Volstagg.

"Try to act like a lizard," Fandral advised, amused when Volstagg stuck his tongue out and gave him a sullen glare. "That's the way. Just flick it out more and try not to blink."

Volstagg marched toward the veldt. "If this does work, I'm telling my mount to bite you both."

The big Asgardian moved out into the grass. Fandral watched with mounting tension as Volstagg waved the banner around, swirling it through the air so that the motion would be noticed by the terror-wings. "Down here, you scaly vultures!" he shouted. "Come down here and test your mettle against Volstagg Buzzard-bait!"

The sharp cries of the flying reptiles rained down from the sky. Fandral noted one of the beasts send a bolt of arcane energy slashing down toward Volstagg, narrowly missing him. The other terror-wings didn't so much as pause, but threw themselves into a swooping spiral, losing altitude with such rapidity that the riders clung to their necks in panic. One man lost his grip and went plummeting to the earth.

Volstagg kept waving his crude banner, the flash of red goading the reptiles to greater fury. The possessed terror-wing didn't spit again, though Fandral was careful to mark it out from the others and keep track of it.

"Here, you reject dragons!" Volstagg roared at the descending creatures. "Let's see if you're all hiss and no bite!"

The onrush of the terror-wings was near enough now that Volstagg stopped waving the banner and instead drove the poles into the ground and stepped behind them. He drew his blade from under his belt and braced himself for the attack.

"Now!" Fandral shouted. He jerked back on the vine cords he held while Hogun did the same with the rest of the ropes. The terror-wings were swooping only a dozen feet above the veldt now, their fanged beaks gaping wide as they converged on Volstagg's position.

Then the trap was sprung. The Asgardians had carefully woven nets from jungle vines and fitted them to frames held taut against the ground. Pulling on the cords they released the triggers and caused the nets to whip up straight in the path of the fliers.

Some of the terror-wings were caught outright, snared as they collided head-on into the nets. Others deviated from one net only to be caught by another. One managed to avoid being snagged, but in avoiding the nets it turned too low and its wing smacked into the ground. The reptile careened through the grass, flinging its screaming rider across the veldt.

A single beast managed to avoid all the traps and hurtled straight toward the banner and Volstagg. The huge Asgardian swung around as the reptile neared him and brought his sword slashing across its beak. The creature's dive turned into a somersault and it slammed into the ground on its back, crushing the rider still clinging to it. Volstagg ambled over to finish the screeching creature.

Fandral and Hogun, the instant they pulled the cords, ran from the cover of the jungle. They charged toward the netted beasts and fought with those riders who remained active. Fandral was more judicious in his use of force this time. Now that he understood the tribesmen were as much victims of Forsung as they were the wizard's servants, he had no desire to hurt them more than necessary. Striking with the flat of his sword, he knocked two riders unconscious before they could free their steeds.

The reptile that had smashed its wing into the ground proved a less tractable foe. It lunged up from the grass, hissing and shrieking as it came. Though its wing was broken and it couldn't fly, it was able to move with skittering bounds. Hogun turned about to confront the enraged beast.

"Hogun! That's the–" Fandral couldn't finish the warning before a bolt of magical energy erupted from the possessed reptile's mouth. The blast slammed into Hogun and threw him back.

Fandral tightened his grip on Fimbuldraugr and charged at the terror-wing. It noticed him and spun around, but he dove aside as it tried to blast him as it had Hogun. Before it could spit another bolt, he was on it, driving his sword down into its skull. This close to the reptile, Fandral could sense the change that swept over it as it died and the evil presence infesting its body retreated back to whatever infernal domain it belonged in.

With the possessed reptile dispatched, Fandral hurried back to where Hogun had fallen. He discovered Volstagg already there, lifting their friend off the ground. Hogun patted the spiked head of his mace. "Hridgandr took the worst of it."

"Next time you should try ducking," Fandral said, unable to hide his relief that Hogun was more rattled than hurt.

"Fangs of Fenris!" Volstagg cursed. He jumped up to his feet with such suddenness that Hogun hit his head as he fell back against the ground. Volstagg pointed at one of the terror-wings they'd netted. One of the riders was freeing it from the vines.

The Asgardians started towards the scene, but it was too late. The rider freed his mount and scrambled onto its back. Before anyone could stop him, he was climbing back into the sky.

"Secure the other ones," Fandral instructed his friends. "And hope they're all still able to fly." He'd wanted to catch all of the fliers in anticipation that some would be injured in the process. Now they had no terror-wings to spare. They had to trust that each hadn't been hurt by the ordeal.

"We also need to hope the prisoner's right about these things being quick to obey anyone who feeds them," Hogun pointed out.

Three Swords 255

Volstagg laughed. "Never underestimate how amiable anything becomes after a good meal. My hope is that they like those salamander-worms we caught so much they don't get any ideas about dropping us once we're riding them."

Fandral shivered. He knew each of them was thinking the same thing, but to hear Volstagg put it into words was something he could have done without.

TWENTY-TWO

Volstagg felt as though his stomach had taken residence in his throat, a sensation that was only made more miserable by the nauseating reptile smell wafting from the terror-wing. Each time the winged lizard dipped or jounced in flight, he gave it a reprimanding tug of the vine leash tied about its neck.

"Just don't look down," Fandral called back to him. With their lighter burdens, the other terror-wings were yards ahead of his own and Volstagg felt regret that he was holding them back. They'd picked out the strongest-looking of the reptiles to carry him, but it wasn't able to maintain the speed of the others.

The moment Fandral spoke, Volstagg's eyes drifted downward again. Like a magnet, the terrifying scene compelled him to keep looking at it. The primordial landscape rushed past thousands of feet below. After nearly an hour of flight the grassy veldt gave way to a harsh land of black rock and smoldering volcanoes. It recalled to Volstagg the fiery wastes of Muspelheim. Any moment he expected to see the fire giant Surtur rear up from a caldera and attack them.

"Faster, you misbegotten dragon," Volstagg scolded his steed as he forced his eyes away from the ground below. The terror-wing crooked its head around and gave him a glance that was entirely too mocking for his liking. He kicked the beast's chest and urged it to refocus on flying.

"Just once I'd like to challenge a wizard who's normal," Volstagg grumbled into his beard. "Builds a mansion on a nice warm island with sandy beaches and a gentle breeze. Tables laden with roast venison and broiled pork. A quick-fingered bard strumming a lively melody on a golden lute."

"There it is," Hogun called.

Volstagg snapped from his reverie and looked in the direction Hogun was pointing. He felt his gorge rise when he saw their destination. Forsung's tower was a grisly-looking spire with flaring buttresses that looked like axe-blades cast from obsidian. The structure was infested with gargoyles, the ugly statues peering from every curve and corner. The few windows that were in evidence each had a spiked portcullis guarding it, their sharp points making them resemble the gaping maws of ferocious beasts. The roof was a flattened expanse dozens of yards across with a spiral stair at its center.

There were no doors that Volstagg could see, and certainly none around the base of the tower. There wouldn't have been any way to make use of such portals, for the building's foundation was a jumble of rock that levitated thousands of feet in the air, situated at the center of a triangle formed by three active volcanoes. The sulfurous reek from the bubbling lava overwhelmed even the reptilian musk of his steed as they flew nearer to the sorcerer's castle.

"Just once," Volstagg scowled. He shrugged his shoulders. "Well, maybe he still has a bard with a lively tune in there."

The terror-wings soared closer to the floating tower. Volstagg had to pull on the leash and kick his steed when it tried to deviate from the approach taken by Fandral and Hogun. The reptile shot him a withering glance. "I don't like it either, but that's where we're going," Volstagg told the creature. "Once you drop me off, you'll never have to see me again." There was something unsettling about the way the lizard looked at him before turning away. If its scaly beak could have managed any expression, he was confident it would have been sneering. He thought of the rider's warning about the reptiles Forsung had infected with demonic spirits. Bigger, stronger, and smarter. All of those qualities applied to his mount. His blood went as cold as that of the reptile's when he considered what else the prisoner had said: that the possessed fliers would rather throw their charges to the earth than return to the Enchanter's lair.

"Too late to worry about that," Volstagg told himself. They'd captured only three terror-wings. If this one was indeed possessed, then someone would have ended up with it. He preferred to be the one exposed to the extra danger than to have either of his friends in jeopardy.

The closer they drew to the tower, the more Volstagg appreciated the enormity of its size. It was such a castle as might have been built by the giants of Jotunheim. The platform at its summit was broad enough that dozens of terror-wings could land there and the spiral stairway that delved down into the levels below was more like a ramp than a set of steps. The gargoyles along the facade...

Volstagg did a double-take. Had that gargoyle just moved? He kept a closer watch. The sculpture twitched one of its wings. There was no mistake this time. His eyes roved across the tower face, spotting more of the statues stirring in their niches.

"Fandral! Hogun! The gargoyles!" Volstagg shouted. "They're alive!"

The Warriors Three each drew their weapons as the gargoyles took wing. As the creatures flew away from the tower, Volstagg saw that they were another kind of winged reptile about the size of a dog. The creatures had no tails, but their fangs were so large that they curled up over their scaly mouths. The black-colored creatures squawked and hissed as they flocked towards the Asgardians and their steeds.

At least a score of the gargoyles converged on Volstagg. The bright blade of his sword whipped around in vicious swings, but he had to be careful not to put too much energy into his attacks lest he hit the wings or neck of his mount. Agile as well as pernicious, the attackers avoided his strikes. Like a swarm of bats, they dove in and around his sword, scratching him with the claws on their feet.

"You might do something," Volstagg growled at the reptile he was riding. He could see that the gargoyles were attacking the terror-wings Fandral and Hogun were riding as well as the warriors themselves. So far none of the creatures had so much as scratched his mount. Further proof that there was something unnatural about it.

Volstagg pulled back on the vine cord while slashing

about to drive off the hissing gargoyles. "If they get me, I'll get you," he promised his steed. The reptile looked back at him, clearly understanding his threat. It opened its beak and an arcane bolt flew out, immolating a clutch of gargoyles. Their charred bodies hurtled earthward.

The sudden attack panicked the rest of the creatures. Volstagg vented his frustration by slashing two of them with Brandrheid Undrsigr and watching them tumble away through the sky. The rest of the flock drew back, burbling their glottal squawks.

"So, you *are* more than just a lizard with wings," Volstagg chided his steed. He pulled at the cord around its neck. "Now don't go thinking you'll just throw me off, because I won't be the only one who falls!" He could see from the hateful look in the reptile's eyes that the demon who possessed it had been planning to do just that. Only the prospect of having its host body strangled restrained its wicked impulses.

The gargoyles recovered their ferocity. Hissing, the flock dove down on the terror-wing. This time the creatures didn't ignore the possessed steed, but attacked it as well as Volstagg. The reptile spat more bolts of energy, but the nimble gargoyles easily dodged its efforts. They wouldn't be taken by surprise a second time.

Volstagg had better luck defending himself. Another gargoyle went hurtling toward the ground when his sword crunched through its wing. Before he could raise his blade again, a sharp pain stabbed into his shoulder. He twisted his head to see one of the creatures clinging to him, its fangs buried in his flesh. Automatically he reached up to pull the thing away.

Three Swords 261

As he did so, Volstagg realized his mistake. He'd let go of the leash. Even as he pulled the gargoyle free and threw it down after stabbing it with his sword, he spotted the cord dangling from the terror-wing's neck. The beast turned its head and despite the fixity of its beak, he could swear the reptile smiled at him.

The next instant, the terror-wing put itself into a rolling dive. Wind whipped around Volstagg, threatening to pull him from the beast's back even as he clamped his legs tight around its body. The gargoyles continued to swarm around him, striving to avoid the wings and talons of the larger reptile as they tried to attack the man it carried.

Despite his best efforts, Volstagg lost his grip. His treacherous mount vented a warbling cackle as it flew away, abandoning him to his doom.

The reptilian gargoyles were all around Hogun and his steed. He'd managed to swat several of the beasts with his mace, but their numbers seemed inexhaustible. At best all he was accomplishing was to prevent them from delivering any serious injury to himself or the terror-wing. During a momentary lull in the assault, he was able to spot Fandral. From the way the gargoyles were shy about darting in at him, Hogun thought they must have learned a healthy respect for Fimbuldraugr.

Then he looked back to see how Volstagg was faring. Hogun's heart froze as he saw the terror-wing his friend was riding put itself into a roll. A moment later, Volstagg was thrown from his back and went plunging toward the earth.

Hogun forgot about the gargoyles harassing him and

compelled his mount into a frantic dive. There wasn't a chance of catching Volstagg and arresting his fall, but there was just a possibility that he might be able to change the Asgardian's trajectory. Fandral wasn't the only one who understood something about hitting a target on the move, but seldom had Hogun put his skills to such a severe test.

The speed of his steed's descent was such that for a moment Hogun feared he'd overshoot his target. Then he saw that he'd judged his timing perfectly. By all the Aesir, it was going to work!

The terror-wing slammed into Volstagg as he fell, knocking him leftward and changing the line of his descent. Now, instead of hurtling toward the ground, the warrior was falling toward the roof of Forsung's tower!

Hogun winced when he saw Volstagg strike the roof. A cloud of black dust erupted into the air, evidence of how fierce his impact was. Hogun could only hope it was nothing an Asgardian couldn't endure. At any rate, it was less disastrous than plunging several thousand feet more onto the volcanic plain.

Worry for his friend had to be forgotten. Hogun now had his own crisis to confront. His steed was dazed by the collision and flew in a confused, lurching fashion. Any moment he expected the creature to fold its wings and send them both careening to the destruction he'd tried to spare Volstagg. Worse, the reduction in speed allowed the pursuing gargoyles to catch them. Once again, he was forced to ward off the beasts with Hridgandr, only this time with less success. Because of his mount's distress he lacked the momentum that had enabled him to strike down the reptiles as he had before.

Hogun made the grim decision to stake everything on joining his friend on the roof. It took a cruel jerk of the leash to get the dazed terror-wing to turn. The gargoyles were thick around them now. One was clawing at his chest, trying to work its fangs up towards his neck. Another was worrying at his mount's wing, gnawing its way down to the bone.

Hogun hugged the gargoyle against his chest with one arm, increasing the pressure until he heard its ribs snap. He let the thing spin away and fall toward the ground. Another gargoyle dove at his face, but a swat from Hridgandr broke its skull.

A strangled cry from his steed told Hogun that it had reached the limit of what it could endure. Letting go of the leash, he twisted about and dove from the back of his failing terror-wing.

Hogun hurtled through the sulfurous air, eyes stinging as the wind whipped past his body. He saw the roof of the tower getting closer with each second. Though he'd jumped from a far lower altitude than Volstagg, he knew his landing was going to be brutal.

It was. Hogun slammed into the roof as though he'd been launched from a catapult. The impact drove the wind from him and made sparks dance before his eyes. Every bone in his body screamed at him in agony.

Nor was his ordeal over. Hogun's descent had lacked the momentum of Volstagg's. While his friend had slammed into the tower with enough force to gouge a crater in the black rock, Hogun bounced off the surface and went tumbling across the roof. He saw the edge nearby but his stunned body refused his frantic demands to grab onto something and arrest his motion.

The edge yawned before Hogun, and he found himself with only emptiness below him. Before he could hurtle down the side of the tower, a powerful grip closed across his chest and drove what little breath was in him out of his lungs.

"Got you." The voice was so haggard that it took Hogun a moment to reconcile it with the hearty tones more commonly associated with Volstagg. The big Asgardian slumped back against the roof, arms still wrapped around Hogun. He was battered and bruised, his face bloodied and his body caked in black dust, but at least he was alive.

"Now we just need Fandral to get down here," Hogun commented as he staggered to his feet. He was surprised to find that the gargoyles were wheeling around twenty feet above them, but made no effort to draw any closer. It was an ominous sight, as though the reptiles were too hungry to leave, but too afraid to swoop down on them.

A veritable cloud of the gargoyles drew close to the tower. Hogun could make out a shape behind the flying reptiles and was certain it could only be Fandral's steed. Once the terror-wing was close enough to the tower, the ravenous gargoyles broke away and joined those already circling overhead. When they cleared away, Hogun could see that Fandral and his mount were bloodied by their descent. The reptile managed an awkward landing and the Asgardian was able to drop off its back onto the roof.

"I wonder if Forsung is expecting us or if he greets all his visitors this way," Fandral said as he ambled over to join his friends. When he moved away from it, the terror-wing started dragging itself toward the stairs. From the way

Three Swords   265

it moved, Hogun imagined it had been here before and expected it should go below.

What none of them, most of all the terror-wing, expected was the gout of green fire that billowed up the stairway the moment it dipped its body below the level of the roof. The reptile didn't even have a chance to shriek before its body was reduced to glowing cinders.

"Looks like taking the stairs is a bad idea," Hogun stated.

Volstagg shook his head. "Then what do we do? Wait up here until those blood-hungry buzzards decide to come down?"

Fandral fixed them both with a resolute gaze. "We find another way inside. While one of the Enchanters remains, while one Living Talisman hasn't been cast into the void, the threat to Asgard remains. We have to find another way inside."

Volstagg pointed to the crater where he'd smacked into the roof. "I hit it with full force," he said, wincing as he spoke of the impact. "If that couldn't crack it, there's no way we're going to dig our way in."

Fandral looked over the edge of the roof. One of the angled buttresses was just within reach. "We could climb down," he said. "Try to get to one of the windows."

Hogun frowned as he looked at the distance they'd have to cover. "I don't like the looks of it."

"Now, there's sanity talking," Volstagg chimed in. "Besides, those gargoyles don't like the roof, but we know they've no problem roosting on the sides of the tower. We try to climb down and they'll be on us like flies on a carcass."

"Do you have a better idea?" Fandral challenged.

266 *Marvel: Legends of Asgard*

Volstagg started to frame a reply, but he was leaning against the top of the buttress when he did so. Hogun noticed the spiderweb of cracks that spread from the impact crater across the roof. One of those cracks snaked its way to the buttress.

"What we should do…" Volstagg's words trailed away in a shout. The swarming gargoyles dove down as the buttress gave way and precipitated both it and Volstagg down the side of the tower.

Part of the facade cracked away, spilling down on its journey to the volcanic plain. Hogun rushed over, horrified by what he might see. He was relieved to see Volstagg's clothes caught on a jagged section of the broken buttress. The warrior was swinging his shining sword to keep back the gargoyles flying around him.

"Hold on! We'll get you!" Hogun called to him.

Fandral grabbed his arm and directed his gaze to where the facade had cracked away. Light was shining out. "We'll do more than that!" Fandral laughed. "Volstagg's stumbled on a way to get inside!"

TWENTY-THREE

The opening Volstagg exposed was broad enough for all of the Asgardians to fit through. Fandral was able to shimmy down to the gap by wedging himself between the side of the tower and what remained of the buttress. As soon as he did, some of the gargoyles wheeled away from Volstagg and came after him. He could only grit his teeth as the flock ripped at him with their claws and teeth. The pain lent a fresh haste to his maneuver and he had to constrain himself lest in his hurry to get away from the reptiles he should make a mistake and go hurtling to destruction.

"Filthy vermin! Fight me!" Hogun snarled at the beasts. While he was able, he swung his mace below the lip of the roof and managed to hit a few of the gargoyles. The pressure on Fandral lessened slightly. Enough so that he could see the opening.

His hand slipped as blood made his palm slick. He skidded dozens of feet before he could catch himself again.

The jarring strain of abruptly arresting his fall jolted him and he had to summon all his strength to maintain his hold once he regained it. The gargoyles, hissing and squawking, were all around him again, tormenting him with their vicious attentions.

Blood from a slash across his forehead dripped into his eyes. Fandral could see the last length of the descent. It still felt so far away. Too far to endure the ordeal. He had to take a desperate move.

Fandral let himself go. As he started to fall, he kicked his foot against the buttress and gave direction to his descent. Wind whipped through his hair as he hurtled down the side of the tower, but the twist he'd added was enough to turn tragedy into triumph. His body arced and hurtled through the hole.

The gargoyles pursuing him broke away in a terrified, raucous retreat. A tremendous relief rolled through Fandral not to suffer their claws further. He wiped the blood from his face and watched as the reptiles crashed into one another in their frantic haste to withdraw from the tower. Several were knocked to the floor in the chaos, only to pick themselves up and skitter over to the opening in a series of overlong bounds.

"Run all the way to Niffleheim, you dogs," Fandral spat. He looked around at the chamber he'd dropped into. It was some sort of library, its walls lined with shelves that stretched to the ceiling twenty feet above. The room was lit by a dull crimson light that pulsated from a hollowed sphere of some bronze material. There were several large stone plinths on which were arrayed gigantic bones. He thought

Three Swords 269

if there were still flesh on the skeletons some of them might be recognizable as the same kind of beasts as those they'd seen in the swamps.

Fandral took only a quick survey of the room, long enough to ensure there weren't any guards lurking about. Then he turned and rushed back to the opening. Drawing Fimbuldraugr, he readied himself for any gargoyles that might fly at him when he poked his head outside.

"I'm in!" Fandral shouted up at Hogun. He turned to where Volstagg was poised on the cracked buttress. His friend's situation had improved marginally. The frightened cries of the reptiles fleeing the tower had infected those attacking Volstagg. The swarm broke away and scattered, retreating into the distance.

"You can get inside here," Fandral called to Volstagg.

The big warrior studied the state of the buttress and what remained of its connection to the facade. He pointed up to the roof. "I'll stay put until Hogun joins you," he said. "When Volstagg the Inspiring makes an entrance, he wants an audience." His tar-stained, blood-soaked beard drew back in a grin. For all his bravado, Fandral knew why Volstagg stayed where he was. He was afraid any shift of his position would further compromise the buttress and cause Hogun to lose his angle of descent. That it would also mean Volstagg lost his perch was a point he'd already resigned himself to.

Fandral glanced up and saw Hogun copying his method of shimmying down the side of the tower. There wasn't anything he could do to help Hogun, but Fandral was determined to find a way to aid Volstagg. He turned back to the library and started a closer inspection of the contents. Some of the walls displayed large tapestries and there were rich rugs scattered about the floor. An idea started to form, one that was finalized when he saw the gilded ropes that acted as a border for the largest of the tapestries, a scene depicting an army of men in strange hats firing on one another with guns more sophisticated than those they'd encountered recently in England. Smiling, he ripped the tapestry down from the wall and began cutting the border away.

Hogun joined him soon enough in his task. Together they ripped away the ropes and began cutting the rugs into strips. The largest of the tapestries was used to bundle the collection of saurian bones. This weighty assimilation they poised at the edge of the hole with one end of their rope fastened to it.

Fandral looped the rope around the base of the bronze sphere. It looked securely fastened to the floor. For what he had in mind it would need to be. Hogun helped him push and pull at the fixture, but it didn't budge.

Taking the other end of the rope, Fandral looped it through the eye sockets of a reptilian skull and threw it from the chamber. "Catch," he told Volstagg. The warrior managed to grab the skull on the third toss. "Now tie the rope around you. Make sure it is secure," he instructed.

Volstagg gave the rope a tug once it was wound about his body. He had a bemused expression when he saw Fandral and Hogun move over to the bundled bones. Then his eyes went wide with alarm when he realized what they intended.

Before Volstagg could voice a protest, Fandral and Hogun shoved the bones over the edge. The weight of the bundle drew on the rope and wrenched Volstagg from his perch.

The sudden motion caused the buttress to crumble and go crashing down to the ground far below. Volstagg was dragged across to the side of the tower and then whipped up through the hole and into the library as the rope snaked around the bronze sphere.

Once Volstagg was inside, Fandral swung his sword and severed the rope. The truncated cord finished curling around the sphere and went spooling away after the falling bundle.

"You might've explained your plan," Volstagg bellowed, visibly shaken by his ordeal.

Fandral clapped him on the shoulder. "After the way you complained about flying on a terror-wing I didn't dare try to explain this ploy to you."

Volstagg squinted at him. "I was right about the lizard-bat," he said. "Blasted thing tried to throw me off."

"Well, at least you have solid ground under your feet now," Fandral said. "Certainly that's better than staying out there."

Hogun shook his head. "That depends on what we find in here. It's certain Forsung has more tricks yet to play."

"Then the sooner we find the Enchanter," Fandral declared, "the less chance he'll have to work his spells. I suggest we get looking."

The Enchanter's tower was a massive structure, but Hogun's theory that they'd find the wizard near the summit where he'd more easily be able to consult the stars was borne out once again. Volstagg almost wished it hadn't been. Because when they found Forsung, their enemy was far from alone.

Cautiously climbing the spiral stairway that ran through the structure and which, as they'd seen, was hideously trapped where it opened onto the roof, the Warriors Three passed through two levels above the library without sighting the sorcerer. Volstagg couldn't make any great sense of the rooms they moved through, but the accouterments had an unsavory air about them. There were carcasses in varying stages of preservation, some mummified while others were pickled in great crystal vats. All were examples of the great reptiles they'd seen along with many more unlike anything they'd encountered in this primordial world. Strange as the scaly creatures were in their wild array of colors, shapes, and sizes, Volstagg felt a weird energy clinging to the remains. They weren't natural, even for this primitive realm.

Advancing through these laboratories, the heroes moved to the third level above the library. By Volstagg's rough reckoning they should be near the roof now, though Hogun warned against trusting conventional ideas of space and distance within a wizard's lair.

The stairs opened into a colossal chamber that encompassed the whole level. Bronze spheres like that in the library sent their pulses of light from niches in the walls. An infernal glow exuded from a five-pointed design cut into the floor. Symbols carved within the pentagram seemed to writhe and squirm as though to cast off their profane meanings and reshape themselves into less caustic words.

These details Volstagg noted only in passing, for his attention was soon riveted by the menagerie of terrible creatures that squatted against the walls. Each seemed more immense than the next. He saw a giant lizard with bony plates running down its back and a wicked array of spikes on its tail. There was an armored thing that looked

Three Swords 273

like a colossal pangolin with a battering ram fitted to its tail. One of the long-necked, long-tailed behemoths they'd seen biting the tops off trees in the swamp represented the largest of the group. A toothy monster, of the same breed as the red devil-beast that was the enemy of the riders only with black scales, represented the most menacing of the assortment.

"They're possessed," Hogun whispered, awe in his tone.

Volstagg could see the malicious awareness in the eyes of the saurians, recalling to him the gaze of his treacherous steed. More than that, however, there were visible alterations in these reptiles that differed from those they'd seen before. The long-necked lizard sported curled horns like those of a ram. The armored brute had ghostly fires crackling between its shell and its body. The devil-beast's scales were so impossibly dark that it blotted out the light around it, causing it to reside in perpetual shadow.

The reptiles stared at the Asgardians with undisguised hate. Volstagg could tell the beasts wanted nothing more than to rend them limb from limb.

"What are they waiting for?" Volstagg wondered as he brandished Brandrheid Undrsigr.

"They are waiting for permission." The voice was deep and resonant with evil. The warriors shifted their gaze to see a man walking between the giant reptiles. His powerful frame was encased in blue armor, the sides of the helm flaring out into sharp points that reminded Volstagg of a fox's ears. Over his armor, the man wore a jade-colored robe that drooped almost to the floor. The robe flared open at the breast, exposing the jewel he wore there. The vicious face of the Living Talisman glared at them with an expression of unspeakable malevolence.

"You are quite terribly persistent," Forsung scolded the heroes. "Anyone of intelligence would have accepted the madness of defying me, much less daring to challenge me in my own home." His eyes glittered from the openings of his helm. "Your meddling has been a nuisance. It was my intention to harness the experiments of my brothers and combine them with my own."

"You sound quite distressed," Fandral commented.

Forsung frowned. "I can make do without Magnir and Brona, but I regret the loss of their powers. It is troublesome to lose something that still has utility." He waved his armored hand at the menagerie. "I planned to combine Magnir's studies into automation and Brona's experiments into fecundity with my own research and create the ultimate army." He patted the leg of the nearest beast. "The sages of Midgard call – or will call, time is such a fluid thing – these creatures dinosaurs. An odd name for such dragons, don't you think?"

"What I think, you wouldn't like to hear," Hogun returned, his hands clenched about Hridgandr's heft.

Volstagg saw the amused disdain evaporate from Forsung's face. In its place there came a look of murderous severity.

"Of course, I forget myself," the Enchanter said. "It has been so long since I conversed with another Asgardian that I forgot. You didn't come here to talk. You came here to die."

A mere flick of his hand and whatever magic Forsung was using to restrain the dinosaurs was banished. In a growling, roaring mob, the reptiles surged across the room. Volstagg could feel the tremors of their thunderous charge ripple through the floor.

"Stop the sorcerer and his creations will fall with him," Fandral told them. With a veritable wall of giant reptiles between themselves and Forsung, that was going to be easier said than done.

Hogun met the first of the dinosaurs, bringing his mace crashing down on its head as it tried to bite him. The beast reared back and crashed to the floor, stunned by the mighty blow. Hogun swung about to meet the attack of a second reptile. Again the mace cracked down, but this foe wasn't so easily phased as the other. The spiked mace slammed against the thick plates that shielded its head and glanced off. The saurian responded with a swing of its clubbed tail. Flames crackled about Hogun's body as he was sent flying across the chamber.

Fandral was beset by the long-necked beast. It tried to swat him with its long tail and when he leaped away from its quaking impact it drove its horned head at his back. The warrior spun around, lashing out with his sword and clipping one of the curled horns down to a mere stump. Before he could attack again, a second reptile rushed at him and forced him to dodge between his colossal foes.

"You'll wish you'd picked easier prey!" Volstagg howled as he slashed the nasal horn from a charging brute. The reptile kept on coming and he was forced to grasp the bony frill around its neck. It was like wrestling a titanic bull. He dug his feet into the floor and twisted his body, trying to force the dinosaur to choose between stopping or having its neck broken. The creature chose to stop. When it did, it reared up onto its hind legs and lifted Volstagg off the floor. As he dangled from the brute's neck, he kicked it in the chest with both feet. The reptile crashed backwards, slamming hard against the ground.

Before Volstagg could engage the stunned reptile, he felt an icy atmosphere envelop him. The light drained away and he was cast into shadow. "Aren't I the lucky one?" he scowled as the black devil-beast loomed over him.

The possessed monster kicked at him with its clawed leg. When he avoided the strike, it snapped at him with its massive jaws. Volstagg's nose was filled with the reptile's rancid breath as he was caught between its fangs. Before it could bite down, he pressed one hand against the roof of its mouth and pushed for all he was worth. For an instant he held the mouth open. Long enough for him to stab the reptile's tongue with his sword.

Volstagg was knocked back as the devil-beast writhed in pain, blood from its tongue spilling over its fangs. The monster glared at him with infernal rage. It swung around and brought its tail whipping toward him. Volstagg intercepted the strike, chopping the tip from its tail.

The devil-beast roared at him, spattering him with blood from its tongue. It brought its clawed leg kicking out again. Volstagg jabbed his blade into the descending foot. It wasn't a deep cut, but he guessed he'd hit a tender spot when the dinosaur jumped back and uttered a pained hiss.

Another pained hiss sounded from behind him. Volstagg caught just a hint of motion. It was the thunder horn he'd kicked returning to the fray. He felt the tremor of its pounding feet. Throwing himself into a sprawl, he let the enraged lizard storm past him. Its momentum was such that it couldn't stop itself before colliding with the devil-beast. Both dinosaurs fell in a heap of hisses and roars.

Volstagg saw his friends still embattled by other creatures from the Enchanter's menagerie. Strangely, Forsung merely played the part of spectator. It explained why he'd let them get so far. Like Magnir, he was availing himself of the opportunity to test his monsters against Asgardians. "And if we start to win, then you'll take a hand and tip the balance," Volstagg growled. If Forsung created another manifestation from the Living Talisman, he knew they were finished. There wouldn't be any tar pit to dispose of the entity this time.

"Hogun!" Volstagg shouted when he saw the grim warrior swatted once more by the club-tailed dinosaur. Again, his friend was flung across the room to slam against one of the walls. Volstagg knew Hogun couldn't endure that kind of punishment for long. Even an Asgardian had his limits.

"Try that on Volstagg the Colossal!" Volstagg roared at the armored beast as he sprinted toward it. The reptile turned from chasing after Hogun and fixed him with a hateful glare. He saw it swinging its tail from side to side, demonic fire crackling around it.

A scheme developed in Volstagg's mind. He glanced over to where Forsung stood. Volstagg only hoped what he had in mind would hurt the Enchanter more than him.

"I've seen dwarves who were bigger than you," Volstagg fumbled for an insult. The reptile blinked at him, but then decided to take offense anyway. Bellowing, the saurian rushed at him. Volstagg clenched his teeth as it swung its tail.

The impact was almost as bad as his collision with the tower roof. At least then he hadn't felt the frozen burn of demonic fire. He was sent sailing through the air, the breath driven out of him by the dinosaur's attack. He struggled to retain his focus, but it was only when he felt his shoulder slam into something that he was able to ignore the pain that assailed him.

Volstagg struck the chamber wall, but the hit was absorbed somewhat by the body he'd struck on the way there and which had been propelled ahead of him. Forsung crumpled to the ground alongside Volstagg. The sorcerer shook his head, trying to make sense of what had just happened to him.

Before the Enchanter could collect his thoughts, Volstagg grabbed the man's chest and with an effort that strained every muscle in his battered body, wrenched the Living Talisman free from his armor. Forsung glared at him, the theft of the talisman snapping him out of his daze. Volstagg expected to be blasted by some withering spell.

Instead, Forsung leaped to his feet and sprinted across the room. Volstagg was at a loss to explain the sorcerer's retreat. At least until he heard the furious roars of the dinosaurs. He turned his head and saw that the giant reptiles had abandoned battle with the warriors and were now charging after the wizard. He recalled Brona's serpent and how the snake had immediately turned against him the moment his spell was broken. It seemed the same applied here. The dinosaurs were clearly still possessed by the demons

Forsung had summoned, but it was also clear they were no longer under his control. A control for which they now sought revenge.

The Enchanter practically threw himself at a spot some distance across the room, reaching it just ahead of the enraged dinosaurs. Volstagg saw that it was some sort of circle, similar in some ways to the astral circle used by Onund.

Only this circle didn't teleport Forsung elsewhere. When he reached it, he made arcane gestures with his hands and a wall of force enveloped him. The possessed dinosaurs snapped and clawed at the barrier, but were unable to penetrate the circle. The Enchanter glared back at his rebellious creations as they paced around his refuge, testing it for any sign of weakness.

Volstagg lifted himself off the floor. He tucked his sword under his belt and tapped his finger against the Living Talisman. "And you make three," he told the inhuman visage locked within.

Fandral and Hogun hurried over to Volstagg. "An unconventional use of force," Fandral smiled. "The last thing Forsung ever expected, I'm sure."

Hogun, as usual, was more serious. "The last of these cursed talismans," he said. "Now Asgard has nothing to fear from the Enchanters."

"Just as soon as Onund brings us back and this thing is locked away with the others," Volstagg agreed. He looked around, expecting any moment for their surroundings to vanish in a blinding light and for them to be transported back to Asgard.

Instead, there was a shimmering distortion and a portal opened before their eyes only a few yards away. The warriors readied their weapons, but relaxed somewhat when they recognized the figure who stepped through the portal. It was the very man they'd been talking about. Onund the seer.

"I almost attacked you," Volstagg reprimanded the seer.

Onund smiled at him. "Quite impossible," he said. "A protective property of that salve you've used to mend your wounds." A sinister light shone in his eyes. "You can't lift a finger against me thanks to that spell."

Volstagg found himself unable to move anything except his eyes. He could see that Fandral and Hogun were similarly beset. He could offer no resistance as Onund stepped over to him and plucked the Living Talisman from his hand.

A dramatic change swept over the seer once his hand closed around the artifact. From the humble aspect of the old mystic, he was transformed into a much younger man arrayed in Asgardian armor and wearing green robes edged in gold. "No need for the glamour now," he chortled. The wizard made a mocking bow in the direction of Forsung. The trapped sorcerer glared back at him.

The wizard pressed the Living Talisman to his chest and the artifact sizzled as it fused to the breastplate. "I wasn't quite truthful, you may have gathered. Oh, to be sure, the Enchanters do threaten Asgard. But there aren't three of them. There are four. Only I, as the youngest brother, was deemed too weak in my magic when the others created their Living Talismans." He glowered at Forsung from behind the mask of his helm. "They dismissed Enrakt as unworthy of their art. Now, thanks to your efforts, they know better."

Three Swords 281

Enrakt – the deceiver who'd posed as Onund the seer – brushed his fingers across the Living Talisman, a wicked smile on his face. "I was truthful when I said my magic was too weak to recover anything sent into the chest. But with this to augment my power, I will easily regain the others you've collected for me. And with all three Living Talismans in my possession, all Asgard will tremble."

Volstagg struggled to move, to strike, to do something to stop the gloating madman. Enrakt noted his efforts and laughed.

"In helping me, you've brought about the very doom you thought to prevent," Enrkat declared. "The conquest of Asgard!"

Still laughing, the fourth Enchanter opened another portal and vanished.

Twenty-Four

Hogun railed against the magic that paralyzed him but he wasn't able to move so much as a finger. The duplicitous Enrakt had baited his hook well, lulling even some of his suspicions. He should have known better than to trust anything that smacked of sorcery. He'd let himself be so focused on defeating the Enchanters and breaking their power that he'd forgotten the most dangerous aspect of defeating any villainy: the jackals that would swoop in once the wolf was gone.

They'd been used by Enrakt. That was a humiliation that stung Hogun more keenly than the bite of a dagger. He'd played on their heroism to feed his own lust for power. There was no denying the awful scope of that power, either. The Warriors Three had been sorely pressed by the other Enchanters and each of them had access to only a single Living Talisman. Enrakt now had all three to tap into to further his schemes.

Three Swords 283

Hogun shifted his gaze from where Enrakt had vanished. He could see Fandral, frozen in place as rigidly as himself. He couldn't see more than one of Volstagg's feet, and even that only from the corner of his eye. All of them were frozen. Utterly helpless. He wondered how long it would be before one of Forsung's dinosaurs grew weary of trying to force its way into the sorcerer's protective circle and turned to make a quick snack of the Asgardians.

"It doesn't have to end that way." The voice was Forsung's but Hogun couldn't tell if he actually heard the Enchanter's words or if they were only inside his head.

"We share an enemy now," Forsung stated. "I know the enchantment Enrakt has placed on you. I can break the spell, but if I free you, then you must likewise free me."

Hogun could see the disgust in Fandral's eyes. It was a mirror to his own revulsion. They'd just been tricked by one wizard and here was another one trying to bargain with them.

"There is no bargaining," Forsung stated, plucking the thought from Hogun's mind. "If we don't come to an agreement, then all of us will die here. What will become of Asgard then? Enrakt will be at liberty to cast his spells, only now with the boundless power of the Living Talismans at his command! With only my own Living Talisman I was almost able to overcome Odin. Think what kind of power Enrakt now has."

To enter a compact with the sorcerer went against Hogun's entire being. With Enrakt there had been the deception of the virtuous seer, but with Forsung there was no illusion. The man was evil. Hogun would rather die than be responsible for setting such a villain free. At the same time, he knew the Enchanter spoke truly when he said it wasn't merely their own lives but all of Asgard that was in jeopardy.

"Promise only to let me escape the protective circle," Forsung's words rippled through the mind of each warrior. "Only make me that vow and I'll break Enrakt's enchantment."

The desperation in Forsung's tone surprised Hogun. From his arrogant self-assurance of a moment before, now the wizard was all but pleading with them. He wondered if the barrier holding back the possessed dinosaurs was as strong as the Enchanter wanted them to believe. Even now it might be on the edge of dissolution. A few minutes might see Forsung slaughtered by the huge reptiles and the vengeful demons within them.

Only freed from the circle. If Hogun could promise no further aid to the sorcerer, perhaps he could justify dealing with Forsung. He shifted his gaze to Fandral and saw his friend flick his eyes downward, almost as though trying to approximate a nod.

Suddenly Hogun was able to move again! There was no gradation of liberty, just an abrupt shift from paralysis to freedom. He clapped his hands together and stamped his feet, reveling in his release. Fandral and Volstagg cheered as they too escaped the shackles of Enrakt's spell.

"Free of one wizard," Hogun growled. He fixed his eyes on the embattled Forsung. The black devil-beast was trying to chew its way through the invisible shell that surrounded the Enchanter. "All we need do is stand idle to be rid of another one."

Three Swords 285

"We swore an oath," Fandral pointed out, his disgust making the words seem like poison on his tongue. "We have to help him escape from the reptiles."

Volstagg shook his head. "How do we do that? We didn't exactly overwhelm them when we were fighting."

Hogun gestured with his mace at the enraged dinosaurs. "We don't need to beat them, we just need to lead them away."

Fandral nodded. "Precisely. Since I'm the fastest runner among us, that'll be my job." He scratched his chin and pondered the next problem. "Somehow I need to get their attention." He smiled as he looked up at one of the bronze spheres. "I wonder if we could use one of those to give the lizards a hot foot."

Hogun helped Fandral and Volstagg break one of the spheres free from its sconce. It felt blistering to the touch and they had to use extreme care to keep from being burned as they lowered it to the floor.

"Give it one good swat with Hridgandr," Fandral instructed Hogun. "Then both of you get to cover. I'll lead the dinosaurs down the stairs. If I'm lucky I can lose them in one of the lower levels."

"You trust to luck too often," Hogun stated. "I don't like this scheme, but I can't think of another."

"And since this is the plan, you know I'm the best one to play decoy," Fandral said. He glanced at the trapped Enchanter. "Let him get away from the circle, but don't let him get away. He's our only chance to get back to Asgard."

Hogun turned away and walked to the sphere. Again, he knew Fandral was right, but he didn't like it. Any portal Forsung opened was as likely to send them to Muspelheim as it was Asgard. Still, the Enchanter's magic was their only recourse.

Raising Hridgandr high, Hogun brought it cracking against the sphere. The blazing vessel was hurled across the chamber. Hogun threw himself flat against the floor alongside Volstagg as the burning orb crashed among the dinosaurs.

The beasts swung around, hissing and bellowing in surprise. The one with a spiked tail rolled about on the floor, trying to smother the red flames that clung to its scaly body.

"Over here, you misbegotten monsters!" Fandral shouted at the dinosaurs, waving his arms over his head so that the creatures couldn't fail to spot him. Enraged roars burst from the giant reptiles. Tremors rumbled through the floor as the beasts stampeded after Fandral. The warrior waited only a moment, then spun around and raced down the stairs. The dinosaurs trampled one another in their murderous haste, clawing and biting as they plunged down the wide steps in pursuit.

"By Odin, it worked," Volstagg gasped as he stood up.

Hogun faced toward the circle. He watched as Forsung stepped out from his refuge. Springing to his feet, Hogun raced across the chamber, mace at the ready. He rather hoped the wizard would resume hostilities. They might need his spells to leave this primordial world, but Hogun doubted he needed his legs for his conjuring. A solid hit from Hridgandr would break them regardless of the armor the Enchanter wore.

Forsung, however, made no threatening move as Hogun approached. The wizard gave him a thin smile and an even briefer bow. "We can treat with each other as equals now. I have freed you and you have freed me."

Hogun's fingers tightened around the heft of his mace. "Fandral's leading that menagerie of yours away. He might get killed by them. We're anything but equal."

Volstagg circled around to flank the sorcerer. The big Asgardian's eyes were like flecks of steel. "He dies, you die." There was no brag in his voice, only the promise of death.

"Then I'd better do something to ensure that doesn't happen." Forsung started to walk away. Volstagg pressed the tip of his sword against the Enchanter's breastplate, tapping the spot where the Living Talisman had been. "We need each other now," he scolded the warrior.

"You'd better start being useful," Hogun advised.

The wizard gestured to the large pentagram on the floor. "I need to go over there to work my magic. The loss of my talisman has… restricted my abilities."

"So you can call more demons," Hogun snarled. He was well aware of the purpose to which wizards put such arcane symbols.

Forsung gave him a weary stare. "What can be summoned can also be banished," he explained. "If you don't trust me, you can join me inside the pentagram."

Hogun eased Volstagg's sword away and motioned for the Enchanter to proceed. As he marched toward the pentagram, the warriors fell into step beside him. "We don't trust you," he said, "and if you try any tricks, I promise you'll die first."

The Enchanter nodded in understanding. The three of them entered the pentagram. The moment they stepped into the design, Hogun felt a chill sweep through him. A clammy, foul sensation that slithered into the very recesses of his being. He could faintly hear the sound of scratching claws, as though there were creatures all around him trying to tear their way into his flesh.

"The threshold between ourselves and the infernal dimensions is thin here," Forsung warned. His eyes gleamed malignantly. "If you are careless you'll invite something in, so I advise you think only of Fandral and ignore the unseen denizens around you."

"I wish he hadn't said that," Volstagg grumbled. He glanced over at Hogun. "Have you ever tried *not* to think of something?"

It was a question Hogun could have answered, but didn't. Simply to function he had to lock away his memories of his vanquished homeland, partition them so that he didn't allow them to consume him utterly. Often – far too often – they'd bleed through his defenses, but that he still walked among the living and not the dead of Valhalla was testament to his ability to drive back the shadows of his own mind.

Forsung's hands curled into clawed fists as a stream of eldritch words crawled across his lips. The tips of each arm of the pentagram began to glow with a hellish light. Hogun felt the things scratching at the edge of reality recoil, fleeing to the dark recesses of their profane realm.

Roars boomed through the Enchanter's tower, fierce cries of debased savagery. Hogun felt a vile wind billow up from the stairway. He thought he could see spectral shapes borne upon that wind. Things with horns and fangs that howled in protest as they were drawn back. The tempest swirled around the outside of the pentagram, gyrating faster and faster. Finally, when Hogun thought its speed could become no greater, the storm vanished. At once the air felt clean, the demonic pollution that had tainted it was gone – sucked back into the black pits where it belonged.

Hogun started to step from the pentagram when a thunderous bellow rang out. He felt the floor quake as a huge creature charged up the stairway. It was the long-necked dinosaur, its flank bleeding from a vicious bite. He could see at once the change that had come upon the reptile. The horns were absent and its eyes lacked that infernal intelligence from before. It was now only a beast rather than a monster.

Close upon the trail of the long-neck came a second dinosaur. Though its scales had lightened to a charcoal gray and the aura of shadow was no more, Hogun recognized it as the devil-beast. The enormous predator roared as it bounded after the long-neck. Its jaws clamped tight about the behemoth, catching it by the throat. Twisting its own head and kicking out with its clawed leg, the devil-beast forced the other dinosaur down onto its side. The long-neck struggled to throw off its attacker but it was losing too much blood to escape those crushing jaws.

"Without the demons, they revert to mere animals," Forsung explained. "Simple brutes with the instincts of the jungle." There was a regretful note to the wizard's voice as he watched the dinosaurs battle.

Hogun gave small notice to the feuding reptiles. His attention was riveted by a much smaller shape that ran up the stairs. He tapped Volstagg and directed the warrior's attention to the steps.

290　　　　　　　　*Marvel: Legends of Asgard*

"Fandral!" Volstagg shouted, dashing from the pentagram to greet their friend.

Hogun wanted to join them, but kept his place near the sorcerer. "It looks like you get to live a little longer," he told Forsung.

The Enchanter shook his head. "I'm pleased Fandral survived," he stated. "It will take all of us if we're going to defeat Enrakt."

"Us?" Hogun bristled at the Enchanter's use of the word.

"Of course," Forsung said. "We share the same enemy, and to defeat him will need all of our powers."

The Warriors Three followed Forsung down through the layers of his tower. Fandral expected the structure to go plummeting earthward at any moment, its enchantment vanishing with the loss of the Living Talisman the way Brona's fortress had started to rot the moment he was vanquished.

"My brother was always too dependent on his talisman," Forsung explained as they entered a cramped chamber that resembled some sort of deranged museum. "He drew so deeply on its energies that he was quite lost without it."

"And what about you?" Fandral wondered. "What are you without your Living Talisman?"

The Enchanter glowered at him. "Diminished," he conceded, "but far from helpless." He gestured at the collection around them. "I can still conjure powerful spells; I simply need my apparatus to do so."

Volstagg picked up a large tome from one of the shelves they passed. He frowned as he ran his hand along its leathery binding. "You're saying this holds some of your magic?"

Three Swords 291

Forsung smiled at him. "It should. That tome is bound in the skin of a Jotunheim witch. You can still smell her screams if you concentrate." Volstagg tossed the book back onto the shelf as though it were a live serpent.

"What about this?" Hogun drew a simple iron sword from a rack of similar weapons.

"Elfbane," Forsung named the blade. "I won an argument with Malekith with that sword." He shook his head. "Unfortunately, the dark elf was able to recover." He scowled as he watched Hogun tuck the weapon under his belt.

"You say you can return us to Asgard?" Fandral asked, trying to divert the Enchanter's attention away from Hogun's appropriation of the sword.

"Enrakt is an amateur at the art of crossing between worlds," Forsung stated. "If I had my Living Talisman, I could easily bypass the borders between this land and Asgard. As things stand, I will need the Wand of Kalumai to summon the power I'll need."

The wizard hastened through the racks of arcane devices. Finally, he spotted the object he desired. It was a rod about as long as Fandral's forearm. It appeared cast from some red-hued metal and its top was shaped into a goat-like head. There was a dark energy about the relic that disturbed Fandral.

"Only the bold can master the black arts," Forsung said, amused by Fandral's uneasiness. "To defy the laws of the cosmos, a wizard must have courage…"

The Enchanter's face went pale and he dashed past Fandral. He stopped a pace away from where Volstagg was inspecting another item from the wizard's collection. The big Asgardian had what looked like a skull shaped from crystal in his hands and was slowly turning it from side to side to study it.

"Set that down," Forsung implored, gesturing at Volstagg with both hands. "That skull contains the essence of the necromancer Yoshinaga. Were it to break, his dark powers would be unleashed and destroy us all."

Volstagg tried to discard the object even faster than he had the grimoire. In his haste, it slipped from his grasp and would have hit the floor had Hogun not intercepted it. The grim warrior shook his head as he gave Volstagg a stern look.

"Maybe we should get out of here before there's an accident," Fandral suggested.

Forsung turned toward him. "The Wand of Kalumai is all I require to get us to Asgard." He held his finger up in warning. "I can sense Enrakt the same way I could sense my other brothers. I remind you that my arcane abilities are greater than his. When he sent you to this domain, he lacked the precision to place you within my tower." A smirk tugged at the Enchanter's mouth. "I possess the skill to transport us precisely to where my treacherous brother is. When the portal opens, you must be ready to fight. Don't hesitate."

Something in Forsung's tone alerted Fandral that the wizard knew more than he was letting on. "You have some idea of what we'll find when we cross back into Asgard."

Forsung nodded. "I suspect I know the ritual Enrakt intends to execute. He's a fool! It is beyond his abilities! He thinks he can harness the Living Talismans to accomplish a thing over which he has no mastery. He'll destroy himself."

Three Swords 293

The Enchanter's expression darkened. "But first he will destroy all of Asgard!"

Volstagg pointed at the Enchanter, an edge of panic in the warrior's eyes. Fandral knew his friend was thinking of Gunnhilde and their children. "Then stop talking and open the portal!" he demanded.

Forsung motioned the warriors to gather around him. "Each of you set your hand on the next man's shoulder," he instructed. He held the wand out into the center of the ring they formed. His other hand worked in arcane passes. The reddish metal began to glow as he coaxed its magic into action. Fandral saw a cruel gleam in the eyes of the goat-head, then the gleam expanded into a blinding radiance.

There was a deafening tumult, the shriek of reality being pierced. The sensation was far worse than that caused by Enrakt's astral circle. Fandral felt as if every inch of his skin was being flayed from his bones.

Then the sensation was past. The light vanished and Fandral could see again. But what he saw was stranger than any of the realms to which the Enchanters had gone. Only the familiar positions of the constellations convinced him they were indeed in Asgard.

What stretched before the Warriors Three was a cracked and shattered landscape. Great blocks of stone hung suspended in the blackness of cosmic space. Fandral saw the rubble of a once mighty castle, its gates and battlements hovering in the void.

"The edge of Ringsfjord," Hogun muttered.

Fandral shuddered. They were gazing upon the edge of

Asgard itself, the spot where the Realm had been frayed by terrible magics and spilled away into the sea of space.

"And there's Enrakt," Volstagg growled, pointing at the cusp of the shattered terrain, the last place where the ground remained solid.

The youngest of the Enchanters stood on a spit of broken masonry, his arms raised above him, his fingers splayed as he called upon eldritch forces. Around him, levitating in the air, were the Living Talismans, each of the stones acting as the point of a triangle. Poised at the center of the triangle, Enrakt drew the energies of the talismans into himself.

It was what was happening behind Enrakt that commanded Fandral's attention. A nimbus of darkness, blacker even than the cosmic vastness, boiled into sight. It seemed to fold in upon itself while at the same time expanding outward.

A figure moved within that darkness, a hulking shape that lumbered out onto the jagged rubble of the ruined castle. It was a massive humanoid creature, taller and bulkier than a troll. Its gray skin had a stone-like quality. The creature's head simply sprouted from its shoulders without any semblance of a neck. The head was featureless, lacking mouth or nose or ears. There was only a long gash where its eyes should have been. A dull yellow light emanated from the slit as the creature strode into Asgard.

"He has opened a doorway to the Dark Dimension!" Forsung cried, genuine terror in his voice. "He has summoned the Mindless Ones!"

Twenty-Five

"Asgard already has enough monsters!" Volstagg shouted. Gripping his sword in both hands, he charged the Mindless One as it marched over the broken flagstones. The creature wasn't quite so oblivious as its name implied. It reacted to his approach and turned to face him.

Before Volstagg could close on the creature, the light shining from the single, visor-like eye grew even more intense. It erupted from the monster in a concussive beam that slammed into him with the force of a frost giant. Volstagg was sent spinning through the air, his momentum broken only when he crashed into a section of ruined wall. The masonry crumpled around him and he crashed to the ground with debris raining down on him. One block cracked against his helm and made his head ring.

"Won't be making that mistake again," Volstagg promised himself as he painfully got back onto his feet.

Enrakt, the fourth Enchanter, crowed with triumph as the

Mindless One lumbered onward. "No force in all Asgard can defy me now!" A trace of the sorcerer's arrogance slipped away when he saw that Forsung was standing with the Warriors Three.

"You're a fool, brother!" Forsung shouted at Enrakt. Volstagg saw that the portal Enrakt had created was opening wider. Dimly perceived shapes stirred in the corridor to the Dark Dimension. The glowing eyes told him what those shapes belonged to. More of the Mindless Ones, a veritable army of the mighty brutes!

"Abandon this madness while there's still time," Forsung cried.

Enrakt sneered at his eldest brother. "You should have stayed with your lizards." Energy crackled from the three Living Talismans and swept into the wizard. He pointed his hand at Forsung and from his fingers a coruscating beam shot towards the Enchanter. Forsung hastily conjured a shield of blue light, but it shattered under the force of Enrakt's spell. The older wizard staggered back, flames crackling about his robes and smoke steaming off his armor.

Volstagg noted something when Enrakt refocused his attention onto Forsung. The portal receded slightly, its proportions contracting. "Traitor!" he yelled at Enrakt. "Do you have the spine to do that to Volstagg the Impenetrable!"

The sorcerer did. Glaring at Volstagg, Enrakt spun around and used the might of the Living Talismans to blast him. For the second time he was knocked into the wall. Rubble crashed down around him as the remainder of the construction collapsed.

Volstagg painfully shifted the broken stones. Through

Three Swords 297

his pain, he managed a smile when he saw that the portal had grown still smaller. He was far from a magician, but it seemed to Volstagg that whatever ritual Enrakt was using to open a door to the Dark Dimension, it demanded his concentration. If they could just keep him distracted, they might be able to collapse the portal entirely.

Fandral and Hogun appeared to have reached the same conclusion. The two sought to converge on the young wizard, but in their dash to confront Enrakt they drew the attention of the Mindless One. The monster sent one of its optic blasts flashing toward Fandral but the nimble Asgardian was able to divert from its path. The beam exploded the flagstones where he'd been running and sent slivers of stone in every direction.

Hogun spun about and dove behind a section of inner wall. The Mindless One didn't send a blast after him. Instead, it reached down with its massive hands and ripped a huge block of stone from the ground. Hefting the cumbersome missile above its head, the brute sent it hurtling toward the ruined wall. Hogun scrambled from cover just as the block smashed into his refuge and reduced it to a pile of rubble.

"I can see this is going to be a three warrior problem," Volstagg grunted. He rushed across the broken courtyard to aid his friends. Fandral and Hogun were on opposite sides of the monster and the strategy was clear. However frightful its strength might be, there was no way it could react to a simultaneous attack from all sides. Volstagg joined the ploy, positioning himself so that he could charge the brute from a third angle.

Fandral spotted him and grinned. "Attack!" he shouted.

At his command all three of the warriors rushed the monster. The Mindless One turned and sent an energy beam slamming into Hogun. He tried to block the force of the beam with Hridgandr, but the mace was unequal to the might of the creature's assault and he was sent tumbling across the ruins. Fandral managed to reach the brute and slash it with Fimbuldraugr, but the blade merely scratched the gray skin and no blood oozed from the cut. A swat from the Mindless One's fist caught the Asgardian and threw him a dozen yards away.

Seeing the ineffectiveness of Fandral's sword against the Mindless One, Volstagg tucked Brandrheid Undrsigr under the wire belt. Instead of trying to slash the monster, he lunged at it from behind. His arms wrapped about its head, approximating where the thing should have had a neck. The brute was only a few inches taller than the big Asgardian, so he was able to keep a firm footing as he tried to choke the invader from the Dark Dimension.

"Go to sleep, you ugly pig," Volstagg hissed as he strained against the gray monster. The hold he was using was one that had knocked the fight out of trolls but the Mindless One didn't even seem phased by his choking grip. After a moment, it reached back with both hands and grabbed him. Volstagg's arms slipped away from the brute's head as he was lifted off the ground. As though he weighed no more than a child, the Mindless One threw him.

Volstagg slammed into the ground twenty feet away and slid across the cracked flagstones, scraping his face and arms in the process. The moment his slide ended, he scrambled into the trench-like declivity where a moat had once been.

Three Swords 299

He was just dropping into the trench when he heard the impact of an optic blast and felt shards of stone glance off his body.

"The people you meet in the strangest places," Fandral joked as he helped Hogun pull Volstagg into a sitting posture. Like him, they'd sought cover in the dry moat.

"We can't let that maniac bring an army of these things into Asgard," Volstagg swore, wiping at his bleeding scalp. "I don't even think they are capable of appreciating the fame of the warriors they're fighting."

The levity brought a laugh from Fandral, but Hogun just peered over the lip of the moat. "We can't get to Enrakt with that monster in the way."

Volstagg nodded. "So much for Forsung's help. I thought he was going to keep his brother distracted."

"He is," Fandral said. "Look."

Volstagg peered over the edge of the moat. He spotted Forsung using the toppled length of a tower for cover, ducking behind its crenelations as Enrakt sent bolts of magic crackling toward him.

"This ritual is beyond your power!" Forsung shouted at the younger sorcerer. "You can summon the Mindless Ones, but you can't control them!"

Enrakt gestured and a bolt of green lightning vaporized a section of the tower. "So speaks the coward who lacked the determination to achieve what I have done!" He made a chopping motion and the broken sides of the tower split apart as though gripped by gigantic hands. Forsung was exposed as his cover was drawn away. The eldest of the Enchanters stood his ground and glared back at his sibling.

"You thought to conjure an army to serve you, but all you've summoned is your own executioner!" Forsung's voice trailed away in vindictive laughter.

Volstagg saw why Forsung had taken such a triumphant mood. A second Mindless One had crossed through the gate. Only this brute didn't march to join the first. It turned instead toward Enrakt.

Enrakt spun about, his eyes going wide when he saw the truth of Forsung's words. He pointed at the Mindless One, shouting commands at it. The monster simply kept plodding towards him. Realizing his peril, the wizard unleashed his magic against the monster, drawing upon the energies of the Living Talismans and causing the portal to diminish to a mere speck at the edge of Asgard.

The Enchanter's spells staggered the Mindless One, but they did not stop it. The brute grabbed Enrakt in both hands. Volstagg saw it lift the sorcerer as he'd been lifted. Only instead of tossing Enrakt across the courtyard the monster turned and faced the Sea of Space.

Enrakt screamed as he was carried away from the triangle formed by the levitating talismans and flung out into the cosmic void beyond Asgard. Forsung's warning was fulfilled. The ambitious Enchanter had conjured his own executioner.

"That takes care of one problem," Volstagg said, unable to repress a shudder. "Now we just have to deal with the Mindless Ones Enrakt let into Asgard."

Hogun clenched Hridgandr tight as he watched the first Mindless One lumber toward the dry moat. He was eager

Three Swords 301

to avenge himself after the almost casual way the monster had brushed him off. No demon, whether it came from the infernal realms or the Dark Dimension, was going to get the better of him.

"What's the plan?" he asked Fandral. Hogun could see that the other warrior was already trying to devise a strategy.

"Hela's horns!" Fandral suddenly cursed. He pointed at Forsung. After disposing of Enrakt, the second Mindless One was focusing on the remaining Enchanter. The spells he cast against the monster were even less effective than those of his brother, lacking the added power of the Living Talismans to strengthen them. "We'll have to divide our forces. Someone has to help Forsung."

Hogun scowled. "Leave the wizard to fend for himself," he said.

"We can't do that," Fandral countered. He nodded at the ripple where the door to the Dark Dimension remained and the crackling triangle formed by the Living Talismans. "He's the only one who knows how to undo what Enrakt's done." Fandral laid a hand on the shoulders of Hogun and Volstagg. "You two take on the monster here. Distract it long enough so I can help Forsung."

"Distract it?" Volstagg pulled a clump of tar from his beard. "The only way we can distract it is if it trips when it walks over us."

"We'll try something else," Hogun said. "If it doesn't work, we can always go your route." Volstagg grimaced at the remark. "You draw it to you. I'll rush in and smack it with Hridgandr. Try to buckle its knees."

"Are you sure it even has knees?" Volstagg asked. He

patted his sword. "I'd like a more substantial weapon. Like a mountain to drop on that thing."

Hogun locked eyes with Fandral. "We'll keep it busy. You go help the sorcerer." He moved around to a curve in the trench. Once he was in position, he waved to Volstagg.

The huge warrior scrambled up the side of the trench and shouted at the Mindless One. "If you're looking for Volstagg the Marvelous, you've found him!" He slapped his hand against his chest. "Come and get me, you lumbering oaf!"

Volstagg dropped back down into the trench as the Mindless One sent an optic blast at him. Volstagg was neither fast nor agile – if Hogun was blunt he'd call his friend outright clumsy – but falling back into the trench didn't require grace. The beam overshot him as he fell, exploding against the flagstone several yards beyond the moat.

Hogun sprang from cover as the brute marched towards Volstagg's position. He was on the monster before it noticed him. His mace smacked into the Mindless One's leg with such force that he felt the impact pulse through his arms.

The Mindless One was unhurt by the strike. It didn't even stumble, but simply turned and glowered at him with its slit-like eye. Energy crackled as it unleashed another optic blast. Hogun was struck by the full fury of the beam, tossed backwards by the brutal energy. He could smell his flesh burning and smoke billowed from his singed clothes.

As he lifted himself off the ground, Hogun saw Volstagg charge back up from the moat and attack the Mindless One before it could press its attack further. Grabbing its arm, he pivoted the monster so that a second eye beam failed to hit the sprawled warrior.

Three Swords 303

Hogun also saw Fandral sprinting across the courtyard, hurrying to aid Forsung against the other Mindless One. The distraction, at least, had worked. Now there was just the problem of defeating their own monster.

Volstagg's grapple with the Mindless One ended in a sprawl. He cried out as the brute stamped its foot down on him, pinning him to the ground. One of its craggy hands closed around the warrior's face. Hogun could see the thing start to squeeze. In a moment, Volstagg's head would be crushed to pulp.

"Hey! Forget about me?" Hogun shouted as he charged the Mindless One. Hridgandr smashed into its back with all the might he could summon. He managed to stagger the brute this time. It released its hold on Volstagg and glowered at Hogun.

This time Hogun was ready for the optic blast, darting aside as the beam left the gash in the creature's face. Having succeeded in drawing the monster's attention, he sprinted back to the moat. "Volstagg, let it chase me!" he called to his friend.

A plan had formed in his mind. He let Hridgandr swing from its thong as he jumped down into the trench. When they'd entered Forsung's vault, he'd taken the sword Elfbane with an idea of using it against the Enchanter if he tried any tricks. Now he saw a different purpose for the sword.

Hogun felt the ground tremble as the Mindless One pursued him. His attack must have agitated it more than he'd expected, for its rush toward the trench was the first indication the creature had given that it could muster any sort of haste. Instead of feeling dread, he was eager. The sooner they disposed of their enemy the quicker they could help Fandral.

Crouched against the side of the moat, Hogun judged how close the Mindless One was by the sound of its footfalls. He held his breath as the monster reached the edge of the moat. The instant he saw it looming over him, he sprang into motion.

The monster tilted its body so that it was gazing down into the trench. Another second and the Mindless One would have unleashed another optic blast from its eye. Instead, the cold-wrought iron of Elfbane pierced the gash-like slit as Hogun thrust the sword into the monster's face.

The Mindless One reared back, its hands pawing at its head. Light crackled around the sword. Sparks of energy spewed from the monster's pierced face, steaming as they struck the ground. The brute staggered, flailing wildly as power continued to spill from its pierced eye. Hogun found the display ghastly, for despite its obvious agonies, the Mindless One uttered no sound at all.

"Get down!" Volstagg shouted as he dove into the trench.

Hogun didn't ask his friend why. He saw that the energy escaping the Mindless One was reaching a critical state. Just as he ducked back under the edge of the moat there was a calamitous explosion. Shreds of the Mindless One's gray hide showered the moat, hitting the ground like hailstones. Hogun saw a larger piece slam into the opposite wall of the moat. It took him a second to recognize Elfbane. The sword was corroded down to a mere fragment by the force of the detonation.

Three Swords

"Well," Hogun sighed, "we won't be using that trick against the other one."

The Mindless One chased after Forsung with a deliberateness that spoke of its minimal intellect. The monster doggedly followed the wizard around the toppled remains of the tower, tearing through whatever rubble got in its way. Fandral thought he could have walked right beside the brute and not garner any sort of response.

What he intended was far more practical. Following the Mindless One at a distance, Fandral caught Forsung's eye. He motioned to the Enchanter, hoping he understood the visual cue. For his plan to work, he needed Forsung to bring the monster where he needed it to be.

Fandral withdrew from the chase and scrambled up onto what remained of the tower's wall. He focused on the spot he wanted. A balcony, half destroyed when the castle crashed into ruins, acted as a kind of overhang. He'd noticed it when he ran to help the Enchanter. It wouldn't take much to knock the rest of the balcony loose. A ton or two of stone slamming down was bound to make for a bad day, even for a monster summoned out of the Dark Dimension.

Fandral got into position. He braced his legs against the tower and pressed his back against the weakest part of the balcony. He dug the point of Fimbuldraugr into the join between two of the immense blocks. He hoped the sword held fast. He would need it to anchor him so he didn't fall along with the balcony.

The sound of Forsung's spells crackling against the Mindless One alerted Fandral that his quarry was close. He waited while the Enchanter dashed past the danger spot, then strained with all his strength against the balcony.

The platform cracked with a loud snap. An avalanche of stone went crashing to the ground. Fandral grabbed the hilt of his sword before he could join the cascade he'd unleashed. From his perch he could see the Mindless One the instant the rubble slammed down on it. The brute vanished beneath the tide of destruction.

"That won't hold it long," Forsung cautioned. The Enchanter turned and gestured to the edge of Ringsfjord where the Living Talismans continued to blaze with arcane power. "Keep guard while I close the portal." Forsung ran toward the site of Enrakt's folly.

Fandral hesitated for only a moment, then jumped down and took off after the Enchanter. He'd seen enough of Forsung's ruthless evil that he wasn't about to let him reclaim his Living Talisman.

What Forsung had in mind was far worse. The instant he was aware Fandral was chasing him, he spun around and unleashed a storm of lightning. The wizard's spells might not have phased the Mindless One, but even without his talisman he had enough magic to bring Fandral to his knees.

"Stay there and watch as Asgard gains a new overlord," Forsung sneered. He looked utterly drained by the spell he'd used against Fandral, stumbling over the broken blocks as he climbed toward the Living Talismans.

Once he stood within the triangle, however, the Enchanter was replenished. He seemed to swell with power.

"Enrakt was a presumptuous idiot," Forsung said. "His ambition exceeded both his power and his knowledge."

Three Swords   307

There was pitiless cruelty in his eyes as he looked down at Fandral. "I, however, have both the power and the knowledge to achieve what my brother couldn't. He was too weak to control the Mindless Ones. I am equal to that feat!"

Forsung pointed and the pile of rubble fell away. The Mindless One that had so recently been trying to destroy the wizard now marched at his command. "I must thank the Warriors Three for their help," the Enchanter snidely declared. "It would have been difficult for me to take the Living Talismans from my brothers, and hard for me to usurp Enrakt's plan without you."

A malignant grin spread over Forsung's face. He pointed his finger at Fandral. "For your assistance, I bestow on you the honor of being the first victim of my reign!"

The ground shuddered as the Mindless One lumbered toward Fandral.

Twenty-six

"Nidhogg devour all sorcerers," Hogun cursed as he saw Forsung poise himself in the same spot where Enrakt had been. It was obvious that far from stopping his younger brother, the Enchanter was simply taking his place.

Volstagg shook his head as they sprinted toward the scene. "We've the same problem as before," he growled, pointing at the Mindless One. "To get at the wizard we first have to get past the monster."

"Let's first keep it from crushing Fandral," Hogun stated. He felt his stomach churn when he saw the doorway to the Dark Dimension begin to expand once more. The Mindless Ones still imprisoned there must have lost interest once the opening was too small for them to cross, but now he could see the monsters gathering once more, their eyes blazing as they answered Forsung's summons. Whatever else happened, they had to break the Enchanter's spell before that hideous army descended upon Asgard.

Three Swords   309

Volstagg stopped to wrench a slab of stone from the ground. In a display of his incredible strength, he heaved it at the Mindless One just as the brute was about to blast Fandral. The block slammed into the monster, knocking it prone.

Hogun hurried to Fandral and picked him up. "I told you not to trust sorcerers."

"Next time I'll pay more attention," Fandral said. "For now, let's just try and stop this one."

The two of them dodged as a blast from the Mindless One's eye scorched the ground. The monster rose from where it had fallen. It picked up the block Volstagg had thrown and sent it sailing at Fandral, the stone missing him by mere inches. The ground fragmented where it struck, pieces being drawn away to join the debris drifting on the edge of Asgard.

A fiendish directive caused the Mindless One to tear another block from the courtyard and hurl it after Fandral and Hogun. Another pit opened when it struck. Hogun could see the black void of space yawning at the bottom of the hole. The ground under the ruins was thin, fragile enough for the monster to fracture it and cause it to collapse into the Sea of Space.

Another block went sailing past and crashed against the courtyard with devastating force. Fandral shouted in warning as he realized what the Mindless One was trying to do. "It's trying to herd us into the Sea of Space!"

Hogun shifted and started to run back to the more solid ground, but the monster cast another stone and gouged a hole directly in his path. He knew the creature's improved speed and accuracy stemmed from the Enchanter. While

Forsung maintained control of the Mindless One they had little hope of overcoming it.

Volstagg tried everything he could to distract the monster. His efforts to divert it were futile, but then a wise look came across his features. Hogun guessed the big Asgardian had reached the same conclusion he had. He turned and threw the stone he'd been ready to use on the Mindless One and cast it instead at the sorcerer.

"Impertinent fool!" Forsung snarled. The Enchanter gestured with his hands and a wave of magic caught the stone before it could reach him. The block crumbled into dust as the sorcerer exerted his power.

But in exerting his power, Forsung had to focus his energies. Hogun saw the door to the Dark Dimension retract somewhat even as the monstrous army was starting along its path. The Mindless One attacking them didn't pick up another block to shatter the ground but instead lumbered forward to bring them within range of its optic blasts.

"Forsung might be more powerful, but he has the same weakness his brother did," Fandral said. "We have to keep him occupied on anything but that portal."

Hogun joined him as they hurried toward the sorcerer. For now, Volstagg held Forsung's attention. Lightning crackled from the Enchanter's fingers and seared the warrior. Volstagg sought cover in the one place the wizard never expected. He dashed around the Mindless One. A sheet of electricity crashed into the monster, staggering it.

The Mindless One instinctively turned to confront its attacker. "Obey!" Forsung snarled, and at his word the monster did just that. "Kill Volstagg!"

Three Swords 311

The brute shifted and tried to smash Volstagg with its fist. The big Asgardian ducked the clumsy blow and withdrew across the courtyard. The Mindless One started off in pursuit.

"We have to stop him before Forsung calls his monster back," Fandral declared.

"I have an idea," Hogun said. He quickly explained a desperate strategy. "Keep him busy," he told Fandral. "Leave the rest to me... and the sorcerer."

Fandral stopped behind a broken battlement. Using Fimbuldraugr, he pried loose a few of the stones. Hogun could see he was keen to play his role. Attracting Forsung's attention would prevent the Enchanter from giving directions to the Mindless One and provide Volstagg with a necessary respite.

"Over here, traitor!" Fandral shouted as he threw one of the blocks at Forsung. The sorcerer shifted around and used his arcane powers to shatter the missile as easily as he had the block Volstagg had thrown.

"Pathetic," the wizard sneered. He laughed when Fandral threw another stone at him. He exploded it just as he had the other. "Is this what the Warriors Three are reduced to? Throwing rocks as though they are naught but children?" Forsung smiled as he destroyed a third stone. "I will savor destroying you," he promised.

While the Enchanter fixated on Fandral, Hogun slipped around to the opposite flank. He started to climb up towards the wizard's perch. As he did, his foot contacted loose rubble and sent it clattering down into the courtyard.

Forsung swung around. "The third fool," he snarled, loosing a spell to destroy the projectile Hogun threw at him.

Hogun leaped down into the courtyard. Elfbane wasn't the only relic he'd appropriated from Forsung's collection. The wizard's eyes were wide with alarm when he saw exactly what it was Hogun had thrown. The object he'd just shattered with his spell. The crystal skull, the artifact that housed the destructive energies of a long-dead necromancer. It was this which disintegrated under the Enchanter's magic.

The detonation was of such force that Hogun felt as if his teeth were going to be shaken from his jaws. He saw a ball of black flame explode before the Enchanter. Blocks of stone were pulverized in the discharge. The entire spire was lifted up and cast away, hurled toward the Sea of Space.

Or not quite the Sea of Space. Between the edge of Asgard and the cosmic void stood the doorway to the Dark Dimension. Into this gulf was drawn Forsung and the Living Talismans. The Enchanter shrieked as he was sucked into the realm of the Mindless Ones. As Forsung was pulled through the doorway, the portal collapsed in upon itself, vanishing with a sound like a thunderclap.

Fandral came out from behind the battlement and hurried over to Hogun. "Destroyed by his own magic," Fandral said, awe in his tone.

"A fate Forsung richly deserved," Hogun replied. His hand tightened around the heft of his mace. "Now we'd better help Volstagg with the last of the Mindless Ones."

Volstagg felt sick when he saw the cosmic void yawning at his feet. "A brilliant plan," he chided himself as he quickly changed his path. Unfortunately, the monster chasing him did the same. "The Mindless One will fall for anything," he grumbled. "I mean, it's in the name. Just lure it out to one of the pits and let it fall into space."

An optic beam scorched the ground and Volstagg had to scramble to avoid falling into a newly blasted hole. It galled him to think the monster had the same idea he did. It galled him even more to think the brute might kill him after his friends had triumphed over Forsung. There was nothing so bitter as being the last casualty in a battle.

"If you give up now, I'm prepared to call it a draw," Volstagg shouted at the Mindless One. The monster just kept plodding after him. It wasn't the fastest enemy he'd met, but the cursed brute seemed tireless. And trying to avoid the growing number of holes was making it impossible to put any real distance between himself and the monster.

Volstagg stumbled as a blast from the Mindless One's eye slammed into him. He rolled across the ground. When he scrambled to his feet, he felt the earth give way. He was uncomfortably reminded of the fight in the Sssthgar's tower on Golden Star. Reeling, he threw himself forward, landing in a sprawl.

The sound of the Mindless One's lumbering steps caused him to look up. The monster stared down at Volstagg and energy crackled from its eye. He tried to roll away from the blast, but as he did the already weakened ground gave way.

Volstagg flailed as he pitched over the edge of Asgard and into the Sea of Space. He felt the void drag at him, pulling him away from the firmament. His hands seized on a jagged spit of stone, a clump of rock poised at the cusp of eternity.

Relief rushed through him as he secured a grip on the

stone. Then Volstagg looked up. The Mindless One, with the fearless tenacity of a machine, glared down at him from the edge. Again, its eye crackled with destructive energy. "You've got to be kidding me," he sighed.

The optic blast sheared away a section of the stone. Volstagg was almost knocked free by the violent impact, but his hands now had a death grip on the rock. It would need much greater force to dislodge him.

Unfortunately, the monster was prepared to provide that force. Volstagg doubted the most crazed berserker would willingly have climbed down from the edge of Asgard, yet that was precisely what the Mindless One did. Hand over hand, it clawed its way down the cliff-like edge of Ringsfjord.

"You just don't give up, do you?" Volstagg told the monster. Its descent brought it within ten feet of him and slightly to his right. He knew once it was level with him all it had to do was pick him off with one of its beams.

"I don't give up either," Volstagg declared. He slashed Brandrheid Undrsigr along the stone the Mindless One was descending, opening a narrow fissure. Thrusting the blade back under his belt, he secured his own position with both hands and brought his legs kicking at the crack he'd made.

Volstagg could see the stone shudder from his impacts, but the Mindless One wasn't swayed. It continued its way toward him. He knew only a matter of heartbeats lay between himself and the monster's optic blasts. The force from even one of those eye beams would knock him loose and send him hurtling into the Sea of Space.

He kicked the stone again, but was rewarded with only a few splinters that drifted away into the void. Volstagg

Three Swords 315

blanched as the Mindless One drew nearer. Soon it would be level with him and turn its eye on him.

As he braced himself for disaster, Volstagg saw that the Mindless One's weight accomplished what his kicks couldn't. The monster was almost level with him when there was a loud crack. The face of the stone sheared away and went sliding off into the Sea of Space, taking the Mindless One with it. For a moment he could see the monster and the rock trailing off into the void.

Then Volstagg's own perch shifted into horrible motion. He scrabbled desperately for a handhold as the rock face, as though in sympathy with the Mindless One, fractured and went sliding free. He cried out as he hurtled towards infinity. The black vastness of space loomed before him, but strangely didn't rush up to engulf him.

Volstagg ran his hands down his body and found the cause of his sudden stop. The wire belt had hooked itself onto a spur of rock, catching him before he could hurtle into infinity. The nearness of his doom was such that he barely dared to breathe. When he heard voices at the edge of Asgard, he could scarcely find the courage to reply. Only the thought that he would be left where he was finally made him dare to put any volume to his voice.

"You can start grieving for me after you pull me up!" Volstagg called to Fandral and Hogun.

"I knew we couldn't be that lucky," Fandral commented with mock despair. "Volstagg's the one who has all our luck."

"Well, I'll feel a lot better when I have solid ground under my feet," Volstagg replied. As though in warning, a few pebbles clattered past him. After that, he decided if Odin himself called to him, he wasn't going to so much as whisper back.

Once they drew Volstagg back from the precipice, the Warriors Three made their way from the broken castle and the daunting vista of the Sea of Space at the edge of Asgard.

"We've a long walk ahead of us," Fandral advised his companions. "Ringsfjord is a vast land and far from hospitable. Especially for three adventurers in such condition as we're in."

Volstagg winced as some of his beard came away with a clump of tar. "We've nothing to show for our ordeal," he agreed. "We took no plunder from the Enchanters. There's no glory since the only ones who witnessed our victories were the wizards and their monsters."

Hogun frowned and shook his head. "Wealth and glory are fleeting things. It should be enough that we've thwarted a great evil and brought ruin to a cabal of sorcerers who spread misery and destruction wherever they fared." He fixed each of them with a somber look. "That, at least, is all I need to be satisfied."

"And you've quite the story to add to your saga," Fandral reminded Volstagg. "You've journeyed across space and time to see things perhaps no other Asgardian has seen. You've fought aliens and robots and dinosaurs and demons. Such a chronicle!"

Volstagg smiled. "Aye, a great chronicle indeed… if anyone would believe it."

Fandral laughed. It took some time for him to regain his

Three Swords 317

control. The bemused looks from Hogun and Volstagg only made it harder for him to compose himself.

"I shouldn't worry on that score," Fandral told Volstagg. "Half of Asgard knows Volstagg the Loquacious stretches the truth."

"And the other half hasn't met you," Hogun added.

Volstagg joined in the laughter. "Truth is forgettable. A legend endures."

"Speaking of which, we'll need to find mounts that can carry us across the desert," Fandral said. "We've unfinished business in Skornheim with King Gunnar."

Fandral's eyes sparkled as he pictured their return to the people of Gunnarsfell. "After what we've been through, helping the rebels depose their tyrant might not seem like much, but it means everything to them."

"After vanquishing the Enchanters," Volstagg said, "Gunnar won't know what hit him."

About the Author

C L WERNER is a voracious reader and prolific author from Phoenix, Arizona. His many novels and short stories span the genres of fantasy and horror, and he has written for *Warhammer's Age of Sigmar* and *Old World, Warhammer 40,000*, Warmachine's *Iron Kingdoms*, and Mantic's *Kings of War*.

AMAZING SUPER HERO ADVENTURES

WORLD EXPANDING FICTION
Do you have them all?

Marvel Crisis Protocol
- ☐ *Target: Kree* by Stuart Moore
- ☐ *Shadow Avengers* by Carrie Harris (*coming soon*)

Marvel Heroines
- ☐ *Domino: Strays* by Tristan Palmgren
- ☐ *Rogue: Untouched* by Alisa Kwitney
- ☐ *Elsa Bloodstone: Bequest* by Cath Lauria
- ☐ *Outlaw: Relentless* by Tristan Palmgren
- ☐ *Black Cat: Discord* by Cath Lauria
  (*coming soon*)

Legends of Asgard
- ☐ *The Head of Mimir* by Richard Lee Byers
- ☐ *The Sword of Surtur* by C L Werner
- ☐ *The Serpent and the Dead* by Anna Stephens
- ☐ *The Rebels of Vanaheim* by Richard Lee Byers
- ☒ *Three Swords* by C L Werner

Marvel Untold
- ☐ *The Harrowing of Doom* by David Annandale
- ☐ *Dark Avengers: The Patriot List* by David Guymer
- ☐ *Witches Unleashed* by Carrie Harris
- ☐ *Reign of the Devourer* by David Annandale

Xavier's Institute
- ☐ *Liberty & Justice for All* by Carrie Harris
- ☐ *First Team* by Robbie MacNiven
- ☐ *Triptych* by Jaleigh Johnson
- ☐ *School of X* edited by Gwendolyn Nix
- ☐ *The Siege of X-41* by Tristan Palmgren
  (*coming soon*)

EXPLORE OUR WORLD EXPANDING FICTION

ACONYTEBOOKS.COM
@ACONYTEBOOKS
ACONYTEBOOKS.COM/NEWSLETTER